# The Book of
# Knowledge

# The Book of Knowledge

## A NOVEL

*Doris Grumbach*

W. W. NORTON & COMPANY
*New York   London*

Copyright © 1995 by Doris Grumbach
All rights reserved
Printed in the United States of America
First Edition

The text and display of this book is composed in Century Old Style.
Composition and Manufacturing by The Haddon Craftsmen
Book design by Charlotte Staub

Library of Congress Cataloging-in-Publication Data

Grumbach, Doris.
The book of knowledge : a novel / Doris Grumbach.
p. cm.
I. Title.
PS3557.R83B66 1995
813'.54—dc20
94-37901

ISBN 0-393-03770-3
W. W. Norton & Company, Inc., 500 Fifth Avenue, New York, N.Y. 10110
W. W. Norton & Company Ltd., 10 Coptic Street, London WC1A 1PU
1 2 3 4 5 6 7 8 9 0

*For my friends in Maine:*
  *May Sarton*
  *Helen Yglesias*
  *Robert Taylor and Theodore Nowick.*

*And for my main friend in all places*
*and seasons:*
  *Sybil Hillman Pike.*

They say that "time assuages"—
Time never did assuage—
An actual suffering strengthens
As sinews do, with age—

Time is a test of trouble—
But not a remedy—
If such it prove, it prove too
There was no malady—

—Emily Dickinson

# The Book of
# Knowledge

# 1

# Far Rockaway

*The ceremony of innocence is drowned . . .*
—W. B. YEATS

FOR MOST PEOPLE, childhood is remembered as a continuous seam, a long, happy fabric of time, until it is broken by the fierce rips of adolescence. But for the Flowers children, both childhood and early adolescence were Edenic, undisturbed by any familial harshness or by the nation's ruinous financial crash in the fall of 1929. In the summer of that year, they made two friends, Roslyn and Lionel, who were not to be so fortunately spared.

It happened in this way.

The children of the three families came together early that summer. Kate and Caleb Flowers lived in Far Rockaway year-round, a long journey, as they thought of it, from the City. They lived alone with their mother, their father having died in the Great War. Theirs was the largest house on Larch Street. Lionel Schwartz and Roslyn Hellman arrived at the seaside resort in June with their parents, occupying adjoining houses on Linden Street, a block away from the Flowers.

The fathers of the summering families drove to the City every day during the week in a black sedan. Caleb, a close observer of automobiles and knowledgeable about their manufacture and design, identified it as a De Soto Six. The Flowers children stood on the curb with their new friends, watching with admiration its ceremonial morning departure. There had never been a car in their family, for a very good reason, their mother pointed out: they had no need to leave the peninsula on which they lived. They walked or sometimes bicycled to school, to the library, to the beach, to the stores, and to the Gem, the motion picture house on Mott Avenue, all of these places a few blocks from Larch Street.

Warm ceremonies accompanied the City fathers' evening return. Whatever they played together, all the children stopped their game to see the two men, dressed in somber City suits and brown fedoras, step down from the running board and wave to their wives and children. To Caleb they resembled the generals he had seen in newspaper photographs returning for the celebration of a great victory. Even their hats, positioned squarely on their balding heads, seemed akin to officers' headgear. His own father, he had been told by his mother, had worn a private's narrow, boat-shaped cap.

In the evening in the house on Larch Street, their mother, whose hearing was poor, strained to catch Caleb's account of the enthusiastic greetings, the hugs all around, the tousling of their children's heads by the happy fathers. Emma concentrated on the lower tones of Caleb's excited voice, unable to quite catch what Kate was saying. After many repetitions of the narrative about the felicitous homecomings, she began to feel her children must feel deprived of such significant rituals.

So Emma would remind them of her carefully constructed version of their father's death.

'He was a true hero,' she said.

14

Caleb was unfailingly polite. He never revealed his boredom with the story. He was twelve and had heard the story many times. Kate was fourteen months younger: she loved the old, heroic tale and did not care how many times Moth, as the children called her 'for short,' repeated it.

'He was a true hero,' Emma said again, and waited for their full attention. 'It was exactly four days before the Armistice was declared. A German sniper hiding in a trench saw him stand up. Your father was under orders to look about on all sides to locate the position of the enemy. So he was shot, through the head.'

At this point in the narrative, in his strong, loud voice, Caleb always asked:

'But Moth, didn't the American soldiers wear helmets?' He thought all combat soldiers must resemble the ones he had seen in newspaper cartoons of the Beastly Hun who wore a round metal hat covering a large portion of his thick, piggish head. Were not Americans similarly equipped?

'Oh, no,' Emma said. *'Never.* They were too brave. They were given small caps like little folding pouches with pointed ends. They carried them in their belts. Our soldiers wore them to have their pictures taken. And for parades.' By establishing this distinction Emma managed to suggest that only cowards and Huns wore hats of any kind to fight in the trenches.

She would then interrupt her story to take down from the mantel a brown-tinted, wood-framed photograph of an American soldier standing at attention, his fingers touching his cap in a smart salute.

'This is how they looked.'

As she handed Caleb the picture, Emma never said: 'This is your father.' The children assumed the noble figure was Private First Class Edmund Flowers. The pictured soldier had light hair like theirs, and he wore the little cap they believed

15

had been taken from his belt when he fell. He was very handsome, as they knew a true hero always was.

The truth was otherwise. Because she no longer wished to look at his face, Emma had destroyed their wedding pictures and the few boardwalk pictures taken on their honeymoon in Atlantic City. No photographs of the fabled father existed. The anonymous one now enshrined on the mantel had been cut from the Sunday section of the *Daily Mirror* on that cold winter day when the soldiers came home in triumph to New York City. She surrounded it with brown velvet matting and placed it in a wide frame to disguise its common rotogravure finish.

Kate enjoyed thinking of herself as the only daughter of a dead war hero; Caleb was uncertain about his feelings. His father's death seemed somewhat precipitate to him, poorly planned in a way he could not define. Why had he died only a few days before the war ended? Could this have been carelessness? Shortsightedness? Bad luck? The presence on the mantel of the photograph and, lying beside it, the European theater medal with its faded ribbon was not, to his mind, sufficient evidence of valor. Still, these apparently concrete reminders of Edmund's existence served as satisfying, if distilled, evidence that he too had a father.

Both children had been so persuaded by their mother's vivid account of their father's heroic death in the war that they were without any sense of paternal deprivation, even when they watched their new friends' fathers come home in seeming triumph from the City. His absence seemed to them to signify a more noble inheritance.

As for Emma: the history she wove about their father was a barren invention. The Army never informed her in detail of the circumstances of Private Flowers' death. His body was never returned to her (buried as he had been with the thousands of other soldiers who died in the Spanish influenza epidemic in the last days of the war). The brown medal arrived at the house on Larch Street by mail, together with his veteran's papers. Emma, a skilled fictionalist on this subject, created a parent (always referred to as 'your father') who had come home twice from his training at Fort Dix, a leave just before America entered the war, and then again just before his departure for 'over there.'

The children accepted these meager details without question. From them, Caleb then wove a gratifying story which he told Kate during one of their early make-believe games. It proceeded in this way:

During each of his visits, their father had descended into the Far Rockaway house from what, in Caleb's imagination, seemed a great height. To him New Jersey was situated vertically, high above New York; he was unacquainted with geography beyond the borough of Queens. After coming down he had performed the two mysterious acts that resulted in their births.

Kate saw her father clearly, dressed in his brown, belted uniform and high-laced boots, standing at attention in her mother's bedroom, patiently awaiting the arrival of Caleb, the first baby. But Caleb, claiming to be better informed about such matters, described graphically their blond father lying in their mother's bed, and depositing into her open hand the makings of babies. He saw their parents as wearing no clothes during this exchange, of that he was very sure. The mechanics of the transfer were unclear to him, as well as the nature of the 'makings.' But he did not communicate his uncertainties to Kate, and she did not think to ask about it.

To hear their mother tell it, their conceptions had been the most significant accomplishments of their father's short life. Having performed these acts, in one flash of enemy fire, in the coda of the saga, he had died and ascended into a special habitation of heaven reserved for war heroes, with space set

17

aside for bereft windows. Satisfied by the glory of this dramatic account, the children lived securely without their father.

'Someday,' Caleb assured Kate, 'Moth will join him there.'

Kate looked horrified.

'But not for a long, long time,' he rushed to assure her.


As Emma pictured him to her children, their father had looked like the slim, blond, handsome, hardworking, dependable young man in the rotogravure. He had made a very good living in the City manufacturing play clothes for children, especially overalls and jumpers. His factory was a series of lofts in the garment district, a place which Caleb, who had never been to the City, imagined to be an immense street fair where his father's products hung on tree branches along the edges of a country lane. This image stemmed from his assumption that his mother, whose poor hearing made her sometimes misspeak words, had meant to say 'garden' when she said 'garment.' So he envisioned City children strolling along, pointing out to their parents the knitted coats, or knickers, or bloomers, of their choice.

Emma added a few details to the history. With his profits Edmund Flowers had bought his bride a many-roomed, wide-verandaed, comfortable country house two hours by train from the City, in the poetically named seaside village of Far Rockaway. The children believed their father had provided them with the best house in the village. Five blocks from the ocean, it occupied the center of a pleasant quarter-acre of grass edged by very large old oak trees. In winter the house's shutters were closed against the cold and the stiff ocean winds, making a warm cocoon, almost a sheltering hollow, of the downstairs rooms.

In early May a carpenter came to hang fringed, dark green

canvas awnings over the veranda and the many windows. Now shielded from the summer sun, the rooms became cool caves into which, Emma's story to the children went, their father hurried after his hot days in the City and his dusty train ride to the country. On Friday nights he was always very late. Sometimes, he said, he had to remain in the City until early Saturday morning because of the pressure of work and his dislike of the overcrowded weekend trains.

At this point Emma's story always ceased. She provided her children with a very sparse autobiography and never hinted at her loneliness and disappointment during the early years of her marriage. Born in a crowded section of Brooklyn, she was the only child of aging parents who feared for her safety on the streets and wanted her with them whenever she was not in school. Although they were Methodists, they sent her to St. Ignatius's high school because it offered her strong discipline, an education in Latin and History, and the appearance of morality.

Emma's few acquaintances in her class admired her good looks and Protestant freedom from the strictures of catechism instruction. They envied her flair for Reading and Latin, but rarely was she invited home to their parties or study sessions. She was an amiable, good-natured girl who taught herself to disguise her hurts at rejection by her classmates because her parents were so clearly pleased always to have her with them.

Emma McDermott had great expectations. She accepted her isolated existence with the calm born of her fantasies. She agreed with the nuns who taught her that the best callings for a young woman of her unfortunate Methodist origins were marriage and motherhood. After graduating first in her high school class, she was offered a position (as she termed it) as secretary to the head of a company that specialized in the manufacture and selling of corsets for ladies of fleshy propor-

19

tions. She herself was slender, so she found her eight-year-long employment at Figurine Emporium for Undergarments a source of income and some amusement.

In a few years her parents died, within weeks of each other, and she was then free to begin her hungry search for a husband who would be her companion, her friend, her support, and, if need be, her lover.

Emma's work in the garment district served her well. It was there that she met Edmund Flowers, seated beside her at a lunch counter where, by chance, they both ordered the same things—egg-salad sandwiches and Dr. Peppers—and then turned to smile at each other at the coincidence. By the time of their encounter Edmund had advanced to vice-president of Flowers and Sons.

Good-looking, ambitious, and more hardworking than any of his five brothers, by the time of his marriage Edmund was favored by his aging father to head the flourishing company. Edmund assured Emma that he made a very good salary and was regularly 'putting a fair amount away' for the future. As a wedding present his father turned the company over to his industrious son and happily retired to weekends at Belmont Park racetrack, and late afternoons at Mulligan's Bar and Grill.

At the start, Emma considered her life with Edmund perfection itself. If his demands upon her at night, after the children were put to bed and their late dinner consumed, when she wished to sleep and he wished her to serve his nightly needs, were at first tiring, painful, and unrewarding, she tried to hide the fact from him and from herself. She submitted to his invasions, regarding these inconveniences as a small price for his provision of the good life she enjoyed.

But after a while, awakened slowly to the pleasures he provided, almost unwittingly, she began to enjoy lovemaking, and then to be eager for it, a contributor to it. In addition, she loved

Edmund for their fine house, and for her long, satisfying, empty days in the porch swing or on the sofa while a lady from the village cleaned the house and prepared the meals. On warm afternoons in summer, she read the sentimental novels that she borrowed from the lending library and cared for the flowers that grew in beds in the back garden. She was especially fond of the hydrangeas growing around the house; at their base she planted and watered pansies and nasturtiums, hardy blooms that required little care.

All in all, her life was effortless, her husband generous and uncritical. To be sure, his absence from early morning to late evening was a contribution to her comfort, to her fondness for lazy inactivity. Of all this, of course, she said nothing to her children. She told them only that they had all lived in this same house since she and their father had married. Her account always ended with the same coda:

'And then the Great War was coming. It was already on in Europe. And your father volunteered to be a soldier. . . .

'You were just a baby, Caleb. And Kate came very soon after.'

She did not add that their father was twenty-four when he joined the Army, and she was almost thirty.


As the children were to remember their early years, until the summer before the Crash, they were without incident, serene and private, composed of sun-filled days, soft, late dusks, croquet games on the lawn with Moth, evenings on the veranda looking out at the lawn lit with fireflies, and hydrangea heads lazily awaiting the arrival of moonlight.

Always the children spent their evenings together. Although they were unconscious of their seclusion, they enjoyed it. They were shielded from interruption and close observation by their mother's deafness. Most of the time it shut her off from what she expected to be childish conversations in which she had no interest.

Occasionally it occurred to her that, even during the school year, they never brought friends home from school. Caleb said the boys in his class were interested in nothing but playing hockey, trading baseball cards, and building racing cars out of old wheels and fruit crates.

'Aren't you interested in those things?' his mother asked, having no idea of what properly constituted a boy's recreation. Vaguely, she wanted Caleb to be like other boys. There must be a standard way of being a boy, she thought. But having no brothers, and having been educated by nuns throughout her school years; she had always found the male experience a mystery. It never occurred to her that Caleb was more like Kate in temperament and interests than the boys who skated or bicycled by their house on the way to the sandlot or the beach.

Occasionally she wondered about her children's absorption in each other. But their mutual contentment made life easier for her. So she put the question aside. There was no extra cooking to do for friends they might have invited. She never had to strain to hear the high, sharp voices of other children, and, in fact, since she had few friends of her own, there were no unaccustomed sounds to break the bland tenor of her days. Naturally reclusive and self-absorbed, she never inquired into the content of her children's lives. To do so, she thought, might disturb their comfortable familial peace.


In the evenings, to seem more companionable than she felt, Emma sat near her children in order to appear to be listening to their conversation. Rarely could she catch very much of it. The children would lie on their stomachs on the living-room rug, their heads in their cupped hands, their shoulders almost touching. Now and then their legs swept the air, and they murmured to each other, like actors rehearsing their parts. Emma noticed that their eyes often closed as they spoke as though they had entered another world and were imagining a foreign geography and encounters with unearthly people.

Caleb was an avid reader of the *New York Herald Tribune,* the newspaper his mother brought home every day from the village cigar store. The paper was always a day late, but she did not mind, and Caleb never noticed. He was indifferent to the news of the world or the nation or the City unless it pertained to particular persons, heroes and murderers, presidents and generals, titans of industry, starlets and movie moguls. What he read during the day he summarized for his sister and his mother at the dinner table. He excelled in combining stories so that details from one were cunningly inserted into another. This creative act transformed dull newspaper fact into lively personal fiction. Emma strained to hear his recountings, and Kate smiled with pleasure, accepting without question his résumés of human-interest stories, knowing that, later, they would serve as subject matter for their private games.

It was a warm evening in late June, just after the arrival of the summer children on Linden Street. Emma sat near her children reading *Sorrell and Son,* a novel she had obtained after a long wait from Stark's lending library. Warwick Deeping was her favorite writer; she had read all of his many novels at least twice. But this evening her attention to the book flagged. She concentrated on listening to her children's conversation.

Caleb asked Kate: 'Were you flying the plane, Amelia?'

'No, Charles. I was the passenger.'

'But weren't you the first to fly over the ocean?'

23

'No. *You* were. I was the first *woman.*'

'Yes, of course, I forgot. The first woman.'

A long pause.

Then Caleb asked: 'Was the weather bad the whole way?'

'Oh yes, it was. Especially over Newfoundland. The weather is always terrible there. And then over the mighty Atlantic. I hated that part of the trip. Thirty-three and a half hours. And then we landed in Wales. It was very foggy and very wet. We could hardly see the landing field.'

'Oh, I know. It was like that in Paris when I came down there two years ago.'

Silence. It was as if they had lost themselves in the high adventure of the past and did not know how to get back into the present. When they spoke again their voices were low: Emma surrendered to her deafness. As it was, she had not heard enough of their talk to understand its references. She opened *Sorrell and Son* at her place and began to read. Caleb's voice dropped to a whisper.

'Don't you think famous aviators like us ought to be married to each other, Amelia?'

Kate smiled and reached over to put her hand on Caleb's shoulder. She whispered:

'Yes, I do. I do. We would be the most famous flying couple in the whole world. But I think I'm married already.'

Caleb tried to remember what he had read about Amelia Earhart's life. Was she married? He had no idea. In his reconstructions from newspapers, details like this were often moved from one story to another to make the truth serve his inventions. He whispered:

'You are not married. You are going to marry me. We'll fly two planes across the Atlantic, one after the other, but very close together. This time we'll go the other way, from Le Bourget to New York. Round trips, for both of us, when you add the two together.'

'How long will that take?'

'A day and a half, like the last time, if the weather and the winds are with us.'

'Who will lead?'

'I will. I know the way.'

Kate said nothing. Caleb took her silence for agreement. He went on:

'There'll be a huge crowd waiting for us at Roosevelt Field. As it was two years ago in Paris. Only this time there'll be banners with our names on them.'

'Both our names?'

'Sure. They'll read, "Welcome Charles and Amelia Lindbergh."'

Kate sighed at the obliteration of her famous last name. But she decided to accept the inevitable demotion and dwell on the pleasures of the event.

'It will be wonderful,' she said. 'I can't wait.'


It is another warm evening. They sit on the veranda after supper. The bloated white faces of hydrangea bushes on each side of the steps shine up at them in the moonlight. Emma occupies the swing. Stretched out on the coarse hemp rug, the children are filled with unexpressed contentment. Once again they are renewing the ritual of their happy lives with their absorbed, silent mother.

Emma gets up.

'I must do my needlepoint by a better light,' she says, and goes inside.

Relieved of her presence, although they always feel sure she hears very little of what they say to each other when she is near, Kate and Caleb move to the swing and take up their game.

Caleb creates their fictions. Kate listens, learns her assigned part, and feels pleased that her brother gives her a role. Often, persuaded by the bare facts of their mother's often-repeated history, they start their pretending by assuming they are happily married to each other.

Caleb begins: 'Now about our daughter, the Samoan child ...'

At dinner Emma had told them about a book review she had read in the *Tribune*. It was of a book by a lady who had lived among the Polynesians, a native people who wore almost no clothes.

Caleb's foot pushes on the floor to keep the swing moving. He asks Kate if she thinks their daughter—he calls her Polly—would consider covering herself with a blouse if they brought her from the South Seas to Far Rockaway. For some time, before the light dies away and Emma sends them upstairs, they debate the virtues and the dangers of permitting Polly to be partially unclothed in public. Would she lead a happy life playing croquet on Larch Street or walking down Main Street with them to get ice cream?

When Emma calls to them that it is bedtime, they make no protest. They kiss their mother and climb the stairs, Caleb leading the way. Taking advantage of the unlocked door between their bedrooms, they meet in Kate's room and lie side by side, fully clothed, on her bed. They continue the discussion of South Sea Island customs. But verbal invention does not satisfy them for very long. To illustrate the reality of their story, Caleb removes his blouse and undershirt and Kate her blouse and chemise. With pleasure, they inspect each other's similar flat chests. Caleb's small pink nipples are surrounded by golden hairs. Kate wets her finger and teases them into wayward patterns. Tickled, Caleb laughs and squirms but does not remove her hand.

Once Kate has replaced the little hairs, they begin to explore the intricacies of each other's ears. They play with their hands, admiring the elegance of their long fingers and pale, tapered nails. Entwining their legs, they raise their heads to examine their straight toes, their slender knees, the tender, inner curves of their ankles. Lying down again, they turn their attention to the little bunched fleshy knobs of their elbows and then the fine lines of their identical blond eyebrows.

Out of an unexpressed delicacy, the regions between their thighs remain untouched. They acknowledge a reticence about the single difference of which they are aware. It is that, but it is more. They do not wish to acknowledge any variation in their bodies that might distinguish them from each other. United by birth little more than a year apart, and by the circumstance of a single, uninvolved parent, into what seems to them a twinned sensibility, their love enables them to think of themselves as alike.

All this gentle, limited exploration, these excursions into the shallow declivities of their bodies, are accompanied by low, wordless sounds of pleasure. The two are amazed by the discovery of their physical similarities. The realization always delights Kate, who thinks it a wonderment that her body, inferior in strength to her brother's, should resemble his so closely in every other way. And Caleb: for him these nightly reminders of his sister's likeness to him are to become the foundation of his burgeoning sexuality. Those he will seek out and love as a young man will be like Kate in their slenderness, their small-boned elegance, their soft, blond hair and skin.

So it was in late June of 1929 that the Flowers children made their new friends from the City. School had provided them with few congenial companions, and the neighbors on their street were elderly, or childless couples or spinsters and bachelors.

Emma thought perhaps Kate and Caleb's preference for each other had discouraged children from approaching them.

Their new friends, Lionel Schwartz, whom they called Lion despite the unsuitability of the nickname to his gentle nature and small, unassertive frame, and Roslyn Hellman, were vacationing a street away. The four children discovered each other almost at once, the way children do, by means of an uncanny, generational sense that made them move toward one another.

No such attraction operated among the adults. They made no efforts to become acquainted. Emma thought:

'Summer renters. From the sound of their names they must be Jewish. I have no reason to get to know them.'

But she was pleased for her children. This summer, she decided, it would be good for them to have playmates other than themselves. Comfortable as she found their contented exclusivity, occasionally she wondered about it. Then she dismissed her moment of concern as foolish. She knew she preferred having them always at home with her and with each other. Their quiet mutuality suited her own fondness for quiet and order. But still . . .

Roslyn Hellman was a little older than Caleb. She was taller and more solidly built. Her straight black hair reached down her back to her waist, her eyes were large and black, her nose was high-bridged and prominent, giving her an air of natural superiority. She had spent the summer before at a girls' camp in the Catskills, where she had acquired a taste for playing the main part in the Saturday-night plays and an active dislike of all sports on land and in the water if she was not selected as captain.

Almost from her first day in Far Rockaway, Roslyn became the leader of the children in their games, the self-appointed president of their club. Indeed, it had been her idea to form a club, which she named 'the Talkies,' a word she came upon in the *New York Times* to describe a new kind of motion picture. When they were all together, in midmorning, and seated cross-legged in a circle on the Hellmans' grass, she would call the Talkies to order and announce the game for the day. This strict scheduling she had learned from the head counselor at her camp. She found that coming to the circle with a plan awed the others. She would allow no challenge to her choice of entertainment. Only Caleb occasionally got up his courage to question her authority. But in the long run her firm posture of certainty defeated him.

Lionel, the youngest of the four, was shy. His hair, eyebrows, and lashes were white, as if even slight coloration would appear to be too assertive. If he had not been so young he would have been taken for an albino or regarded as a child struck a great blow by the sun. He was almost a head shorter than Roslyn. Perhaps because of this disparity, or it may have been her manner of superiority, she was the object of his unquestioning admiration. The two had been friends in the City. They lived in the same apartment house on West Eighty-sixth Street and played stoopball against the facade of their building. In the late spring they squatted in the little square of earth that surrounded the plane tree to the side of their doorway and aimed their immies against a root in hopes that they would rebound and strike another marble out of the square. It was Roslyn, with her natural sense of the ironic, who had nicknamed him Lion. She relished his willingness to be her obedient follower.

Their fathers both worked 'in the market' in the City, Roslyn informed the Flowers children. Lion phrased it differently:

'My father works on the Street,' he told them.

Kate had no idea what sort of work was done in these places. She wondered whether there could be different names for the same place. Perhaps Roslyn's father sold cod and haddock and mackerel; the fish market on Central Avenue owned by Mr. Elderly was the only kind of market she had ever seen. She pictured Mr. Hellman wrapping a flounder in damp newspapers for a customer to take home and keep fresh in the cold water of the bathtub. This, of course, was what Moth always did. She kept it captive there all day until it was time to decapitate it, remove the scales and tail, and bake it in the oven. Kate told Caleb she wondered if the bathtubs in Roslyn's house were filled with fish.

Caleb knew better. He had read about the stock market in the business section of the *Tribune* and he knew that men traded there with each other, although he was not sure what changed hands on Wall Street. Kate thought his explanation of the words most unlikely. She had already conjured up a vision of Mr. Schwartz's street work: he must empty trash-filled gutters with a large dustpan and broom into a tin garbage container on wheels that he pushed ahead of him through the fish markets. Caleb said both surmises were foolish. Men who dressed every morning in black suits and brown fedoras and drove to their work in a touring car did not sell fish or clean streets. Of course, he said, they could be gangsters who went from street to street, and market to market, forcing merchants at gunpoint to pay for protection. He had read about Al Capone in Chicago, whose gang had 'rubbed out' seven members of the Moran gang in a dispute over just such matters: 'turf warfare' it was called.

Whatever it was the fathers did, they left together every weekday morning and returned, saying they felt dusty and weary, and needing a rest and a bath, in the late afternoon. Then Caleb and Kate knew it was time for them to leave the broad lawns that stretched across the two houses on Linden Street and walk under darkening oak branches and colorless sky around the corner to their own house. There they waited in the swing until dinnertime, holding hands, relieved to be alone

30

together, absorbed in themselves and each other.

At dinner they told their mother that Mr. Schwartz had brought Lion a tennis racket from the City. Emma was silent. Then she said she regretted they did not have a father to come home to them bearing presents. The children left their chairs to come around the table. They hugged her from either side and assured her it did not matter in the least to them. She was a good father as well as a good mother, Caleb told her. Emma was pleased by the tribute. She hugged them and called them 'my angels.'


Soon after their arrival on Linden Street that summer, Roslyn and Lionel invented a private means of communication between their houses. Across a narrow strip of grass, their bedroom windows faced each other. They strung picture wire through the bottoms of round Mothers Oats containers. By means of these cardboard receivers they conversed for a while after their bedtimes.

Lionel's shy voice, ordinarily very light and segueing to a whisper at the end of his sentences, became strong while speaking on their wire, much as adult users of the early telephone shouted because they did not understand the operation of sound waves and wire. Roslyn and Lionel spoke very loudly despite their belief that their system worked well. So they heard each other clearly over the distance, permitting them to confide secrets they would not have shared under ordinary conditions, unaware that their parents, enjoying the cool air on their porches, listened to the innocent revelations of their children, smiling at their charming confidences.

After a week of playing together, Roslyn and Lionel spent an afternoon on the veranda of the Flowerses' house reading books from Caleb's collection. Their telephone call that evening centered on their curiosity about their new friends.

'They don't have a father, do they?'

'I don't know,' said Roslyn. 'I've never seen one.'

'Are they orphans?' Lionel had always considered orphans to be both fortunate and very romantic.

'I suppose. My cousin Jean's father is dead and my mother always calls her *that poor orphaned child.*'

'Their mother is very queer, isn't she? All that time out there in the sun on the porch and it was *hot* and she never asked us in, only kept bringing out that sour lemonade and cookies and then going in herself.'

Roslyn said yes, she was very queer. 'I said "How do you do" when Caleb introduced us, but she never said anything. Or even after that. Do you suppose she's deaf and dumb?'

'*I* don't know. Maybe. Caleb kept going up to his room to get his books. I wanted to see his room and his other books. I didn't bring many books from home, did you?'

'Not too many. There wasn't room in the car.'

Roslyn had struck a sympathetic note. Lionel was quick to agree:

'There never is, for my stuff.'

They were silent for a minute, and then Roslyn said: 'I like Caleb a lot, don't you?'

'Oh yes. But I like Kate too.' Lionel thought a moment and then, aware that his declaration might hurt his older friend's feelings, he raised his voice: 'But I like you best of all.'

Roslyn smiled, decided this was a satisfactory time to end the call, said: 'Night, Lion,' and removed the Mothers Oats carton from her ear. It had been a nice day, she thought; she was ready, at last, to go to bed.


The Talkies Club spent some warm afternoons at the beach under Emma's care. She could not rest easy at home if Roslyn were left in charge, as Mrs. Hellman had suggested to her daughter. All the children played too close to the water, she believed, and ventured too far out into the surf. Mrs. Schwartz and Mrs. Hellman disliked the noisy, uninteresting ocean and the dangerous sun. They were satisfied to trust their children to an adult, even so odd a one as Mrs. Flowers, from the reports of their children, seemed to be.

'Behave yourselves,' they told Roslyn and Lionel. Then they went back into the cool parlor of one house or another to talk about their relatives, their husbands, their prospective fall wardrobes that they hoped to find at Russek's or Franklin Simon's, and the pleasures of the City in the season to come. In the comfortable release of a few hours away from their children they drank sugared hot tea from tall glasses, believing that such drinks in summer were cooling. Mrs. Schwartz was much preoccupied with considering the merits of a caracul coat versus a beaver one. Her husband had promised her a new fur for her birthday.

At a short distance from the sea, Emma sat in a low wood-slatted chair. The children played at the edge. To shield her skin from the sun she held a broad black umbrella that had belonged to her husband. Her black silk bathing dress was covered, from wrist to ankle, by a full black blouse and long skirt. She took no chances of revealing her body to a passing glance or her face to the ruinous sun. Her hand was posed on her forehead to shade her eyes from the glare. The children were in her sight.

Caleb and Roslyn played in the surf, leaping over small waves and splashing through the water, pretending to be the heroic rescuers of the hapless victims of waterfalls, storms, and floods. They quickly tired of the weightlessness of their nonexistent sufferers and took the parts themselves, Caleb the drowning boy, Roslyn the brave lifeguard. This game entertained them for some time, until Caleb complained that his head ached from being dragged up on the beach by his hair.

Lionel disliked violent activities like drowning and forcible saving. He spent his time constructing houses in the wet sand while Kate crouched down to watch him.

'Why don't you build castles?' she asked him.

'I like domestic architecture,' he said loftily. 'This is a single-story beach house, ranch style. It'll have many porches and fireplaces in every room.'

Roslyn and Caleb had come over to watch. They were irritated by the horizontal character of Lionel's structure and the absence of dripped-sand towers. So they noted with pleasure the arrival of the tide that wiped out the sand veranda facing the sea. Then they turned back to the ocean.

Standing in the water to her ankles, Roslyn called the Talkies over to her side. She announced that she had decided they now were all to pretend they were lemmings. She would be their queen.

'What is a lemming?' asked Kate.

Roslyn said she knew all about lemmings; she had been reading about them in *The Book of Knowledge*.

'They're little rodents, like mice, and brown-colored. They live in Norway and Sweden. When there are too many of them, for some reason no one knows why, they start moving across the land, eating everything in their way. Some of them are eaten along the way by other animals. But some survive and go on until they arrive . . .'

Roslyn raised her arms dramatically toward the horizon.

'. . . at the sea!'

'Can they swim?' asked Lionel.

'I think so. In shallow water, I guess. But even if they can't, they're so brave they plunge into the water as if they were still walking on land. They go out so far that they all drown. Not a single one is left.'

'Do they know they are going to drown when they go into the water?' asked Caleb.

'How would I know that?'

The three children stood looking at Roslyn, trying not to believe in the truth of her tragic story.

Caleb said: 'How do you know they have a queen?'

Roslyn had invented the part about the ruler of the lemmings. But her quick wits saved her. 'Well, they're like bees in that way. *They* have a queen, don't they?'

'Why should you be the queen?'

'Because I want to lead you all into the ocean to see if you will drown.'

'Not me,' said Caleb. 'I can swim.'

Lionel said: 'I can't. I haven't learned yet.'

Kate said nothing. She was afraid to play the game. But she knew if Caleb followed Roslyn into the ocean she would go in too. Nothing would part her from him, not for a moment. She thought her courage would keep her afloat, or perhaps maintain her at a depth just above her head, or she would be instantly granted the swimming skill she wanted so badly. And if not, Caleb would not let her drown. Of that she was certain.


In the hot sun, Emma dozed off 'for a mere second,' she later told herself. A wheeling gull above her head woke her with its shrill cry. She sat up abruptly and looked for the children. Roslyn's black head was immediately visible. Then she saw Caleb kneeling beside her, his hair dark with water. Both were bent over examining something at the edge of the sea. Then she saw Lionel sitting cross-legged, looking down. Kate was not to be seen.

Emma ran, ignoring the pull of her long skirt. She reached the end of the sand and saw Kate stretched out, her eyes closed and water running from the side of her mouth. Caleb held her hand and with his other rubbed her forehead.

Emma screamed and pushed Caleb and Roslyn aside as she bent to pick up her daughter. Kate opened her eyes, looked up at Emma, spat out water, and then smiled weakly.

'Hello, Moth,' she said.

'What happened, Caleb?' Emma said.

Roslyn said: 'It was her fault. She was a terrible lemming.'

Caleb turned on her angrily. 'She was *not*. It was all your dumb idea. You had to be a queen.'

Emma wrapped Kate in her skirt, exposing her own bathing dress for the first time in many summers. Kate squirmed impatiently in her arms, wanting to be put down, but Emma insisted on carrying her. The other children trailed behind her shouting recriminations at each other, but Emma was unable to hear what they were saying.

'Why didn't she *say* she was afraid of the water? How could I know that?' Roslyn's voice was harsh with fright.

'She's *not* afraid. She just can't swim. Like Lion.'

'Yeah, but he didn't go in. He's not stupid.'

'*You're* stupid, stupid. Very, *very* stupid. And so are lemmings stupid. Maybe you read it wrong. Maybe they go the other way.'

'What do you mean, "go the other way"?'

'Maybe they come out of the ocean for no reason, like hermit crabs, so they won't drown. Even you could be wrong, you know.'

Emma carried Kate back to the chair and sat down, still holding her in her lap. She threw Caleb a towel. Roslyn and Lionel found their towels. For a few moments everyone was silent, occupied with drying off. Emma rubbed Kate so hard she began to cry. Caleb watched them. At this moment Kate seemed fragile to him, almost babylike. His throat ached as he

36

looked at her. Then he knelt down beside her and took her hand. 'Don't cry, Kate. It's over. You're okay. You didn't drown.'

'I'm not crying about that.' She tried to get off her mother's lap, but Emma held her tight.

'No, stay still.' Emma was angry with herself for not having watched her children more closely, and at Caleb for not taking care of Kate when Roslyn, she had surmised, suggested some dangerous game or other.

'Why didn't you stop her?'

'I didn't see her go in. She was behind me.'

Emma put Kate down and took up the wooden chair. They all walked slowly through the sand to a row of narrow, upright bathhouses resembling gray privies at the edge of the beach. Roslyn and Lionel went ahead to where they had left their clothes. Emma and Kate went into the one beside them, Caleb into the other. He pulled off his wet suit. On the other side of the wall he could hear Kate singing 'Apples and oranges and lemmings' over and over.

When the children had changed, Emma still wearing her long wet skirts, which embarrassed her by clinging to her legs, they went to where Roslyn and Lionel were waiting at the Rockaway Beach Boulevard crossing. Without a word to each other they walked to Linden Street. Emma waved to the two mothers on the Schwartzes' veranda, took Kate and Caleb by their hands, and turned back toward Larch Street.

At their driveway she said: 'Are you feeling better, Kate?'

'Yes. But I didn't feel that bad. It wasn't anything. I just swallowed some water, that's all. Caleb and Roslyn pulled me out right away.'

The afternoon ended in reconciliation. Emma hugged Caleb and said: 'Thank you.' Caleb kissed Kate's cold, salty lips and said: 'I'm glad you're okay.' Kate kissed him back and said nothing.

That evening Emma insisted they come early into the warm parlor. She was fearful that Kate had got chilled by the salt water. The children assumed their usual posture on the floor, disappointed that they could not go on with their new pretend-in-progress about the monk and the nun. But their mother's clinging presence—after her fright at the beach, Emma felt the need to stay close to her children—caused them, instinctively, to suspend their play. They sensed that the content of this new game was not for her ears. In fact, they believed it unlikely that anyone else, even someone as dear as their Moth, would ever be able to understand the nature and intensity of their pretending, just as they were quite certain that their delicate exploratory night unions should be kept secret from everyone, forever.

They settled for a more acceptable game. Caleb took the white endpaper from the library book he had been reading. He tore it in half and, holding the ends between his thumb and first finger, carefully compressed them into a small roll and handed it, ceremonially, to Kate. Then he made another for himself.

'Thank you so much,' she said. 'I was hoping to have a smoke. What brand are these?'

'Lucky Strikes, I think. Light up, Kate.' He held an imaginary lighter to the end of her rolled paper and then lit his own. He breathed deeply and blew a ring of invisible smoke.

'Would you care for one?' he asked his mother.

'What was that?'

'Would you care for a cigarette?'

Emma took note of theirs and said: 'I won't use yours up. I'll smoke my own.' Pleased to be included in their game, she put a Camel cigarette into her ivory holder and lit it with her lighter.

Smoking companionably, the three sat and talked about the sunny weather they had been having. For a while no one mentioned the accident of the afternoon.

38

But then Emma said: 'Caleb. You mustn't always do what Roslyn tells you.' She had spent much of the long silences at supper with her children planning a lecture to her son. She intended to impress upon him that his male seniority should make him more vigilant of his sister.

'And also, you must not let Kate follow her.'

'I won't. I won't let her. I'm sorry.'

In this brief exchange, Emma had exhausted her energy for recriminations. No one said anything for a few moments. Caleb knew his mother was quite right. He had not acted in a proper, brotherly, protective way. But still: he then felt it necessary to defend to his mother the reasonableness of what they had pretended at the sea, the logic of emulating lemming behavior to the letter if they were going to play at all. Roslyn had made that clear to them, he said.

'Not to do so would violate the laws of nature,' he told her. Loyalty to Roslyn required him, almost against his will, to defend their leader against parental criticism. He put away the thought that, a few hours ago, he had angrily told Roslyn she might be entirely wrong about what she had read.


That evening Roslyn pulled on the wire until Lionel shouted: 'Yes, what is it?' into his cardboard receiver.

Roslyn shouted back: 'Kate's some dummy, isn't she? Walking in like that.'

'You told her to.'

'Sure. But she didn't have to do it.'

Lionel said nothing for a few seconds. Then he said:

'She almost drowned.'

'She did not. I saved her. And Caleb helped. She's a real dope is what she is.'

On their veranda, seated beneath the mock telephone wire, the Hellmans gasped.

39

The next day Caleb and Kate did not go over to play with the children on Linden Street. They walked into the village with their mother and watched while she examined the new books on the library shelf. Caleb read the jackets of a few and thought Emma should take out a book about children who are captured by pirates in the West Indies. Emma thought it sounded too much like a children's book. But she accepted his suggestion, and added it to *Magnificent Obsession* by Lloyd Douglas, a writer she had not heard of before.

'What is an obsession?' Kate asked Emma.

'What?' asked Emma, using her deafness to play for time.

'An *obsession.*'

'Er . . . something that fills your mind so completely that you can think of nothing else.' Emma looked at Kate as she spoke, suddenly remembering herself at that age when she could think of nothing but becoming a nun and living in what she imagined would be the happy, warm seclusion of a convent.

'Did you ever have an obsession?' Kate asked.

'No,' said Emma firmly.

In the afternoon, while Emma took her customary nap to escape the heat, Caleb and Kate sat on the swing. Kate's head rested on Caleb's shoulder. He read to her from the beginning of *A High Wind in Jamaica*. He had persuaded Emma to let him borrow the book, from which now he was preparing a scenario for some future pretend session. From the idyllic picture of young contentment they presented to any spectator who might have passed by, there was no way of knowing that Caleb was planning cruelty and carnage of the highest order.

One night, weary from an afternoon of hopscotch and king of the hill and hide and seek with Roslyn and Lionel, the brother and sister lay resting on Kate's bed curled in each other's arms. They had decided to embark on a new pretense. In a collection of tales by an Irish writer that Caleb had found in the library was the story of tragic lovers, his favorite subject. At once he recognized its dramatic possibilities. The parts seemed ideal for them. They played at being Héloïse and Peter Abelard until they could no longer stay awake.

The next day, having spent a long afternoon at the beach by themselves with Moth (the parents of Roslyn and Lion had decided it would be wiser if their children did not go swimming unless their fathers were free on the weekend to accompany them), the tired Flowers children ate an early supper, carrying on their usual quiet dialogue. Silent and still absorbed in the Charles Morgan novel she had been reading, and, as usual, unable to hear them clearly, Emma at first made no effort to listen.

'Do you mind being shut away like that in a cell?' Caleb asked Kate. She folded her hands prayerfully and said:

'No, I don't, Peter, not too much. The bed is narrow but quite comfortable. And,' she added, 'I have a very good pillow.'

Caleb shook his head. 'I don't think they have such things in nunneries, do you? I think they sleep on boards.'

Kate accepted this correction as she did all of Caleb's instructions.

'Well, okay. But the board is very comfortable, thank you. I hope you will be able to get out of your monastery to visit me."

There was silence while Caleb tried to think of whether that would be possible given the strictures of his housing.

Changing the subject abruptly, as they often did when the imaginative potentials of their stories, for the time being, were exhausted, they began to talk about Roslyn. She interested Caleb most when they had been apart for some days. He told Kate he admired Roslyn's learning.

'She can think up interesting things to do.'

41

Kate said she didn't find Roslyn so interesting. 'In fact,' she said, 'I think she's boring. Very *boring.*'

'Boring?' Caleb's voice was loud with irritation. 'Not at all. *I* think she's very much like Héloïse.'

Emma, startled, heard him. *'Who?'* Héloïse was a personage who had been much discussed by the nuns in her high school.

Caleb sensed danger and hesitated. But he could think of no way out of an explanation.

'I meant Peter Abelard's lady Héloïse, who went into a nunnery after her husband was taken captive by her uncle and some other evil men. She was brave and very smart, like Roslyn.'

'What have you been reading, that you know about her?'

'There's a story about her in *The Book of Knowledge*. She lived in the Middle Ages. I don't know exactly when that was, but it was quite long ago.' Caleb had the feeling that temporal distance might reconcile his mother to their absorption in the tale.

'What else did you read . . . about those two?'

'Only that when the evil men caught up with Abelard "they perpetrated a most brutal mutilation upon him." '

*'What?* What did you say?'

' "A brutal mutilation upon him," the book said. I guess that means they cut off his hand or his ear, something like that. It could not have been his tongue. They did that to people in the Middle Ages when they were heretics. But Peter Abelard became a monk and went on teaching religion and philosophy for a very long time, so it could not have been his tongue.'

Emma was aghast. But she said nothing, unable to formulate a suitable reproach to an innocent boy of twelve, no matter how precocious.

Caleb continued to praise Roslyn. Kate grew resentful that she should be so admired by her beloved brother. Héloïse indeed. When they were finally upstairs alone together, she told him she felt jealous. Quickly, he reassured her. *She* was the only person he loved.

'Except for Moth, of course. I *do* love her.'

'And you like Roslyn, just *like* her?'

'I admire her. She's so forceful and strong . . . like a boy.'

'And I'm like a girl, I suppose. Weak and . . .'

'No, you're like me, something in between. Whatever that is.'

Caleb reached over to caress the warm, damp crook in Kate's arm. She found the same place in his. It was cool and dry. Their gentle, amorous play began. Lingering at one place, they advanced slowly to the same places on each other's bodies. As always, their explorations ended in giggles, which they tried to suppress for fear Moth would hear them and come up to find that Caleb was not asleep in his own bed.

Soberly they began again, playing follow-the-leader to their underarms, then to the transparent slings of flesh between their fingers, then to the delicate declivities in their bellies, identical in form and depth, as if a branched umbilicus had held them at the same time attached to their mother.

Deaf to most sounds above her head, Emma had caught their laughter. She called to them to go to sleep; she could not tell that they were together. Caleb kissed Kate on her narrow lips. He raised her hand to kiss it as had seen an actor playing a Frenchman do in the movies.

'Good night, Sister Héloïse,' he whispered. Reluctantly he climbed off the bed and left, closing the door between their rooms, and got into his own bed. If he had not worried that Emma would come upstairs in a little while 'to tuck them in,' as she always described it, even in summer when they slept on top of their sheets with no covering, he would have stayed in Kate's bed, his arms around her shoulders, his tongue licking the salt from her eyelids, and then exploring the lovely wet

43

folds of her neck and ears, imagining they were her secret, soft place where he had not yet been.

For two days in late July it rained constantly, a slanting, gentle summer rain that kept the children indoors. On the second afternoon they met in the Schwartzes' parlor. Mrs. Schwartz had set up a card table and then retired next door to visit Rose Hellman.

The children played Slapjack and I Doubt You and then Hearts until they were all tired out by the fierce competition and the accusations of cheating that the losers threw at the winners.

Lionel put the cards back in their box. They all sat, their hands idle on the table, wondering what to do next. Suddenly Lionel said into the air, to no one in particular:

'Do you believe in God?'

Kate was too startled to answer. She had never heard the question raised before and assumed all such belief was universal. Caleb considered a reply. Roslyn said, with firm conviction:

'Certainly not.'

'Why not?' Lionel asked. 'Didn't He make us?'

'*Make us?*' Roslyn repeated, her voice filled with scorn for the very words. 'How would anyone need to make us when we were *made* by our fathers and mothers?'

Lionel: 'Well, how did they do that?'

Roslyn (scornfully): 'Oh, you know.'

Lionel: 'No, I don't. Tell me.'

Roslyn: 'Your father pushes his cock into the hole in your mother's bottom . . .'

Lionel (agitated): 'His . . . *cock?*'

Roslyn (impatiently): 'Oh, for goodness' sake, Lion. Don't

you know *anything*? His . . . his penis. Your pee-er.'

Lionel (defensively): '*I* know what a penis is. I didn't know it was called a . . . a cock.'

Roslyn: 'Yes. At least I heard a boy I know call it that. He even showed me his.'

Kate and Caleb sat silently during this interchange, looking from one speaker to the other as though they were watching a play.

Roslyn turned to Caleb. 'You know what a cock is, don't you?'

Caleb had never heard the term before. He said: 'Of course.'

Kate, equally ignorant, giggled. She decided to make a joke to hide her embarrassment.

'I think it's also a rooster. Like in the nursery rhyme with it: "Cock-a-doodle-doo." '

Everyone laughed. Lionel picked up the box of cards.

'Let's play another game of Hearts. I'll be Roslyn's partner.'

Kate and Caleb nodded, looked at each other, and smiled.


Some afternoons were cloudy, so there was no impetus to go to the beach. On one of these cloudy days, Caleb and Kate went around the block to the Hellmans' backyard, where, it being Saturday, Roslyn's father was outside, setting up a new cro-quet set he had brought from the City. The four children stood on the back steps watching him make his disjointed, ungainly way around the course, setting up the wickets. Roslyn whis-pered to the Flowers children that, as a boy, Max Hellman had lost his leg in a street accident. He had been hanging on to the grille at the back of a trolley car, stealing a ride, when he lost his grip and fell under the metal wheels of another trolley traveling behind. She told them that her father now wore a carved wooden leg which she very much admired.

'It straps onto his stump,' she said, and smiled, as though she thought this singular equipment raised him far above other fathers with the ordinary supply of two legs and feet.

'What's a stump?' asked Kate.

'The piece of his leg that's left. He doesn't even have a knee.'

'Oh,' said Kate. She shuddered and looked down at her small, pink joint.

'But I think the wooden leg was cut off too short. That's why he limps like that.'

Roslyn seemed to be warming to her subject, but Caleb and Kate wanted to hear no more and went down the steps to inspect the nine shining new wickets Mr. Hellman had erected. The wooden stakes had bright red stripes, with none of the flaking paint of the Flowerses' old set. The wickets were set far apart, the distances prescribed for the adult game.

Lion came across the lawn carrying the remains of a piece of divinity fudge, which he put into his mouth when he arrived at the first stake.

Roslyn said: 'I call the Talkies to order. First, we'll play singles.'

Kate and Lion stood together, eyeing the course. They could see that it was going to be very hard, and after their first strokes, it was clear that it was far more than they could manage. Their weak, choppy strokes brought their balls barely halfway to the next wicket. Roslyn decreed that they should play first, pretending it was a kindness to the younger players, but they soon understood the true reason: their balls were open targets for Roslyn and Caleb to foot them viciously toward some distant corner of the lawn. Roslyn's shots were bold, covering the distance but sometimes going far afield of the wicket for which she was aiming. Caleb had a smooth, fierce drive which came very close to his wicket. He won the first round easily.

Then Roslyn announced that they would team up, she of course with Caleb. He was secretly pleased with this suggestion, because, like Roslyn, he loved to win. But his concern for Kate and her inaccurate shots moved him to pity. So he ignored Roslyn's order and invited Kate to be his partner. She gave him her most delighted smile. Roslyn gritted her teeth at him.

Lion was glad to be Roslyn's partner, but unhappy at being assigned the black mallet, a color he hated. Roslyn preempted the blue, the color that always, by rule, led off. By this choice she knew she would make up for her partner's predictably limp shots.

The children used the vocabulary of the game professionally, having been instructed by Mr. Hellman. He was the resident expert on all games, despite his handicap. Kate and Lion loved to call out 'You're *dead* on my ball!' and 'I'm *alive* on yours!'

Lion was usually termed an *Aunt Emma,* the game's mysterious nomenclature for *coward.* Roslyn relished this designation of his timorous approach to his strokes and used it often. Kate liked to say she was *cleaning* herself when she finally drove her ball through the right wicket. Caleb's favorite was *tice shot,* a term he used to invite his opponents to aim at his ball, with the fervent hope they would miss and thus make them more available to his next, lethal shot.

The skill of the two younger players never matched their aptitude for the jargon. But they both enjoyed their alliances to the persons they most admired in the world. To be rescued from almost inevitable disgrace by Caleb's confident strokes was, for Kate, like feeling his hands under her as he pulled her from the surf. She thought of him as her savior in everything, forgetting Roslyn's hard hands tugging on her hair at the same time.

After the accident at the beach, croquet was the one activity

that held the four children together during the long succession
of late afternoons. They kept a running score that did not count
for much, for victory seesawed between the two teams. Pulling
their inept partners along after them, skillful Caleb and determined Roslyn felt they were playing alone against each other,
in hand-to-hand combat. They were handicapped but not
halted by their weak partners as they proceeded to 'peg out,'
the term they had been taught for victory.

Roslyn dubbed the series of games the Talkies Tournament
and announced it would be held annually in the summer.

In the dusk, hand in hand, Kate and Caleb walked home.
Kate was full of compliments for Caleb's accomplished playing; he was sympathetic to her valiant failure.

'You helped me a lot,' she said.

'Not so much. You were just *positioned* right."


On the Mothers Oats telephone, Roslyn berated Lion for what
she considered to be his willful awkwardness. Lion did not
respond. He wished Roslyn liked him better.

Then he thought better of his silence and shouted into the
cardboard receiver:

'You might have won, without me.'

'Right. But don't worry. I'll win tomorrow. I'll kill them.'

She spoke loudly, not trusting to the wire to convey her
determination. On their veranda the Hellmans smiled at their
daughter's resolution. Max Hellman sat back in his wicker
rocker, his left leg thrust out before him.

'She's a go-getter, that one,' he said.

'I guess so,' Rose Hellman said. 'She sure likes to win.'

'Nothing wrong with that. I like to win too.'

'But you're grown up, and in the market. She's a child, a *girl*.
Where will she use all that fierceness?'

'Maybe where I do. On the Street.'

'Are there any women brokers?'

'Not that I know of. Not yet. But who knows, there may be soon. Women can now vote and go to college. And look at the Yeomanettes in the Navy during the war.'

'Well, I can see Roslyn as a sailor, all right. But she's too impatient to be a broker. Too . . . too cocksure, I mean to say'

Max thought about this for a moment. Then he laughed and said:

'Well, no one is more cocksure than Lester Schwartz, God knows. And he's sure a success.'

'And so are you a success, for that matter,' said Rose. 'But you're gentler, thank God.'

Max rubbed his aching stump, and then took his wife's hand.

'That was a nice thing for you to say.'

Rose: 'Sometimes I worry about her. There's nothing feminine about her. Sometimes I think she should have been a boy. Then she could grow up to be a man like Lester.'

Max laughed. 'Do you suppose Lionel should have been our daughter and Roslyn the Schwartzes' son?'

'No, of course not. But still . . . heredity ought to count for something. There's no sign of either of us in Roslyn.'

'Not true. She's hard to manage. You always say I am.'

Enjoying the evening breeze and their uninterrupted time together, they stroked each other's hand. In silence they searched the surrounding darkness for one admirable characteristic of Roslyn's for which they might claim responsibility. Across the way, Lionel's voice had finally given out. It was quiet for a moment. They heard the children say good night to one another. An ocean breeze moved along Linden Street, bringing the odor of honeysuckle to the veranda. The little Amazon's parents pushed their chairs close together and held hands in the consoling stillness.

One Sunday afternoon, the last contest of wooden balls struck through wickets and against staunch posts ended badly. The Hellmans had gone across their lawn to play whist with the Schwartzes. Caleb roved widely, trying to prevent Roslyn from following him through the final wicket. The younger children, already out of contention, stood behind home stake to watch the victor's advance.

Caleb's second stroke was a fierce chop. His red ball flew up and struck Lionel hard on the side of his head, knocking him unconscious.

Kate's screams brought the four parents to the croquet field. Caleb sat on the grass patting Lionel's cheeks. Beside him, Roslyn clumsily wiped a small stream of blood from her partner's broken scalp with her handkerchief, spreading it so that it colored the blond hair on the side of his head. The boy was limp, and very pale.

'Oh, my God, he's dead,' Sadie cried. She threw herself on the grass to look at her son.

Lionel responded to the sound of his mother's voice by moving his head slightly.

'He's *not* dead,' Caleb said, almost in tears, 'Just knocked out. He's better now.'

'*He* did it, not me,' Roslyn shouted. 'The red ball hit him. Mine's blue. Lionel's is black. It was Caleb's red ball.'

Caleb's face was scarlet. 'I didn't mean it. My foot slipped when I was going through to the stake. I hit the ball wrong. It was a mistake.' He stood up and tried to hide his tears with his hand.

The Schwartzes paid no attention to the accusations and defenses. Lester picked Lionel up and said to Max Hellman:

'Start our car. We'll take him to the hospital in Cedarhurst.'

Sadie turned white. Nothing about the accident had affected her as keenly as the word *hospital*. In her childhood, both her parents had died in agony in St. Vincent's Hospital, the victims of a tenement fire. To her, all such places were charnel houses and entry into them put the seal of mortality on anyone unlucky enough to be taken there.

'Oh no,' she moaned.

Lionel's vision cleared. He focused on his mother's face, saw her distress, and heard the note of terror in her voice. He smiled at her.

'I'm okay, Mama.'

Concerned that Sadie might collapse, Rose took her arm.

'Come on to the car, Sadie. He's not badly hurt. The doctor will just check him for concussion.'

Confusion followed Sadie's swoon at the sound of another dire word. Roslyn helped her mother with Mrs. Schwartz, thinking how delicate the whole Schwartz family was, especially Lion, what a baby he was, really, almost like Kate. They were the ones who always got hurt, whatever it was they all played.

'There goes the Talkies Tournament,' she whispered glumly to Caleb, who stood beside her, his arm around his sister. The three watched as Lester carried Lionel across the driveway and Rose fanned Sadie, who regained consciousness almost as quickly as she had lost it.

Rose and Caleb helped Sadie to her feet. They all went in the direction of the Schwartzes' car, Sadie leaning heavily on Rose's arm. Max stood at the rear, holding open the door.

As for Kate: the spectacle of blood on her friend's white face, a pallid mother lying on the grass, colored balls and silver wickets knocked every which way on the usually orderly course, frightened her. She was unused to the mixture of adults and children, two naturally disjoined orders of persons hitherto kept happily separate in her mind. She tugged at Caleb's arm.

'I think we should go home. Moth will be wondering where we are. It's getting dark.'

Caleb agreed.


They reported to Emma that Lion was all right now but had been, as Kate told her, foolishly, 'almost dead.' Emma blanched, her arm around Kate. She pulled her close, recalling the the seaside incident.

'No more croquet,' she said. 'I think it's a dangerous game for children.'

'He was okay when we left,' Caleb said.

'But you said they were taking him to the hospital.'

'For checking,' Caleb said in his most adult voice. 'Only for checking. He was awake before they got to the car.'

'Thank the Lord.'

Emma gathered Caleb to her with her free arm. Positioned in this way, an onlooker might have regarded the family as models for a portrait of devotion. It would have been an accurate view of the reality. The children believed in the universality of their family life. *All* children, they thought, lived with a comfortably distant but devoted mother. All children loved one another. They never questioned that maternity, beyond any doubt, granted to every child the same affection and exclusive tenderness manifested to them by their mother.

But Emma's motherhood was complex, far more than her children knew. She was proud of their beauty, thinking of herself as the sole source of it and ignoring the existence of Edmund. She saw herself in them, and, as she grew older, she saw her young, pure self as she remembered it in their double image. Her children became the objects, the unaware recipients, of her quiescent sexual passion. Her ardent heart, her unused body, yearned for occasions of physical pleasure. Finding none, she spent her fire on love for her children. They were her possessions, her occasions for fantasy, her touchstones that she was alive.

And Caleb: he had no idea that his love for his sister, who looked and felt so much like him, was a form of *amour propre*. He considered it the usual and natural affection for a sibling. To explore her body was to search himself, to learn, through his intimate investigations, some of the pleasurable secrets of his own anatomy.

And Kate: denied by her happy childhood any self-knowledge whatsoever (for children are most apt to discover their inner selves in moments of misery), she unhesitatingly offered her loving little heart to her adored brother, her revered mother, her unknown, sainted father.

After croquet was proscribed, the Flowers children, with little regret, returned to their cocoon of exclusivity. Their pretenses grew in variety and daring, extending to other times in the day, while their mother was shopping or visiting the lending library. So engrossed did they now become in their dramatic fictions that they found it difficult to suspend them, as of course they knew they must, during meals with Moth and their occasional trips to the beach with Roslyn and Lion.

In mid-August, long after Emma had returned the book, Caleb finally gave up trying to use the children in *A High Wind in Jamaica* as roles for their game. The book was difficult for him to understand. It struck him as unbelievable that the children, captured by pirates, came to such curious ends. The oldest boy, John, whose part he had intended to take, died very early by breaking his neck in a fall, and nobody, except his mother at the end, ever thought about him again. He just disappeared from his younger sister Emily's mind. Emily too was strange, lying as she did to everyone, and murdering the Dutch captain without a thought or any backward glance of conscience. To him, both roles reeked of the kind of unacceptable reality his romantic soul denied. He was glad to return the book to the library. It represented his only imaginative failure in that happy summer.

After his rejection of this subject matter, Caleb went up into the attic for his annual survey of the vast, dusty area before his mother began her fall cleaning and the storage of their summer clothes. As he always did, he reviewed the contents of his father's trunk. He inspected the now outmoded City suits, the almost new straw hat, the high, brown derby with a stiff brim, the yellowing flannel trousers, the ties wrapped in celluloid, and three pairs of pearl-gray gloves that matched the elegant spats, all encased in clear, cracking tissue paper. Everything seemed to be arranged in this careful way, protected against dust and decay, as though awaiting the owner's eventual return.

Near the trunk, wrapped in what Moth called a garment bag, was his father's black winter overcoat, with its sumptuous velvet collar. Caleb pictured himself as having attained the age and size of Edmund Flowers and being dressed in this fine haberdashery. He was planning to grow very quickly into the entire outfit so he could wear it proudly into the street. To practice, he put on the coat, the derby, a pair of gloves. Thus clad, he felt he had become his father. He was preparing to call on Emma McDermott during the early days of their courtship.

Caleb went downstairs to find Kate. She was reading a new library book about a boy named Christopher Robin and his teddy bear, a childish story that her brother had scorned when she told him the story.

'Robin! Pooh! What can we do with that silly stuff?'

Now he suggested they pretend being their parents, an old favorite game they had played many times before, with variations. He took her hand:

'Miss McDermott, would you care to come upstairs and be my wife?'

Still wearing his father's clothes, he took Kate's hand and led her upstairs to Kate's room. He took off the hat, the big coat, and the gloves and lay down beside her. He had thought of a new way of being married. He opened the buttons of his trousers, pulled down her silk underpants, and placed his penis gently along her small, damp seam.

For some time they lay there, facing each other and staring into each other's eyes. An unaccustomed warmth suffused Caleb's chest, his throat, his loins. His penis grew larger, causing Kate's small crevice to widen.

It was a revelation to them. Caleb thought of his independent-seeming organ as something apart from himself, a separate object that came to life without his willing it, an extension of some active agency within him over which he had no control. Kate too thought of the moving thing between them as a third party, a new character in their game.

Then, having been assigned no active role in the drama, the member subsided. They were uncertain how to proceed, holding each other tightly in the clasp of confused children. Caleb wet his lips at the thought of the wondrous pleasures Edmund Flowers might soon receive from Emma McDermott, using what he now knew to be his own capable weapon. Kate, having no capacity for such a vision, believed they had gone as far as would ever be necessary to effect a true marriage.

Caleb returned to the attic carrying his father's clothes. Startled by the sound of something stirring, he dropped them on the top of the trunk and walked cautiously toward the noise. Two brown bats rushed past him, their winged arms extended

55

from their furry bodies, their round eyes glittering with astonishment (Caleb thought) at being disturbed in a place they must consider their own. They settled into the rafters, hanging by their webbed forearms, their little heads down, seeming not to see him, not to be watching the intruder. As they hung, their slender bodies touched, their soft coats (it seemed to Caleb) rubbed reassuringly against each other. He put the clothes he had worn into the trunk and sat down on its cover to watch the two bats, who seemed now to be watching him.

He was fired by a new idea: he and Kate could enact the lives of these two warmly connubial creatures.

On Kate's bed that night they played at being bats, according to the new scenario Caleb had devised in the attic.

'We are to wear no clothes at all,' he told Kate.

She lay face down, her arms outspread, her toes pointed down over the edge of the bed, trying to imitate the flattened-out hind limbs of the bat as Caleb had described them. He smoothed himself on top of her, his thin arms and legs stretched along hers. He straightened his toes, like a dancer's on point, so he could align himself to Kate's body. Placing his head sideways on hers, he was able to cup her small ear in his. It was in this way that he envisioned the soft, webbed creatures in the attic coupling. So strong was his vision that he could sense the gauzes connecting his arms to his body and then to Kate.

'Like tissue paper,' he whispered. 'Now open your eyes and stare straight ahead, as they do.'

Caleb lay relaxed upon his sister. His cock—he enjoyed thinking of the new term he had learned from Roslyn—swelled downward, becoming hard and straight between Kate's buttocks. Wishing to recreate the private pleasure he had long ago discovered he could obtain by rubbing this part, he began to move gently from side to side.

Kate, obedient to his instructions, did not move. She concentrated on staring ahead as she had been told to do. She thought his movements were in emulation of the bats he had observed. Unsurprised, she continued to lie still. Then, after a time, he began to weigh heavily on her. She pushed up against him as hard as she could and felt a warm jet of liquid between her legs, in the area from which she peed. Not wanting to disturb the bat trance she thought he was in, she said nothing.

Nor did he. There was a fine satisfaction, a strange novelty, in using Kate's lovely tight buttocks and soft thighs for the pleasure he had hitherto given himself. It was as if she were joined in some magical way to his marvelous release. He heard her sigh and realized that his weight was oppressing her. Moving onto his side, he looked into her eyes. They both smiled, a long, knowing, identical, loving smile.

'Is that what you saw the bats in the attic do?'

Caleb said nothing. Kate waited and then she asked:

'Do you think we will have babies?'

'Bats, I've read, have only one. Sometimes, but very rarely, twins.'

'Well, then, one baby?'

'No, I don't think so.'

'Too bad. I think it would be fun, don't you?'

'No. Not yet.'

Tired from the strain of looking at each other, they closed their eyes and lay still, pressed close, wet, weary, and very comfortable. Caleb was filled with a contentment he had never felt before. He wanted never to leave Kate's bed.

He whispered: 'I love you, Kate. I want to marry you.'

Holding her underpants against the wet that covered her upper legs, she said: 'I accept.'

At summer's end, as if to anticipate the approaching separation, the Flowers children drew even further apart from their
friends. There were no more croquet games and very few excursions to the beach, which by now had lost much of its allure.
The air and sand, even the ocean, having cooled a little, none of
them went racing down over hot sand to be refreshed in the
surf.

The summer parents talked vaguely about a farewell party
to be held the day before they returned to the City. Their children looked forward to ice cream from Huyler's and cake
baked by the Hellmans' maid. But somehow, like so many
adult plans for children, in the press of packing and eagerness
to get back to the City, it never came to pass.

In early September, before Labor Day and the last time the
children would be together in the country, Roslyn and Lion
went to Larch Street. Roslyn wanted to collect acorns from the
bare spaces under their oak trees to take home as souvenirs.

Caleb and Kate came down from their veranda to join them,
bringing wooden pails they always used for the collection of
what Caleb called specimens. The four crawled about, gathering only prime acorns, the best examples of green and brown,
polished-looking seeds, each one set upright in a woody, stiff,
brown collar.

During the collection process, Caleb and Roslyn became
competitive, trying to outdo each other in locating the biggest,
most splendid specimens, pushing against each other when
they thought they had spotted them. At one point, Roslyn held
up a true beauty, perfect except for the absence of its cupped
holder.

'It looks like my father's thumbnail,' she said, and then returned to her search for other superlative examples. Caleb was
irritated by what seemed to him to be a foolish boast. Roslyn's
unconditional admiration of her father extended, he thought, to

58

the tips of his fingers, to his carved leg, to his status, she often said, as the City's most successful broker.

Caleb had never noticed any similarity between acorns and Mr. Hellman's fingertips. But now that Roslyn had pointed it out, he began to imagine that all the scattered acorns he saw were disconnected nails, removed from the poor man's thumbs at the same time as his leg had been taken. He stopped collecting, sat back on his heels, and began to compose a scenario:

Terrible corporeal punishment had been inflicted on a tribe of conquered giants. Now, minus the ends of their fingers, they roamed the dark outer shore of the Rockaway peninsula. Globules of blood fell from their useless hands. Who had committed these atrocities? Retributive animals whose only food was the succulent nails of goliaths? No. Tribal enemies who punished their captives by biting off the ends of the giants' fingers with their sharp teeth, and consumed them as an essential part of their diets.

'Caleb. *Listen* to me,' said Roslyn.

'What?' Caleb disliked having to return from the country of bloody punishments.

'I've called the Talkies to order. We're going to play marbles with the acorns, the ones without their collars.'

'All right,' Caleb said with some reluctance.

Kate and Lion were summoned from scavenging under trees farthest from the house. Their collecting had been indiscriminate, with none of the older children's concern for color, completeness, and perfection of shape. So their pails were full and heavy. Putting them down, they stood waiting to be instructed in the rules of Roslyn's new game.

She placed the largest acorn she could find, a prize picked up unaccountably by Lion, in the middle of a wide space in the dirt and drew a circle with a stick. Each child took up a position on the diameter and tried to hit the prime seed with smaller, less valuable ones. Whoever managed this was awarded the acorn in the center.

'Be careful, Roslyn,' said Lion. 'Don't throw so hard. I don't want my good one to get dented.'

'That's what it's there for,' said Roslyn loftily. As hard as she could she threw her missile at Lion's prized acquisition, and hit it.

The new game, like Roslyn's other enterprises that summer, ended abruptly. Lion started to cry. Roslyn threw his center piece back at him, having to retrieve it from her pile. Caleb accused her of purposeful brutality. Lion started down the street, and Roslyn, angry at everyone, followed the weeping boy.


No farewells were exchanged among the four friends, nor did the Flowers children see the Schwartzes and the Hellmans on the morning after Labor Day when two black sedans carried them and their maids northwest on the Long Island roads. The De Soto and the La Salle (for Lester Schwartz had just acquired a new car) joined the long lines of vehicles leaving the seashore towns for the beloved City, as most of the summer vacationers thought of it. The two families had had enough of sun, fresh air, salt water, and empty evenings and, in fact, of all the ever-green outdoors that the short country exile had offered them. They were delighted to be returning to 'civilization,' a word they used for the cement caverns of New York City.


The remainder of September was unusually warm. The Flowers children found it difficult to return to school, but they were resigned and went dutifully. They did not get home until well after three o'clock and then were sent immediately to their rooms to rest. Emma thought ceaselessly about the polio warnings. She was sure that contact with other children at school, as well as the enduring heat, threatened her son and daughter.

'An hour of rest on your beds before supper,' she ordered from her chair in the corner of the parlor where she sat, fanning herself.

When they came down, they did their homework seated on each end of the cretonne-covered davenport. After dinner they listened to the humorous black talk of *Amos 'n Andy* on the radio, turned up very loud for their mother's comfort. Discouraged by the volume, they decided upon an early bedtime.

With Roslyn no longer there to make demands upon his allegiance, Caleb returned happily to Kate. Their love for each other expanded to fill all the space around them. Whenever they could arrange it, sometimes at odd times of the day, they plotted to be alone, their hungry hands journeying from one stopping place to another on their bodies. Prodding, stroking, exploring, caressing, imagining the pleasures of those they knew about from history and myth, they approached each other courteously, almost deferentially, disguising, or perhaps still not entirely aware of, the depth of their passion.


After the accident-ridden summer, and the catastrophic fall of 1929 that changed their lives, Roslyn and Lionel never returned to Far Rockaway. On the 24th of October, a cloudy Thursday in New York City, the stock market, in which their fathers had worked so profitably, plummeted a disastrous thirty points. Brokers and speculators alike were thrown into a state of confusion. In three days, despair and bankruptcy had spread to businessmen all over the country. Lester Schwartz and Max Hellman, investors like their clients, were wiped out the next day, unable to make full payments for their stocks held on margin. Small brokerage firms, like theirs, closed, 'temporarily,' it was announced.

In December, Max Hellman began to look for employment. For the first time since the Great War his stump caused him much pain as he walked the unyielding sidewalks of the City in search of a job. Almost at the end of his endurance, he was saved by his brother-in-law, a prosperous Brooklyn butcher who had not been affected by the Crash because he had never believed in buying stocks and bonds.

The butcher worked Max hard. In whatever time he had left after he worked on the store's accounts, Max had to help with cleaning the floors covered with bloody sawdust after the store closed at seven in the evening. His misery at being deprived of the stimulating life on the Street was very great, and he was always aware of the butcher's pleasure, his barely concealed gloating, at his relative's downfall, and the unending recriminations of his wife.

He moved Rose and Roslyn from their apartment on the Upper West Side of Manhattan to a much smaller one down the street from Prospect Park in Brooklyn, ten long (for his bad leg) blocks from the kosher meat market where he worked. His walk to and from work was slow and painful; the De Soto Six had been the first of his assets to be sold.

Protesting tearfully, Rose settled into the cramped quarters. The softness and tenderness that prosperity had nurtured in her died under the stress of her now deprived life. She became a constant complainer, a fountain of weeping, a compendium of small illnesses. Roslyn was transferred to a public high school in Brooklyn, one with very few good students and athletes. Quickly she became the star of her classroom and the czarina of the playground.

Together with pride in her academic success, Roslyn began to develop a poorly disguised scorn of her neurasthenic mother. Of her father, she was openly contemptuous. At first he had seemed to her an unjustly deposed hero, of the same stature as a wounded soldier in the war. But as time passed and his spotted apron and straw hat in the butcher store where he scrubbed gory chopping blocks and swept up stained sawdust became his familiar garb, he lost her respect. In her lofty view, his blighted Wall Street career became the deserved sequel to his earlier dismemberment. But now it was the result of ineptitude and worthlessness: She thought of him as a hapless cripple.

Whatever pathos the fall of Max Hellman contained, the fate of Lester Schwartz was even less fortunate. Accustomed all his life to widespread admiration for his money-making prowess, Lester lost his self-esteem along with his holdings and his job when the market crashed. One morning in late November he kissed Sadie goodbye in his usual warm fashion, patted the top of Lionel's blond head as he sat eating his Post Toasties, and picked up his briefcase. He had not been able to bring himself to confess to his wife that he had not looked for employment since his brokerage office closed; his savings permitted him the deception that he still took his usual taxi down to Wall Street, where he did something, Sadie was not quite sure what.

Instead, one day, he took the subway to Forty-second Street, walked two blocks north on Broadway to the Loew's State Building, where, before the Crash, he had visited a client in the theater business. He took the elevator to the top floor, climbed a short set of iron steps, walked out onto the flat tarred roof, and took off his suit jacket, vest, tie, and fedora. He put an envelope addressed to SADIE on the roof beside his briefcase.

With what remained of his old, aggressive self-possession, he climbed over the parapet, pushed his hands against the ledge, and went down into the cold, descending air.


It may have been the cold that had seeped into the straw seats of the train. Or perhaps it was the strangeness of the Jewish service for Lester Schwartz she had sat through, unable to hear very much and understanding nothing of what was audible to her. Or it may have been that the funeral for the dead father brought to her mind Edmund Flowers' memorial service. Whatever the cause for her unexpected and extraordinary departure from myth, her excursion into the truth, Emma told her restless children the true story of their father's funeral.

'It was held in a nondenominational chapel near Inwood, not far from where we live. Because he was a soldier it was a military affair, and very patriotic. Like a lot of his fallen comrades he was buried somewhere in France, I never knew where. Two corporals wearing new uniforms drove from a base on Long Island to bring his parcel of belongings to me, his shaving stuff, comb, fatigue cap, and such. The two corporals stood at attention on each side of the platform, and a minister in an officer's uniform read the service. It seemed very long to me. I didn't hear most of what he said, because I was worried about having left my babies—you two—back at the house with a neighbor's young daughter to look after you. I didn't know her well, so I worried. I never heard the chaplain call your father "Edward," two or three times. An acquaintance told me about that, later. When the formalities were over, and I was leaving the chapel carrying your father's package, I was stopped by a lady, a stranger, who told me she had known Edmund Flowers in the City.

' "Before the war," she said. "I was a close friend." She spoke in a low voice.

'The lady, who told me her name but I did not catch it, wore a large black straw hat with many roses on the brim, a black dress which seemed to me to be tight on her, and a black sable cape. Her black gloves reached to her elbows. To me, her clothing seemed somewhat excessive for the occasion. She told me she had indulged in the extravagance of a Checker taxicab to come from her apartment in Chelsea to Inwood.

' "Where is Chelsea?" I asked.

' "Near the garment district in Manhattan," she said.

'I wished to be polite to someone who had traveled so far. So I invited her back to our house, where a few friends and neighbors were to gather for what I called a requiem supper.

'There, after tea and sandwiches, sherry and Nabisco shortbreads, the flamboyant lady told me that your father had come to her apartment for his Friday nights in the City. With her red-lipped smile, she implied that he had often, um, well, shared her bed—I cannot remember exactly how she suggested this. She made it clear to me that theirs was a most discreet affair, continuing when Edmund stopped in the City at the end of his furloughs on his way back to Fort Dix. It was a very warm friendship, she said, close enough for her to wonder, now that he had passed on, about the contents of his will. Before he left for France, he had suggested to her, she said, that she would not be forgotten.'

Having told this much of the story, to her amazement, Emma realized she had gone far beyond the bounds of propriety. The funeral must have unloosed her tongue, she thought. Never before had she said a word of this to anyone. How could she have told her innocent children the brutal truth about their father? She felt ashamed, and then, after a moment, a new thought relieved her: it was possible they would have understood very little of what she had said.

'Was she, Moth?' asked Caleb.

'Was she what?'

65

'Was she included in father's will.'

'No. Not a penny.'

Having said so much, Emma felt she could not retreat. She decided to finish, as writers of fables always do, with a moral they might understand.

'But it was a lesson for me. Your father always appeared to be so . . . so devoted. He seemed to be . . . an honest man. From what that lady told me, I learned that none of this was so. I learned never to believe in appearances. Nothing is ever what it seems. The surface is always deceiving.'

Caleb and Kate pressed her hands in theirs, kissed her, and told her how sorry they were to learn of the faithlessness of their father. They said nothing about their own feelings, but they were quite sure of them. On the spot they had become disbelievers in their father's myth and absolute supporters of their brave mother. Their games of fictional romances had prepared them for such codas of disappointment and deception, an education their mother was not aware of when she felt she might have foolishly, prematurely disillusioned them.

As the train began to move at last, the three sat very close together on one seat, creating their customary tableau of familial affection. The train made its slow way through the heavy snow that obscured all the windows. The children pondered the cost of replacing the heroic saga of their father's life with the radically revised account. Caleb did not hesitate. He had begun to translate what he had heard into material for a new game:

'Friday nights I will go to visit Kate, the lady in Chelsea who is wearing a black dress and roses on her hat. Although I am married, I will take off my derby and satin-collared overcoat, all my city clothes, and will come into bed with her. . . .' Caleb smiled delightedly at his mother, relishing the prospect of a new fiction between him and Kate.

That night, in Kate's bedroom, the children discussed the lesson Moth said she had learned.

'Do you suppose she loved him . . . after that?' Kate asked.

'I couldn't tell, from what she said. I guess she didn't.'

Kate thought about the curious revelation. Then, with a daughter's characteristically rapid assimilation of her mother's wisdom, she said slyly:

'*Seems*. But you never can be sure. It may only be appearances. She may be deceiving us.'


In these various ways, the four children lost their early, happy visions of their fathers.

# 2

# Camp

*One is not born a woman, one becomes one.*
—SIMONE DE BEAUVOIR

IN JUNE OF 1930, Rose Hellman began sewing name tapes on Roslyn's camp uniforms. Max had told his wife he wanted the summer for themselves. He felt they needed to be free of Roslyn's demands for transportation to the City and movies they could no longer afford. Rose agreed. She went further: secretly, she wished to be left to herself in the small, train-shaped apartment, where she could indulge her resentment against her husband and her intense dislike of Brooklyn. She believed that only the poor, the immigrant, and the Irish lived in that borough. Rarely did she leave the apartment during the day for fear she would be seen on the streets and taken to be one of the newly arrived Polish Jews.

But Max, now away from the competitive demands of Wall Street, found some benefits to his new state. In his prosperous days he had been a lover of spectator sports and had shared a pair of tickets to many events with his client Fire Commissioner John J. Geoghegan. Whenever Max could extricate himself from the demands and the omnipresence of Rose and his daughter, they went to boxing matches at Madison Square Garden and to the baseball games at the Polo Grounds.

After the Crash, the Commissioner was kind to his former broker, with whom he shared an affliction. As a young man, Geoghegan had lost a leg in a warehouse fire in Manhattan. The two cripples liked to joke that side by side, they composed one whole man. Joined by their common disability and by a genuine affection for each other, they continued to attend sporting events, the Commissioner paying for both tickets.

'For the time being,' Max reminded him.

The Commissioner enjoyed his new posture as source of the tickets. He had let it be known among his department's contractors that he was amenable to granting contracts for rubber suits and boots, in return for box-office favors. This summer promised some extraordinary events: the Giants and the Yankees were expected to win pennants in their respective leagues. Max was hoping to be free of his obligations to the despondent Rose and the scornful Roslyn so he could spend his Saturdays at one stadium or another with the Commissioner on their complimentary tickets.


When Aunt Sophie, her mother's sister, offered to send Roslyn to camp again and her parents gratefully accepted, Roslyn understood she was considered an impediment to her parents' private plans for the summer. Aunt Sophie was a widow who had been left 'comfortable,' as Rose put it, when her husband died of a heart attack at the age of forty-two. She had a daughter, Jean, a pretty but somewhat shy girl two years younger than Roslyn who had been sent to camp to her delight since she was eight. Aunt Sophie thought that Roslyn provided her daughter with a useful model of greater self-assurance.

In the nine months since her father's fall, as she thought of it, Roslyn had become an avid, almost obsessed movie-loving adolescent, addicted to the entertainment pages of the newspapers. Without an adequate allowance, she had developed a trick of standing by the back door of the movie theater near her, waiting for the door to open from the inside when a patron left, and slipping in just as the door was shutting. Most Saturdays she succeeded in this free entry. She stayed for hours, sometimes seeing the two features over again. When she left, dazed by the glamorous sets, the lovely clothes, and the suggestive love scenes, she felt herself unfit for ordinary existence and depressed by the fact that, at the moment, she had no way of avoiding it.

Roslyn shuddered at the thought of being sent back to the camp in the Catskill Mountains where the Sunday-night movie was three years old and divided into reels so she had to endure delays while they were changed. Even worse was the realization that she would see few newspapers for two months. For at the same time that her love of movies grew, she had learned to attract the attention of her high school classmates by telling them she was a 'radical.' From the editorial page of the *Daily Mirror* she discovered it was a much-disliked but still *intellectual* thing to be. She bragged in history class about her whole-hearted support of the doctrines of Marx and Lenin, her Communist leanings and anarchist tendencies. But she ignored the front page of the *Times,* where, in the spring of that year, and unknown to her, it was reported that the Soviet government had executed all the old Bolshevik followers of her political hero, Leon Trotsky.

Under duress, Roslyn packed her camp trunk while her mother supervised. Rose inspected every piece of clothing for name tapes while Roslyn rehearsed her resentment against her parents for making her leave the City, the new movies, the entertainment sections of the daily newspaper, for the boring, *boring* mountains.

While, in places far from the serenity of camp, the forces of imperial Japan were preparing, with great show of aerial splendor, to bomb the ancient cities of China, and thirteen hundred banks began their descent into closure in the United States, and Rastafarians in the British West Indies celebrated the elevation of the new Emperor Haile Selassie, thus fulfilling Marcus Garvey's prediction that in Africa 'a new king shall be crowned and then the day of deliverance shall be near,' and in India Mahatma Gandhi started to defy the British forces by leading a march to the coast, Roslyn, the self-styled radical, was arguing angrily with Rose and Max that she was being cruelly and unjustly deprived of her chance to go to the opening of *Anna Christie* with Greta Garbo, a thrill she did not wish to miss because of the promise that Garbo would *talk* on screen for the first time.

Her only consolation was the camp director's promise that she could practice her tennis whenever she wished, if the courts were not being used for scheduled matches. She had taken lessons when they lived near a club in Manhattan. It was the only sport she liked, even if it did involve an opponent.

'Well, if I have to go, I am going to improve my backhand. Then can I have a new racket for my birthday?'

Max sighed and said: 'Not this year.'

'Well, I'm not going to let them make me learn to dive. Let Jean do that. She likes water.' In her last visit to Aunt Sophie's apartment she had seen Jean's bathing suit hanging to air on the post at the foot of her bed. Nastily, she asked her cousin if she kept it at the ready so she could take a quick plunge into the refreshing waters of West End Avenue. Jean blushed and said:

'No, it's there so I won't forget to pack it.'


Camp Clear Lake, familiarly called CCL, was for city girls. It was highly competitive and very athletic. As a result, by the end of the summer two years ago, when Roslyn had been a junior camper, she had grown to hate all group games. If she was not chosen to be captain—and her bossiness precluded that—she did not want to play at all. She believed that team sports detracted from her intellectual energies, and her forehand.

For purposes of orderly competition the counselors had divided the camp into two teams, the Blues and the Grays. To her dismay, Roslyn had found herself on the winning side, although she herself had done very little to contribute to the victory. The campers carried on their noisy celebrations, which, to Roslyn, were vulgar, silly, and childish. Hugs, kisses, handshakes, and high-pitched shouts accompanied the announcement of the Blues' triumph. Roslyn's mood was hardly noticed in the happy confusion.

Roslyn remembered that she had gone back to her bunk to scowl over her unread copy of *David Copperfield*. She lay on her bed, her long, black hair covering as much of her face as she could manage. She was furious at what the rest of the camp was doing, the mindless, loud celebration of, to her, a meaningless victory. She vowed never again to be caught up, even anonymously, with a winning team. She hated the camp, she hated all the campers, she told herself. She vowed she would never let her parents send her back.

All that despised summer, full of interludes when she had turned her back on what she did not want to do and gone to lie on her bunk while the other juniors fought for the team banner, Roslyn had never got beyond the first chapters of Dickens. She brought it back home and put it on the shelf. The margins of page twenty-six were dotted with mineral oil in which the angry swirls of her thumbprints were darkly embedded.

'You're lucky to be getting out of the hot city,' her mother said again, as she had two years ago. 'No polio worries. Think of us sweltering here.'

Roslyn regarded this as a sign of her mother's extreme self-ishness. She herself had never given the disease, or the heat, a thought. Which was strange, because now she always seemed to dwell on the dark side of things. After the Crash, she had turned into a pessimist whose view of the world was colored by her father's fall from eminence and her mother's constant complaints. Now she expected all her plans and hopes to be defeated. At almost fourteen, nothing she wanted to do seemed without its hazards. She lived in dread that no one in the narrow scope of her life would be able to escape catastrophe, including herself. It had already struck down her father and her whining, gloomy mother.

Well, she thought, perhaps there is one virtue to having to go to camp again. The two months might serve as a hiatus in her expectation of misfortune. Everyone at a summer camp was young and healthy and had a job and seemed to have enough money. The air was fresh and cool, and she, fortunately parentless for those two months, and solitary if she resisted being put on a team, might at least for a time avoid all the nameless disasters that were inevitably part of life in the city.

On July 6, a warm Sunday, the Hellman family took the ferry to Hoboken. Waiting on the train platform for the counselors, conspicuous in their uniform skirts and monogrammed CCL caps, to assemble those whose names appeared on their clipboards, the Hellmans grew restless.

'They said eleven o'clock. It's eleven now,' Max said to his wife in his new, impatient tone that Roslyn recognized as dating from the October of his failure. These days he did not speak very much, and when he did, it was to express his dissatisfaction with the butcher business, or the demands of his family, or other people's tardiness.

Rose could hardly disguise her impatience. She put her hand on Roslyn's shoulder. Her affection for her daughter had not diminished. But the prospect of two months' freedom from having to think about her enabled Rose to make a small gesture. She seldom embraced her child any longer or allowed her husband to approach her affectionately. Resentment against what she thought of as the unfair turn of fate had turned her into an emotional recluse.

Max said: 'We'll borrow Sophie's car and drive up to see you on your birthday.'

Pleased as she was to hear this—the visit two years ago on her twelfth birthday had meant presents from her bunkmates and Muggs, her counselor, and a cake from the baker to impress her parents, she thought—Roslyn foresaw only disappointment if she were to allow herself to look forward to their visit. She remembered the last one: they had arrived in late afternoon. She had been called to the gate from the volleyball court to greet them.

Her father had filled the first hour with her by describing minutely the roads he had selected for the trip in the De Soto, the mileage they had consumed, the time the journey had taken from the City to the town of Liberty near the camp, and the stops for nourishment they had made. Then he took his watch from his pocket and inspected it carefully, as if he were studying it for facial flaws. Roslyn knew what that meant. He was ready to go back, now that they had arrived safely and seen that she was in good health. She was sure it would happen the same way this year.

She put her hands on her hips and looked down at her new white Keds.

'Goody,' she said.

She turned so that her mother's hand slipped off her shoulder.

'Bring the movie section of the Sunday paper when you come, will you? And a new racket.'

'No new racket this year,' her father said, his eyes on the large round white face of the station clock.

Rose studied the crowd gathered on the platform. 'I don't see Sophie and Jean anywhere. But over there, look, there's Fritzie,' she said to Roslyn. 'I wonder if you're in her bungalow this year.'

Roslyn looked to where her mother pointed. There she was, her beloved Fritzie. She was plump and soft-looking, her liberal figure seeming to strain her counselor's green skirt. Under her open jacket she wore a white middy blouse held together low on her bosom by a green cotton sailor's tie. Roslyn noted all the details of her uniform and her figure because, two summers ago, she had developed a great fondness for Fritzie. That year her counselor had been Muggs, for whom Roslyn felt nothing at all; Muggs was homely, had a very large nose and a small, fallen-away chin.

Even at the great distance of a junior camper from an intermediate counselor, Roslyn's admiration for Fritzie's elfin grin, her tightly curled cap of black hair, and her capacious bosom was unbounded. Last February, before St. Valentine's Day, she had made her an anonymous, much be-laced card declaring her undying love. But she did not know Fritzie's last name or address and was too ashamed to ask her mother if *she* did. So she could not send it.

Roslyn watched Fritzie, who seemed to be checking a list. She thought: 'She'd hate having me in her bunk. She referees sports, so she won't like me. I know that already.' She felt a burning in her chest. Her mother pulled her over toward the counselor.

'Hi, Roslyn,' Fritzie said, and smiled at her. For a moment Roslyn's life seemed to light up like a stage as the curtain goes up. She thought there might be a midge of hope for her hitherto

75

doomed destiny. She knew the word for the fast beating of her heart as she looked at Fritzie: she had a 'crush' on her. That was not so unusual, of course. Everyone in her bunk two years ago had crushes, or so they claimed. It was very fashionable to have them. A crush, Roslyn had decided, was a cruel blow lowered by pitiless fate upon the hearts of passionate twelve-year-old campers.

What the poor victims felt for the counselor of their choice was intense adoration. But it was against the code, the law governing such things, to mention this passion to the objects of their affection. Having a crush colored their free hours, filling their midday rest period with fantasies, their bedtime moments before they fell asleep with the pains of unrequited love. Their conversations with the similarly afflicted overflowed with their misery; their locked diaries recorded the private details of their suffering.

But it was also true that their young hearts fibrillated with pleasure at the hopelessness of their cause. Captives of love, they enjoyed their profound discomfort.

The Hellmans shook hands with the camp owners, calling them, as it was customary to do, by their surnames. Mr. and Mrs. Ehrlich were pale, amiable middle-aged people, both rotund and fleshy. They looked very much alike. Their white skin seemed to have been immune to exposure to the camp sun. Mrs. Ehrlich was an inch shorter than Mr. Ehrlich, who was shorter than most men. His bald head, as reflective of light as a clear pond, was almost the color of Mrs. Ehrlich's round, pink cheeks. To the parents whom they visited in the winter to sign up their children for camp, they both appeared to be well-nourished testimonials to the excellent meals they would offer their charges. Glowing with health, they were visible reassurances to Sophie and Rose, whose main concern was for the nourishment of their children.

Oscar, the Ehrlichs' beloved, obese only child, now close to his sixteenth birthday, was never present at these winter calls. Had he been, he would have served as further evidence of the camp's good food. But he was always left behind in Winter Haven, Florida, to enjoy the warmth of the Ehrlichs' vacation quarters. Nor was he to be seen beside them now at the Hoboken station as the campers waited for the train to take them to Liberty, their destination, and then by bus on to the camp. If everything proceeded as it had in other years, the fat boy, in his tight black shorts and flower-patterned starched shirt (further proof of maternal attention to every aspect of his pampered existence), would appear at the beginning of July, as if summoned out of the ground by incantation, at the first Saturday-morning religious service, to read the passage from Ecclesiastes:

*To everything there is a season, and a time to every purpose under heaven. A time to be born and a time to die ...*

Roslyn remembered liking the rich roll and thunder of those verses, even in Oscar's rough tenor voice. But, like her bunkmates, she had laughed behind her hands at the fat reader. In her eyes he was both the chosen and the afflicted, an object of her envy and her scorn. Lucky boy: he did not have to play games or write home every other day or share meals at the long mess hall tables. She had pictured him ensconced in the Ehrlichs' dining room, feeding on delicacies from uncommercial china and being privately served by Grete, the wife of Ib the baker, who kept the cottage in beautiful order. Or so Roslyn had imagined. On the other hand, he was an object of ridicule to the campers. Among themselves they called him Fatto, for

Fat Oscar, a portmanteau word they considered very clever.

'Roslyn,' Mrs. Ehrlich said in her high, coy-little-girl's voice. She shook hands with the Hellmans and patted Roslyn's shoulder. She always called campers by their full first names, never descending to the ugly abbreviations so popular at the camp. 'Roz': how Roslyn had hated that nickname. Never using it was the only virtue Roslyn could attribute to Mrs. Ehrlich.

'Roslyn,' she said again, as though to demonstrate to the parents that she knew well who their daughter was and would not, while she was in her charge this summer, confuse her with other girls in her care. She turned away to greet Sophie Lasky and Jean, who had just arrived, breathless and somewhat disheveled.

'We almost missed the ferry,' Sophie reported to Mrs. Ehrlich and the Hellmans. 'Our taxi driver took us to the wrong dock.'

Jean appeared to be on the verge of tears. She avoided her mother's arm, fearful she would not be on the train on time. Roslyn regarded her with scorn.

'She's an Aunt Emma, like Lion,' she thought, believing she was sad to leave her mother.

'Jean,' said Mrs. Ehrlich, her hand on the girl's shoulder. 'I'm so glad you've come back. You'll have a wonderful time. We've rebuilt the diving board.'

Before Jean could express her pleasure at this, Mrs. Ehrlich turned and began to usher those near her toward the train. They all moved obediently at her direction. Rose whispered to Roslyn:

'Did you remember to pack . . . the things?'

Roslyn knew what her mother meant. She nodded, finding it hard to disguise her contempt for her mother's reticence. Never could Rose bring herself to say 'sanitary belt' or 'Kotex,' accessories she had introduced to her daughter some time ago, warning her that her 'period,' as she called it, might arrive at any moment. Roslyn knew what to expect: cramps, headache, irritable disposition, a passion for cleaning (this she found very hard to believe), and blood issuing from a part of her anatomy she had hitherto believed would produce only pee.

Roslyn understood all this. What Rose had failed to explain to her was exactly *why* it all would happen. She was able to go as far as to inform her that the need for the equipment and the abrupt arrival of blood were a sign of being grown up, a woman in fact. This was a surprise to Roslyn. Ever since the children's librarian at the St. Agnes branch of the New York Public Library had sent her upstairs to use the adult-book shelves when she was ten, Roslyn had believed she *was* grown up. It seemed to her extremely silly to have to bleed from her bottom onto a pad every month in order to be recognized as mature.

Now that she thought about it, she remembered that her mother had connected it all to having babies. But Rose had failed to establish a connection between their arrival and what she predicted was about to happen to Roslyn. Too often for her comfort, after Roslyn was twelve, her mother would ask how she was feeling, if she had noticed any sign of 'it.' She told her daughter that 'it' had come early to her, when she was just past eleven. She could not understand Roslyn's tardiness.

The 'things' did not frighten Roslyn: it was the vocabulary. Once, unthinkingly, Rose had called it 'the curse.'

'Why do you call it that?'

'Oh, sorry. I don't usually. But some people do. You'll hear that word used.'

'Why?'

'I don't know. Just a word they use, I guess.'

Roslyn thought it must be more than that. Something was about to happen to her, like all the other terrible events she now anticipated. Curse: the word added a new, ominous tone to the equipment she had in her trunk. But she had thought about it for some time this spring and had worked out a solution that now satisfied her.

She did not tell her mother: it mattered not at all what people called it, or what it was, or what things one should wear when it happened. *Because it was not going to happen to her.* She had devised a clever stratagem to prevent it. At the first sight of a drop of blood in her panties, she planned to exercise the full power of the muscles in her thighs and buttocks. They were to be kept firmly locked against any further bloody display. So buttressed, she would never need the things. The power of the curse would never come upon her. She would not allow it.

'I have everything, yes,' Roslyn assured her mother.

She kissed her goodbye. She saw her unhappy cousin being pushed up the iron steps of the train by Aunt Sophie, and thought:

'She's lucky. She's too little to get the curse.'

Roslyn envied her. She decided to let Jean in on her scheme when it came time for her to be similarly threatened, maybe next winter.

She kissed her father and climbed onto the train after Jean. On an impulse, unusual to her, she took Jean's hand as they walked down the aisle. She felt oddly protective, almost motherly.

'Poor ignorant baby,' she thought. 'I'll save her. I'll tell her exactly how to do it.'


On the dusty, creaking Erie Railroad train, traveling slowly through the flatlands of New Jersey, Fritzie made her six bunkies sit together 'to get acquainted,' and to learn the words of the camp song:

*O Camp Clear Lake, to you we sing your praises.*
*Camp Clear Lake, we'll show that none can faze us.*
*We're out to prove your fame,*
*We'll tell the world your name ...*

Roslyn had learned the song two years ago. She had never been able to figure out what 'faze' meant, and she had forgotten to look it up when she got back home. Two of her new bunkies were very pretty, quiet, identical twins named Muriel and Ruth Something: Roslyn didn't hear their last name. She knew she would never know which was which. Fritzie too seemed puzzled.

'I can't tell you apart,' she said when she introduced them to the others. Roslyn pondered the curious expression 'tell you apart.' What did 'tell' mean, actually? And why did they need to be told who was who? It was all very foolish, she thought. She approved of Ruth's name, noting how difficult it would be to extract a nickname from it. Muriel might not be so lucky. She might be called Murry, or some such dumb thing. Hazeline, the swimming instructor, was called Hozzle, Fritzie had been baptized Frances. And then there was Muggs, who had once been Margaret.

Nicknames were supposed to give an impression of closeness, of family, a false one, Roslyn thought. They were all strangers to each other. These silly tags were meant to suggest comfortable, clannish ties, happy personal relations. It was all a joke. Even the group they belonged to this year, the intermediates, had almost at once been cozily reduced to being called mediates.

The little group sang the camp song through three times until Fritzie was sure they could enunciate all the words of the five choruses. Muriel and Ruth were slower to learn them, but they managed the refrain, which they sang in high, sweet voices, satisfying Fritzie. Jo, Aggie, Loo, and Roslyn, who had all been to the camp before, grew restless. Deciding to show their scorn of counselor authority, they strayed away from the song fest, Roslyn leading the retreat toward the bathroom. The twins were left seated with Fritzie, ignorant as yet of the methods of camper disobedience.

Roslyn considered Jo a giggly, silly girl whose only clear sign of intelligence was that she shared Roslyn's dislike of team sports. Jo's preference was for arts and crafts, an activity Roslyn regarded as evidence of mental weakness. Two years ago the work they had been given to do was tedious and the end products, to Roslyn's way of thinking, entirely useless: snakeskin belts, braided leather lanyards suited only for referees' whistles.

Now Roslyn looked at Jo, her imagination suddenly at work. She decided Jo was destined to study art in college, maybe crafts if they taught such a thing, and then teach old people in retirement homes to make Christmas-tree ornaments and crochet covers for the backs of chairs. She had watched her own grandmother in the Bronx Home for the Jewish Aged make pleated paper lampshades under the instruction of a lady with a foolish laugh like Jo's. Later she'd get married, maybe to a businessman who 'traveled.' They would live beyond the pale, somewhere in New Jersey.

Aggie, an unsubstantial girl with few defining characteristics of her own, aped Jo in everything. Two years ago, for this reason, she had been nicknamed Shadow, an unfortunate, descriptive appellation she would be destined to carry with her (Roslyn imagined) until she was taken away from her college dormitory room, wrapped in a white sheet, to some place for loonies, from which she would never emerge. Roslyn could foresee no other future for her.

Loo (Roslyn could not remember what her given name was:

Lucille maybe?) was the tallest mediate camper. As a junior she had been expert at basketball and playing the backcourt in tennis. But she was so gangly and overgrown that she must hate her body, Roslyn thought. In midsummer two years ago she had refused to talk to any boy when their brother camp, Algonquin, paid its annual visit. Roslyn now envisaged Loo, grown up and married to a college basketball star perhaps, living a very healthy, exercise-filled life as the wife of a coach. Probably in North Dakota.

Roslyn's habit, in the pretenses Caleb had taught her to construct last summer, was to assign everyone she thought unworthy to a purgatorial exile in the worst places she could think of. Such locations increased in frightfulness in direct proportion to their distance from Manhattan.

And Roslyn herself: tall, bony, black-haired, called Roz by those she most despised, this summer destined to be the arrogant, rebellious, fantasizing leader of whatever mutinous act she suggested to the mediates in her bunk, what of her? Her seditious spirit will try to unite the disparate and, to her, wan and characterless bunkies. At the positive, dogmatic, self-assured age of fourteen (the needy and uncertain creature living beneath her arrogant surface being well hidden), she will tell herself that the others are spineless, their minds mirrors, not knives like hers.

Early in that summer of 1930, head counselor Rae (Rae, one of those whose name could not be truncated), who remembered Roslyn's behavior in the past, told her she had to be out of doors more. This summer she had to play hockey whether she wanted to or not. She was not to lie on her bed during the day reading the old newspapers her mother had mailed to her. Roslyn did everything she could think of to get out of such physical efforts, including trying to enlist her bunkmates in her mutinies. Even tennis no longer interested her. That old, flabby racket...

'Do you really want to play hockey in this heat?' she asked her bunkmates in the morning while they were occupied in sweeping under their cots, returning their neatly folded, half-worn uniforms to their trunks, and 'picking up,' as it was called, in their personal area. Roslyn lay stretched on her un-made bed, a little island of indifference amid her scattered belongings.

At first they all decided they didn't want to. When their chores were finished, they too lay down and took up whatever reading matter was at hand: the latest Nancy Drew mystery, secreted copies of *True Story* purloined from their mothers, pieces of Roz's newspapers, especially the old, yellowed ones she had saved from the winter and brought up in the bottom of her trunk. These pages contained little biographies of families in need at Christmastime in New York City. Passed from hand to hand in the bungalow, they satisfied the girls' hunger for poignancy at the same time that they affirmed their own security.

When Fritzie discovered that her bunkies were absent, she stormed up from the hockey field.

'Damm it, you kids get off your beds and get out there. What do you think this, an old people's home?'

They all got to their feet, grabbed their hockey sticks, and followed Fritzie out of the bunk. Everyone but Roslyn, who rose slowly, made a show of leaving, and then, when Fritzie was out of sight, turned and lay down again on her bed. Fritzie might miss six of them, but hardly one, she reasoned. And anyway, she'd never come up the line again to look for her. But if she did, okay: it would be nice to have her all to herself, for a few moments at least.

Rae had had no success with her project for Roslyn. In the Mess Hall at breakfast Roslyn would listen to Rae read aloud the schedule of activities for the day, decide upon her private plan of retreat, and then attend one or two events she liked, either tennis or swimming or, on one of her good days, both. She told Dottie, the dramatics counselor, that she preferred not to be cast in a Saturday-night musical. She wanted nothing to do with playing outfielder on the baseball team, or net player in volleyball, or any other position on any stupid team. Her bunkmates would come back from the hockey field, sweaty and weary, to find her on her cot, disdainful and cool.

This was the summer when prices on the stock market, after a short rise, plunged to a new low, unemployment reached four million, and the country and the world began a decade of severe depression. It was the summer that *The Lone Ranger* took over the airways and Greta Garbo appeared in *Anna Christie*. A musical comedy, *Strike Up the Band*, made the hit lists on the radio with a song called 'I've Got a Crush on You.' Max Schmeling, fouled by Jack Sharkey, won the heavyweight title (Max Hellman was there, in Madison Square Garden with his friend the Commissioner) and became an instant hero to Adolf Hitler. Sliced bread first appeared that summer, and the first supermarket opened in Jamaica, Long Island.

In the newspapers sent to her by her mother, Roslyn immersed herself in such calamities, coincidences, and victories. In this way she was able to escape the mundane details of camp life and enter into the real world of New York City, where she wanted to be.

Throughout July and well into August she went down to the lake twice a day for the mediates' scheduled swim. Never once did she step on the diving board. She had heard from Loo, who was very poor at water sports and so swam with the juniors, that Jean was now a good diver. So Roslyn occasionally went to the lake to watch her cousin practice her half gainer. She was impressed but not moved to try diving herself. She said she thought there was something simpleminded about shocking one's intelligence by hitting the water with one's head from a great height.

July went by without the promised visit from her parents. They wrote that money was short, that Max was needed at his new business, as he called the butcher store, and that Aunt Sophie could not spare her car. Rose sent a birthday present, a box that turned out to contain three used books: an illustrated edition of *Barnaby Rudge,* a battered copy of *Ben Hur,* and an equally worn book called *What Every Young Girl Should Know.* Roslyn stored the box in the dust under her cot and resolved not to open it again.


The eight weeks of the summer seemed to pass very slowly for Roslyn. Stoically she endured it all—the standard, polite letters she had to write home every other day as the price of admission into the mess hall at lunchtime, the games she was made to play when she was too slow to have invented excuses, the prattle (as she thought of it) of her bunkmates, her nagging uncertainty about the retarded functioning of her reproductive system.

She could not wait for August to end, for her exile in woods and meadows to be terminated by the familiar hospitality of paved streets and romantic movie theaters. From her early start as self-confident leader of the little tribe of displaced New Yorkers, she had gradually lost her following, and, what was worse, her confidence in her persuasive powers. Her bunkmates had deserted her, seduced by the more promising rewards, at the end, of medals for being improved campers and good sports.

In the last few days of the camp year, beginning on the 27th of August, Roslyn, the admirer of a counselor unromantically nicknamed Fritzie, was deprived of what remained of her innocence about herself and, more, about those who lived in her world.

Her losses were immediately apparent to her, unlike the hazy recollections that inhabit adult memories when, looking back, it is hard to locate the effects of crucial events in one's early history. During the last days of camp, she felt herself aging. When the inspection of trunks was concluded, when the ambulance had pulled away from the lake road, guided to the gate by lucifer matches and flashlights, when her faith in true love shriveled up under the assault of brutal truth like a pin-struck balloon, and when her body failed her, she knew she had grown up, even grown old.

She had always suspected that very few people were really happy. When, all at once, this proved painfully true, she thought that nothing would ever seem the same to her again. Compared to her end-of-summer-gained knowledge, her father's descent from affluence to near poverty (as it seemed to her) last October was a minor fall. At a stroke, she thought, she had changed, grown ugly and disconsolate, like the mythic hero swept by a wave of a wand into the skin of a hideous frog. Now she was certain of what she had earlier suspected, that life was composed of a series of disillusioning revelations and disappointments.

Most affected was her idea of love. She had thought she knew what it was, but in those last days she discovered its true nature. It was a well-camouflaged phantom, an avid, contemptuous, sneaky mob member, a guerrilla fighter prepared to destroy the natural peace of her heart, always secretly at war with her contentment. More terrible still, when her body betrayed her, she was taught that it was a wild child, capable of tantrums and tempers, furious deeds and appetites, and never *never* obedient to her will.

It happened in this way.


On what was to be a drama-laden day near the end of camp, Grete, fully dressed, woke Ib at six in the morning. A suggestion of light showed over the far side of the lake. In the help's house it was still cool, as if fall had come, unexpectedly, to the summer place. Ib got up at once, accustomed to early rising because sweet buns and soft rolls had to be ready to be served in the mess hall at eight-thirty.

He indulged in his ritual grumbling, followed by his soft, ropy cough.

'From the flour, *not* the tobacco,' he told Grete when she complained about it.

The room the couple occupied in the house smelled of his midnight quart of ale and his badly decayed teeth. Grete reminded him of the birthday cake he had to bake for dinner and the extra loaves for the senior hike.

'I know, I know. What do you think?'

Grete made her escape into the warm, perfumed air of the Ehrlich's cottage. This morning she found the kitchen marred by the remains in the sink of a late meal Oscar must have required two or three hours after his dinner. For the moment she ignored the mess and proceeded to make her own thick, black coffee in the Scandinavian way, and then a small pot of American coffee for Mrs. Ehrlich's breakfast. Mr. Ehrlich had long since gone to Liberty to fetch the mail and provisions.

Grete walked over to the bakery to obtain the fresh rolls from Ib's tray. They said nothing to each other. She carried the little package back to the bungalow.

Grete knocked and then pushed open Mrs. Ehrlich's door

with her firm, uniformed body, holding the tray against her midriff. Mrs. Ehrlich was asleep, curled into the center of her bed like a giant snail. The air around her was sweet and heavy with the effusions of her flesh, perfumed with Chanel No. 5 before going to bed.

Grete pulled the blinds. Mrs. Ehrlich stirred, stretched, and sat up as the aroma of coffee and hot rolls reached her. Into the warm morning sunshine that reached her bed she smiled beneficently, luxuriating in the thought that the administrative tasks of the long summer were almost behind her. Was not the lovely sunshine of their place in Winter Haven about to descend on her? She had always moved contentedly through life, proceeding from one situation of physical comfort to the next—the bed, the sofa, the porch swing, the padded chair at the dining table, the soft armchair reserved for her at all camp events in the Amusement Hall—waited upon and cosseted by Mr. Ehrlich, regarded fondly but lazily by her son, and always certain that the present, demanding as it might be, would turn into easeful release in the near future.

Her sole worry was for Grandmother Ehrlich, who had lived with them since the death of her husband. The details of her care during the summer in the cottage were left to her, Mr. Ehrlich, and a succession of helpers who came in from the village by the day. In winter, Mrs. Ehrlich was entirely free of these concerns. She was able to relax while she enjoyed her eight months in Florida. Grandmother Ehrlich was left behind in New York with a full-time caretaker.

Only the cold February visit to New York to sign up campers for the following summer marred Mrs. Ehrlich's long, hot, slothful holiday, which ended, sadly, in June when they had to return to oversee the refurbishment of the camp. Both directors agreed that it was necessary for them to be on the grounds when the effect of winter storms on the manicured appearance of fields and bungalows, docks and roadways was erased. They knew how important all this was to visiting parents.

Grete poured Mrs. Ehrlich's coffee and buttered her roll.

'Bugle on time today. Campers and teachers are in Mess Hall. Flag is up like always,' Grete said in the pleasant voice she always used to the directors. She felt it necessary to make this morning report to Mrs. Ehrlich as she lay in bed, knowing she was always pleased to hear that all was going well, as usual. Mrs. Ehrlich was the picture of contentment, stretching her short, fat legs under the sheet. Grete considered it important to ingratiate herself, because Ib's drinking threatened their security. Summer jobs were essential to them.

It was not that Grete loved Ib, not in the least, not ever. When he had too much to drink, he enjoyed using his belt on her buttocks and twisting her long hair so tightly it threatened to pull away from her head. Or he would extend her earlobes so painfully during his (never their) lovemaking as a show of force, accompanied by rough assaults on her breasts and thighs.

Every night during the summer, full of drink, he demanded that she lie down under him; every night she wished him dead. After he fell into a heavy sleep, she planned the escapes she might make if cirrhotic death or lung disease did not claim him soon. To her, their union (he was Danish, she Norwegian) was an example of mistaken intermarriage. She had agreed to it because he was about to become an American citizen and she wished to realize the promises of the golden land of America she had come to: high salaries, new automobiles, fur coats, and modern kitchens.

Ib's motives for entering into marriage were equally crass. He had failed to find a woman in Copenhagen willing to submit for any length of time to his distinctive ways of achieving his pleasure, the same attacks he enjoyed inflicting on small animals, and upon men smaller and weaker than he. This uncontained violence, necessary to fire his arid soul and his lax sexual organ, had sent him to jail in Odensee, where he had gone to take a job as an apprentice baker and to find a willing female for his blows and pinches, yanks and drubbings.

His incarceration there had been brief. He had been found guilty of drunkenness and assault upon a prostitute, both very minor offenses. He passed his days in jail baking for the prisoners and his nights methodically, pleasurably battering himself. Freed in a few months, and sick of Denmark, he obtained a berth as a baker on a steamship and sailed to New York. Immediately he applied for his papers.

Almost as quickly he found a job with the Horn and Hardart Company, so easily were American employers persuaded that European-trained bakers must be superior to Americans. In time, he was promoted to supervising the mass production of chocolate-, vanilla-, and strawberry-frosted cupcakes, desserts then much favored in the Automats in New York City. Baked at three in the morning, the cakes were moved upstairs to be placed behind the little glass doors. They were readily available to thousands of thrifty citizens by the insertion of a nickel into a slot.

In the basement kitchen he met Grete. She worked in the vegetable department. 'I do cream spinach, butter carrots, and succotash,' she told him at their first encounter. The next year she agreed to marry him, his impulses and needs having been well hidden from her until the night after they signed a license before a magistrate of the City of New York. Similarly, he was unaware of her avarice, which became apparent later, after an argument about her savings and his nightly ale.

'You are a cold woman,' he told her when she refused to part with her Central Savings Bank passbook so he could buy his necessary drink.

'You are a goat, a pig,' she replied.

Name-calling became their unvarying form of communication. Once, while Grete lay in bed engaged in her customary fantasy of getting free of her life with Ib, he stole her passbook and presented it at the glassed-in teller's window together with a withdrawal slip. He was told he could not use it: her name, her *maiden* name, Grete Olssen, was on the account.

After that, they endured each other in furious silence, broken only by expletives and business communication. They were united in their unspoken resolutions to avenge each other's unbearable behavior. On the morning of the 27th of August, while Mrs. Ehrlich was dressing slowly with Grete's help, Ib was taking his first bottle of ale from the bakery icebox. Now that all the boats had been lifted out of the water and heaped one upon the other in neat piles, he thought he might escape Grete's witness of his drinking, take his bottle, lift down the top canoe, and go out for a peaceful, solitary late afternoon on the water. He might float around in the little hidden cove, the only break in the otherwise perfectly oval lake. There, unobserved from the shore and dock, he could drink his pale fire, dozing if he wished after its analgesic effects had dulled his senses. This would be his last chance for inebriated solitude, he thought. During these last days when camp was winding down, the help could ask permission to enjoy the pleasures of the lake.

'Not at all have I been on the lake, not once all this summer,' he thought, filled with resentment against his job, the owners, the counselors, the campers, even Grete, although he could not have said why.

He gathered up ten long loaves of bread and took them out to the truck that was to follow the seniors on their hike. As he lifted them into the back of the truck, one loaf escaped his grasp and fell into the dust.

*'Jeg er nerves,'* he muttered. Carmen, the driver, free of his usual chores of lawn mowing and garbage collecting, laughed as he picked up the bread, blew on it, and put it with the others.

'Pretty early in the day to be blotto,' he said to Ib.

'Horse. Turkey. Bastar.'

Carmen laughed again. 'Go put your head in the oven, Pop,' the driver said.

'Italian pig,' said Ib.

He went back to the bakery and soothed his rage with a long draw on the bottle of ale. He floured his hands, began work on the dough for lunch rolls, put the layers for one birthday cake for tonight into the oven, expressed his opinion loudly to the hot oven concerning the driver's unlawful origins, and then sealed his view with another insult-quenching drink.

After the water-sports contests of last week, the Grays were twelve points behind the Blues for the summer's total. Roslyn was a Gray and happy not be on the winning side. To her, Gray represented the uniforms of the courageous, radical rebels of the War Between the States, the gallant subjects of a school paper she had written this year. Only a few competitions remained to be played in these final days. They would decide the Blue-Gray struggle: junior field hockey, freshman volleyball, mediate handball. Roslyn hoped she would be overlooked in the final handball pairings-off, for inevitably she would lose, and the winners would gloat. She would hate the whole exultory conclusion, especially the banquet with its stupid awards and medals. And the silly singing of victory songs. Oh jeepers.

But Rae insisted. 'You've done nothing at all for the Grays, Roz. Time to get out and show some team spirit.'

'Jeepers,' Roslyn said under her breath. *'Team spirit.'*

She walked as slowly as she could down to the handball court, bearing witness, she hoped, by her slumped shoulders and clenched fists, to her disdain for the world of competition. For a moment, as she passed the Amusement Hall, where she knew Fritzie was going to meet with other counselors to plan activities for the next day and for the departure, she looked in. There she was, the lovely Fritzie, and here she was, the captive Roslyn. Suppose, by some miracle, she were to win. The Grays would gain a much-needed point, she supposed. But how could this possibly happen? Well, stringbean Loo, who was sure to be her opponent, a Blue who was good at this game, might sprain her ankle and concede to her. Or God would perform a miracle, endowing her own weak right hand and willowy wrist with Amazonian strength. Then, in a series of amazing acts, one *firm* stroke after another, hard palm to rubber ball to cement wall, her game might turn out to be a masterpiece of strategy and strength.

Roslyn sat down on the grass, crouching low, hoping she would not be noticed. On the side bench, sitting with Will, Roslyn imagined she saw her beloved Fritzie. Will was the athletics counselor who refereed most of the games. Roslyn's burning eyes squinted against the sun: her fantasy bloomed. Fritzie will watch her admiringly as she swings and swoops and slams. She will applaud the clever moves that lead to the final point, until Roslyn's heart explodes with love for her generosity. Her life's blood will leak from her palms as a result of glass-hard contact with the ball, coloring her sweat, covering her with the glowing sheen of a victor.

She will bow gallantly to her disabled opponent, nod humbly to Will and then to her beloved, cutting the air with her CCL cap in one glorious sweep of cavalier grace. She will bow again, very low.

Halfway through the match Roslyn tired. The long summer

of relative inactivity had not prepared her for this last challenge. On the bench, Will appeared bored, looking often at her watch. Roslyn lost badly. Good, she thought. Another Blue point, and perhaps ultimate defeat for the Grays to which she had now contributed. Now she had good reason to skip the banquet and celebration by the gloating bad winners and the noisy good losers. She would stay in her bunk and try to finish up all her old newspapers, maybe even take a look at *Ben Hur*. But of course Fritzie probably would not let her.

Will stood up, said she had a meeting, and left abruptly without congratulating Loo, who looked hurt. Roslyn shook hands with her and said: 'Good game.'

Loo raised her clasped hands above her head and said into the air: 'Yessirree bob. Yay for the Blues.'

To Roslyn she said, confidingly: 'You know what? It's a wonder I played so good. I feel lousy. Last night I fell off the roof.'

'Falling off the roof' was the popular camp expression for menstruation. Roslyn had learned it from Aggie. Jo, Loo, Aggie: all of them talked about their monthly troubles in this way. At first hearing, Roslyn had taken it literally and was startled. Then she reasoned it was most unlikely that three kids all would have suffered the same accident. What were they all doing up there, anyway?

'Why do you call it that?' she had asked Jo.

Jo didn't know. Nobody in the bungalow knew. Their disdain for Roslyn's immaturity ruled her out of the suffering sorority. So they made no attempt to invent something or venture a guess at a reason. Roslyn was not offended at their conspiratorial silence. She had already worked out her own explanation. If you fell off a roof you were very apt to bleed uncontrollably. So the expression must be yet another description of the cursed affliction. It was all so stupid, really. Because, her plan locked firmly into place, she would never have any part in the whole mess.

Grete made beds and scrubbed the bathrooms and kitchen while Mrs. Ehrlich in her fresh white dress sat at her dressing table and applied powder and rouge to her cheeks.

'Nothing like a Swede for cleanliness,' she had told Amiel Hoffer, the camp doctor, at the start of the summer. He agreed, wanting to stand in well with the directors and so not correcting her about Grete's place of origin. To Mrs. Ehrlich all persons from Scandinavia were Swedish, and surely the doctor must respect that nation's reputation for hygiene.

Dr. Amiel, as Mrs. Ehrlich called him, had come to the camp this summer as a result of chance. A June graduate of Bellevue Medical School, he had filled in at the last moment for the regular doctor, whose skill at treating poliomyelitis through the winter would keep him busy in the City during the threatened epidemic summer, sadly depriving him of his usual Catskill vacation. So relieved were the Ehrlichs to be able to fill this essential position that they did not inquire into the inexperienced young graduate's credentials. (For what parents would permit their child to be away from them for any length of time without the firm promise of on-the-grounds medical attention?) And Fate had been kind to Dr. Amiel: no difficult-to-diagnose ailments had developed during the eight weeks of camp. The most serious was Oscar's gastritis, caused, the doctor was quick to see, by the boy's overeating.

'But he eats like a bird,' his mother protested.

'Then why is he so fat?'

'It's all glands. It runs in the family.'

Dr. Amiel, who possessed common sense, even if his medical experience was limited, repressed his disbelief. Oscar's first stomach ache had occurred on the fourth day of camp. Even then the doctor had suspected him of being a secret eater. But he knew he had the rest of the summer to get through peaceably, so he made no comment on this diagnosis. Oscar continued to have spells of constipation, pain, and nausea all summer. The doctor prescribed diet, exercise, and milk of magnesia. Oscar refused to change his diet and avoided all physical effort. But he did allow himself to be dosed periodically, in this way garnering his mother's loving sympathy and care.

To the doctor's immense relief, no one had ever had to remain overnight in the Infirmary. Complaints expressed at morning sick call were limited to shin bruises from hockey sticks, splinters, and headaches caused by the arrival of 'my period.' There were a few cases of tennis elbow and a number of occurrences of baseball fingers and bee stings, scraped knees and toes. But nothing happened that could not be treated with Midol, aspirin, Band-Aids, Ace bandages, and tongue-depressor finger splints.

'My future practice should be this easy,' thought the doctor, knowing the impossibility of this wish but still grateful to the Gods of Summer for their forbearance in not putting his ignorance to a test.

At the end of the summer his record was clear, thanks to his one fortunately prescient action. In late July, Ruth Kress, one of the twins, developed a persistent fever. When it did not respond to aspirin and rest in her bungalow and when, on the fourth day of her fever, she complained of arm and leg pains and a stiff neck, Dr. Amiel suggested that she be sent home, 'as a precaution.'

Mrs. Ehrlich agreed, having been assured by Mr. Ehrlich that Ruth's parents would not be due any refund, since the first three weeks of the season had passed. At August's end, with camp about to close, no word had reached the directors about

Ruth's state of health. Muriel was told by her parents that her twin was all right. Everyone else knew only that she had not returned.

The silence made good, self-serving sense for everyone. The Kresses did not wish Muriel sent home to a polio-infested City. So they did not alert the camp to its danger. The Ehrlichs and the doctor had been blessed with luck—no fevers or other suspicious symptoms developed among Ruth's bunkmates. The fearful disease had departed from CCL with Ruth, leaving none of the dread viruses behind. They had concentrated themselves in the twin, who was taken from the train to the Lenox Hill Hospital in the City, where she fought hard for life and, in mid-August, breathed her last in an iron lung.


Seated on camp chairs in a semicircle at the front of the Amusement Hall, Rae and the upper-group counselors held their final meeting for the season. While they waited for Mrs. Ehrlich and the doctor to arrive, they planned their private celebratory outing into Liberty (a town well named, Fritzie thought) tomorrow evening after the banquet. Then, when Muggs arrived, they changed the subject and began to decide about the medals and pins to be bestowed upon their thirty campers tomorrow night. Loo would receive the 'gold' for general athletic prowess. Another gold would go to Frannie in Bungalow Fourteen for being the most improved camper.

'That's an easy one,' said Hozzle. 'Last year she couldn't learn to do the dead man's float. Now she can paddle on the top of the water pretty well.'

Will said: 'Yep. She used to get so tangled up with the hockey stick I had to take her out of every game. Last week she played wing. It's true she never managed to hit the puck, but at least she stayed on her feet.'

Rae said: 'I recall an inning of softball I watched last year. She beaned one hitter and struck another in the chest while she was running to first base. Then Will retired her to the bench. But fine. Most improved camper she is.' She wrote Frannie's name on her clipboard.

Vivvie, in Bungalow Twelve (there was no Thirteen, for superstitious reasons), would be given the medal for best swimmer. Jo would be rewarded with a gold for her skill in arts and crafts. The other twenty-six mediates were to receive copper-colored pins, in recognition of their 'efforts': Mrs. Ehrlich was always firm in her view that not a single camper should return home undecorated. She wished to guard against resentments that might fester during the winter, adversely affecting the decision of parents to re-enroll their offspring in February.

Rae went to the porch to look down the line, as the road between the directors' cottage and the farthest bungalow was called, to see if Mrs. Ehrlich was on her way. They'd all been waiting more than an hour for her, and there was a great deal to do now that the end, thank God, was almost upon them. When Rae saw her approaching, as wide as a sail in her white dress, teetering over the rough path on her tiny white high-heeled pumps, Rae waved, and waited. She helped her up the uneven wooden steps and linked her arm with hers as they walked to the circle of counselors. Mrs. Ehrlich was fond of Rae, because she had run the camp without any help from her for fifteen years. If she ever failed to return, the directress thought, the whole efficient and profitable enterprise might be threatened.

Rae was aware of this. But she was a gentle, kindly, unassuming woman who used her power discreetly to benefit her friends, many of whom she hired regularly from the faculty of an athletic college in Maryland where she had taught for many years. She took care to remain in Mrs. Ehrlich's good graces, enjoying her right to hire congenial athletic counselors who happened to be of her own sexual persuasion.

It was left to Mrs. Ehrlich to hire three counselors, for nature, arts and crafts, and dramatics. Unlike Rae, she had a poor eye for capable and amiable teachers. Muggs, hired to do arts and crafts, had disappointed her with her continued cantankerousness through three summers. She had decided she would look elsewhere next year. The new nature counselor, Amanda, called, inevitably, Manny, had developed a repugnance for snakes, bugs, and salamanders and had to be replaced in midseason by a more intrepid camper-counselor. And Dolly, the longtime dramatics counselor, who was responsible for providing the Saturday-night entertainments, grew less ambitious each week, doing revues and 'an evening of skits' through most of the summer until the last Saturday night, when she mounted an elaborate Gilbert and Sullivan operetta. She believed this last effort would leave the Ehrlichs with an impression that the whole theatrical season had been an unvarying success, a notion, she hoped, that would carry over to the next hiring period.

The directress searched in Greenwich Village for these teachers. But her choices usually ran counter to Rae's, creating a subtle division in the staff between her artsy choices (as Rae's friends called them) and Rae's sturdier, more athletic types. Other, more subtle splits often occurred. This year Dolly, a good-looking unemployed actress, had become close friends with the camp doctor, thus alienating herself from the teachers of sports by what seemed to them to be a perverse interest in men.

The subsidiary member of the medical staff, Nurse Jody, as Mrs. Ehrlich insisted on calling her, had been badly disappointed in her hopes for a summer romance by the doctor's choice of another partner. She then developed a noticeable disaffection with camp life. She had 'turned odd,' Mrs. Ehrlich told

Mr. Ehrlich in mid-July. Any day they had expected to hear that she was leaving. Indeed, she had threatened the doctor with premature departure, hoping to redirect his interest to her. She did not succeed, but she stayed on, secretly enjoying her displays of bad humor and her status as one of the upper people, above the rank of counselor, almost on a par with the directors, the doctor, the visiting parents. Having little to do in this healthy place, and no opportunity for dalliance, she made herself useful as the camp spy, Mrs. Ehrlich's secret agent. She sought out instances of malfeasance and reported them promptly when she could get the directress's ear. If she could not, she went to Rae.

Thus, the good-natured head counselor became the reluctant recipient of steamy summer secrets. Nurse Jody saw who failed to fulfill her duty policing the line during rest hour and, most urgently now, what camper or counselor seemed a likely suspect for the rash of missing objects people had reported all summer: scarves, compacts, pocket knives, small sums of money. But her gossip rarely led to action by camp officials. Harmony and a peaceful surface of life were too highly prized.

By summer's end, Nurse Jody's avidity in her role of reporter of small thieveries led to a gauze of suspicion falling upon almost everyone. Mr. Ehrlich was immune: he was absent from the camp grounds most of the day. Dr. Amiel too was safe, by virtue of the elevated nature of his profession protected against evil reports and immune to denigration.

As usual, the doctor was the last to arrive at the meeting in the Amusement Hall, followed closely by the nurse. Mrs. Ehrlich called for order.

'We need to talk about the search,' she said. 'Before everything is packed away.'

Rae nodded. 'I think it might be a good idea to allocate a few hours tomorrow just for packing. Then one of us can walk around and inspect trunks for the missing stuff.' Rae's solution to a problem always involved allocation of 'space' on her schedule chart. Results were achieved, she thought, in blocks of time in the present, today, not be vague projections into an unscheduled future.

'Good idea. Yes,' said Mrs. Ehrlich.

Everybody nodded in agreement.

'Second thing,' said Mrs. Ehrlich. 'The banquet. The awards. Have you thought about them?'

Fritzie said: 'We've settled on a few, the mediate ones. Loo. Frannie. Vivian. The gilt medals.'

'Gold, not gilt,' Mrs. Ehrlich said testily. 'And of course, the bronze pins for everyone else. You haven't forgotten the names of all of those?' Fritzie grinned broadly but said nothing, suggesting that once again she was willing to overlook the foolishness of indiscriminate pinning.

Rae noticed and said quickly: 'No indeed, we haven't. Although we haven't decided what we will give them *for* this year.'

'Good sportsmanship,' said Muggs glumly.

'That was two years ago,' said Rae. She had total recall of camp events as far back as her first summer fifteen years ago.

'What about "participation"?' said Will, the stern, broad-shouldered young woman who was a no-nonsense authority on field sports. She had introduced the newly laid down rules for girls' softball to the camp, and she captained one of the warring counselor teams that gave exhibitions after services on Saturday. Her name was Millicent Williams: since grade school she had demanded that everyone call her by the abbreviation of her last name.

'Very good,' said Mrs. Ehrlich. 'I like that.'

Rae smiled at Will. 'Leave it to you to think of that. All those team members and all those substitutes *did* participate.'

Will smiled back. Her smile was rare, although she always felt comfortable at camp, relaxing every summer into the precise daily routine because she helped Rae with the scheduling. It was a favorable spot for her, since she was firmly on the side of land games and felt no sympathy for water sports. She was deathly afraid of the water.

The usual scheduling argument began. Hozzle wanted extra periods today at the waterfront to complete junior lifesaving tests. Will made her customary protest against them, appealing on theoretical grounds.

'Human beings were meant to walk on land,' she said in her low, flinty voice. 'Not to move by thrashing around in water.'

'Water was first, I believe,' said Hozzle happily. She had spent the warm, sunny summer in perfect contentment at the waterfront. Eight hours of the day she wore her yellow, belted tank bathing suit, her flat bare feet always wet, her short blond hair plastered behind her ears, her bloodshot eyes glued to the lake where pairs of little swimmers—'buddies,' she called them—paddled about. She took swimming and diving very seriously. In her zeal, she wanted to convert everyone at the camp to exercising in aquatic ways.

'Only for the lowest forms of life,' said Will. 'The higher ones showed their superiority by crawling out of the muck, standing up, and entering civilization. They never went back.'

'Nuts,' said Hozzle. It was her most daring public expletive.

Rae assumed her concilatory role. 'Why don't we divide the time equally? That's what the juniors are going to do. And the seniors are off on their hike. And all the little kids can have free time to finish their lariats and belts.'

'Oh let's.' Mrs. Ehrlich was always in favor of activities that called for safe, sedentary effort.

'I do like "participation," Will,' said Rae. She wrote the word on top of her schedule form. 'It makes it sound like everyone has been included in everything, all summer.'

'Wonderful,' said the directress.

Fritzie decided not to let the matter pass that easily. 'Or it could mean we are rewarding everyone, even those who thought about participating but didn't. Or Roz, who probably should have a pin for steadfastly *not* thinking about it, and not participating.'

'Of course, of course,' said Mrs. Ehrlich, who was, at season's end, quick to agree. Her flabby powers of comprehension continually rode piggyback on the definitions and distinctions others made, making her seem amiable by nature. In reality she could not distinguish between ideas, precise meanings escaped her entirely, and implication was too subtle for her ever to catch. Without Rae at her side, the loose material of her mind never hardened into understanding.

'Now about the medical reports for parents . . .' Rae looked at Dr. Amiel, who was occupied in tying his overlong sneaker laces into triple knots. 'We need a slip for each camper. General health, weight, that kind of thing. Can you get those ready quickly so I can hand them out at the depot when we deliver the little darlings to their eager folks?'

The doctor looked up, startled. For the first time all summer he had been awakened from his Eden of idleness.

'Guess so. Send them to be weighed this afternoon and tomorrow. But *general health?* Wow. Do they all have to be different?'

'I should hope so,' said Mrs. Ehrlich primly. 'They're all separate persons, aren't they? We pride ourselves on developing their individuality.'

'No, Doctor,' said Rae softly, over Mrs. Ehrlich's voice. 'Just three categories. *Good. Excellent.* And *Improving.* That sort of thing.'

In a loud whisper, Fritzie said to the doctor: 'How about a fourth? *Participating* in health?'

'Okay,' said the doctor, and laughed. He stood up to indicate that his part of the meeting was over, afraid that someone would suggest another terminal activity that would occupy the time he was planning to spend with Dolly. Nurse Jody stood up.

'Okay,' he said again. 'I can do that.'

Rae said: 'Fine. I'll schedule the girls to come to the Infirmary.'

Mrs. Ehrlich said to the doctor: 'I'll go down the line with you. I want you to take a peek at Oscar's sty.'

'Another one?'

'Yes. This one looks very angry to me.'

Mrs. Ehrlich went down the steps, her tiny hand on Dr. Amiel's arm. Her feet looked inappropriately small under the vast, starched canopy of her white dress and her thick, tubular, white-stockinged legs.

The counselors pushed back their chairs.

Rae said, 'And, oh yes, one other thing. About the trunk inspection. Who'll volunteer to do it?'

'I will,' said Muggs.


Born Margaret Stewart, Muggs was the only wealthy counselor on the staff, a fact unknown to all the others. She had grown up in a brownstone house near Washington Square in New York City with her father, her mother having died at her birth. Peter Stewart was a corporation lawyer who, as a desirable bachelor, dined out a great deal. He attended a great many conventions and professional meetings and sat on a number of corporation boards which met in various parts of the country.

People told Margaret that her life history was somewhat comparable to that of the heroine in a famous Henry James novel. She made it a point not to look it up. An only child of a single parent, she wanted to feel the uniqueness of her lonely state, only dimly connected to a series of distant aunts, indifferent housekeepers, and cooks.

So she had relished the idea of going to a camp, a community in which her usual state of isolation and her solitary habits could be suspended for the summer. She had grown weary of walking the small, crooked streets of Greenwich Village and studying American Indian Arts at dingy nearby New York University. During her junior year in college, she answered a newspaper ad and was offered a job as arts and crafts counselor at Camp Clear Lake. She was pleased.

Once there she made no friends. It was her conviction that her appearance was her trouble. Her long, forbidding nose seemed to point far out into the space before her. Then her face fell away precipitously to her neck, her thin mouth having, it seemed to her, too little force to command a chin. This combination of too much nose and too little chin made her appear stupid and vulnerable.

She was, of course, neither. Her dearest wish was to convince others that she was worthy of their interest and affection, but she had never succeeded. For three years now, as a junior counselor who taught crafts, she was not able to acquire even a small following of admirers among the campers, unlike the other counselors. She mourned her inability to rise above the misfortune of her looks.

One thing about her physical self *was* interesting: she was the proud possessor of a distinguishing feature, the high arch of her feet. Fritzie once said to her, watching her pose her feet at the dock: 'You ought to be a ballet dancer.' Muggs stretched again and waited for notice to be taken of her even, unmarked toes and the exalted span of her arches. But after the first admiring remarks, her feet came to be accepted as the normal, if curious, appendages to an unusually homely woman, an odd inclusion rather than an ameliorating fact.

Muggs had hoped to shed her ugly nickname. In a weak moment she once suggested to Fritzie that if she had to have a nickname, she be called Archie. Agreeably, Fritzie tried this moniker a number of times within earshot of campers. But it did not stick. Muggs she remained, homely bearer of what sounded to its victim like the name of a comic strip character.

At the arts and crafts bungalow a diverse gathering of campers—freshmen, juniors, and mediates—waited for Muggs to unlock the door. They were unaccustomed to her being late. Indeed, some of the younger freshmen thought the dour, funny-looking counselor lived in the A&C building: she seemed always to be there. The campers stamped around the front door, trying it again and again and finding it closed against them as if it were protecting their precious half-finished presents.

'She's late,' whispered Muriel to the absent Ruth, the one person to whom she always spoke these days. Ruth's departure from camp had never stopped Muriel from communicating with her. She believed that she and Ruth were combining their efforts to finish the purse for their mother, having caught, skinned, tanned, and sewn the skin of a large garter snake. As the purse neared completion, it had become smaller and smaller, until now even coins as small as dimes might turn out to be too great a burden for it.

Nonetheless the twins (as Muriel thought of herself) were impatient to finish it. It was the first time they had ever made anything for their mother. Jean, standing beside Muriel, had left the hockey field early (she was her team's best right wing) so that she could complete the belt she was making, secretly, for her cousin, to whom she had become devoted. Away from her mother, Jean had turned into an agreeable, charming child, attractive to her friends, a good sport and a well-coordinated, natural athlete and swimmer. But she set little store by these virtues, regarding Roslyn, her dark, *smart,* glowering cousin, as the model of perfection.

'Unlock the door! Let us in!' the campers shouted as Muggs approached the bungalow. She told them to step aside. The freshmen squirmed their way past her as she opened the door. The others followed, filling the long benches at the work tables. Quiet settled over the intent young workers in rawhide, birch bark, leather, and snakeskin.

Muggs walked around behind them, helping them with difficult corners and tying hard knots. She tried to hide her boredom with the awkward processes that produced the misshaped objects: too small, too short, too fragile to hold together. But, still, they were love offerings to be given to parents who would regard the worthless gifts with loudly expressed admiration. She foresaw the scene day after tomorrow at the Hoboken station:

'Look, Mom, what I made. I did one for Dad too. *Look.'* The prophetic vision somehow managed to sour Muggs's disposition, underlining her already strong sense of exclusion from family and friends, from, indeed, the human race in general.

'Not that side,' Muggs said to Jean's bunkie, Laurie, one of the few non–New Yorkers among the campers. She came from a coal-mining town in Pennsylvania and was the only daughter of the town's banking family.

'That side stays open. So money can be put in it.'

Laurie blushed, realizing that she was sewing up the fourth side of her mother's coin purse. Muggs started to help her rip out the heavy leather lacing, and then thought better of it. She decided against altruism.

'What the hell,' she said to herself. 'Let the dopey kid struggle with it. Such is life.' She laughed to herself. 'A purse with no opening might be just the thing for the spendthrift wife of a banker.'

Work proceeded in silence. The sense that they were nearing the end of this activity for the summer drove the young campers forward without their usual chatter. Only one girl, Cindy, from Brooklyn, worked noisily, whispering to the girl beside her, who did not reply. Cindy Maggio's geographic origins created much amusement among her Manhattan bunkmates, who told her they thought they would need to be vaccinated before they could come to visit her in the winter.

Cindy was tooling a second belt for her portly father, whose occupation as an influential member of a vast smuggling and bootlegging 'family' her parent believed had been carefully kept from his daughter. The girls at her private school and at camp asked her what her father 'did.' At first, she did not say, but later, to ward off suspicion at her apparent ignorance, she told them he was a stockbroker, an occupation her mother, daughter of another gangster family, had always spoken of with respect. Cindy knew that periodically her mother turned over her husband's lavish gifts of pearls and gold jewelry to her broker for what she called 'liquidation,' thus allowing her to invest secretly in blue-chip stocks.

Cindy's grandfather, Joseph Durante, had met with a tragic, sanguinary death, a violent end that had deeply affected his daughter. So her transactions with her broker acted as a hedge against a time when her husband might suffer a similar fate. Even the broker himself was an investment of a sort, Cindy suspected, since he was very close, 'personally,' as her mother said, and useful, should catastrophe strike her father.

Cindy was well versed in the tangled, precarious lives of her parents, and knew all about the fate of her grandfather. But she said nothing about any of it to her bunkmates. She was a heavyset, hot-tempered girl with a deeply suspicious nature. Recently she had found good reason to vent her indignation. Her red leather belt, completed in July, had been displayed on the wall of the A&C bungalow as evidence of her skill and her admirably early completion of a craft work. It had disappeared.

'Stolen,' she had reported to Muggs.

The counselor showed very little interest in locating the belt.

'You must have misplaced it,' she told Cindy.

'No, I didn't. I left it where you said to hang it.'

'Maybe someone borrowed it and forgot to return it.'

'Who?'

'I don't know. Ask around.'

Cindy told Liz, her bunk counselor, about her loss. Liz offered her condolences but was too busy making scenery for *The Pirates of Penzance* to pay much attention. Not one to abandon a grievance, Cindy went to Rae. The head counselor listened sympathetically, adding the belt to her list of things already reported missing.

Muggs told Cindy she could start another belt if she wished and gave her the necessary materials. She did want to, and she worked feverishly at the new belt, and Muggs reported the cost of the replacement to Mr. Ehrlich, who kept the camp accounts. He added it to the Maggio's bill. Now Cindy was close to completing a more elaborate belt in two tones of red. She intended to stay in the A&C bungalow until she finished it.

At eleven-thirty, Muggs began to clear off the work tables, sending the freshmen campers back up the line to wash for lunch.

'You've got tomorrow morning to finish. Come back then.'

Heartened by the prospect of food—Cookie's lunch was always good, and the baker, called by the campers Cookie Too, usually provided fruit tarts or chocolate cookies—everyone left, except Cindy, who was determined not to move from her task.

'No,' she said. 'I want to finish now. It's a half hour at least till Mess Hall, isn't it?' True daughter of a man renowned for his tenacity to assignments, she was not going to be told by ugly old Muggs to desert her filial belt.

'Come on, Cindy. It's time. Now.'

'No,' Cindy said. Muggs sat down on the bench beside her as if to stir her bodily. She was angry, but impotent against the girl's arrogant will.

'All right. Fifteen minutes. After that, I'm going to lock up whether you're here or not.'

Cindy glared at the counselor's big gray nose.

'Bitch,' she said clearly, spitting out the consonants.

Muggs stood up. She could not believe what she had heard. In her whole time at camp no one had used such language in her presence. Cindy, on the other hand, was accustomed to it. Her father always talked to her mother in this way, using vulgar language edged with what sounded to Cindy like genuine affection.

'Bitch,' he would say, 'get the hell out of my closet.'

Her mother would reply, not unpleasantly, in the clear-edged tones of calm retribution:

'You lousy bastard. I'm collecting all the snotty handkerchiefs you drop on the floor after you've wiped your filthy schnozzle.'

May Durante Maggio was a distant relative of the famed comic. She took advantage of this connection to use an occasional word from the revered Jimmy's familiar vocabulary, thus giving her insults a humorous tone. Cindy was used to exchanges of this nature at home. So her chatter with her bunkies was filled with expletives taken from standard Maggio conversations. After the first shock, the campers grew to admire and then emulate her vulgarity.

Cindy was usually careful of her speech before counselors. Last February, when the Ehrlichs made their enlistment rounds, they were horrified to learn that Cindy's bunkies had incorporated the juicier and more graphic words into their homecoming narratives. Because her parents paid so promptly, and tipped the staff so generously, they decided to give the child one last chance, having asked her parents, in a kindly way, if they could please tell Cindy ... But of course, the mild reproof had little effect.

Muggs shook her keys. 'It's time,' she said grimly.

'But I'm not finished.'

'Tomorrow. Nothing else is scheduled that I know of.'

Cindy made a rude fish face at Muggs, crossing her eyes and drawing in her lips into a Cupid's bow. 'I think you take ugly pills,' she muttered. Then she got up and left.

Muggs put Cindy's well-made, two-thirds-braided belt on a shelf, locked the door, and went to the Mess Hall, where the campers had lined up, through habit, in mail lines. Of course, no mail was required today, it being so close to going home. Monday, Wednesday, and Friday had been letter-home days. The price for going in to lunch on those days was a stamped letter addressed to Mr. and Mrs. Whoever, containing (Mrs. Ehrlich hoped) exciting news about athletic triumphs, gourmet meals, counselor tender care, and close medical attention. Campers were required to leave their letters open. Mrs. Ehrlich sealed them after she made note of complaints and resentments expressed to parents, and unreported (to the Infirmary) cases of diarrhea or constipation.


Roslyn, late to arrive, said in a loud voice to those near her:

'No lines, stupid. We're going home before letters can get there.'

Freed from the customary retraint, everyone broke out of line and milled around the flagpole where each morning the bugle was blown and the Stars and Stripes slowly drawn up the pole. Left hands over their hearts, the campers would recite the Pledge of Allegiance, their eyes fixed patriotically on the rising flag. An honor guard of the 'best' campers for that week was entrusted with the ropes.

In two years Roslyn had never been asked to raise or lower the flag. She attributed the omission to her rebellious spirit, her 'attitude,' as Muggs had called it. Roslyn thought her exclusion might be due to her oft-expressed devotion to Leon Trotsky, although it didn't seem that anyone at the camp knew who the great man was. Roslyn herself knew only that Trotsky represented brave rebellion in the political life of the Soviet Union. That seemed to her an excellent thing.

What did she care about being denied the honor of flag-raising? At first she had, especially two years ago, when she was stricken with her crush. If she had been chosen, Fritzie might have noticed her. This year she had come to think of it as a sign of her superiority to the jingoistic masses who swore allegiance to the flag of a nation too stupid to recognize the genius of Karl Marx.

The cook came out on the porch and rang the bell for lunch. Everyone rushed to the doors, everyone, that is, except for the seditious Roslyn, who put her hastily written postcard to Lionel, the first she had written all summer, into the counselors' mailbox and was the last one into the Mess Hall.

At the Infirmary, Dr. Amiel and Nurse Jody ignored the noon bell. They had been invited to a farewell lunch at one, with the Ehrlichs in their bungalow. It was Jody's first such invitation all summer. She felt it elevated her, belatedly, into the camp's upper class. The doctor, of course, had been a constant guest. Today he hoped the meal would be over quickly so he could join Dolly in their usual trysting place, the costume room behind the Amusement Hall, for a final roll in the hay, as he put it to himself.

At the moment, the medical personnel were engaged in packing up most of the contents of the Infirmary's glass cabinets: rolls of adhesive bandages, gauze, bottles of aspirin and milk of magnesia, tubes of cold cream and other palliatives, analgesics, and placebos. It was done quickly. Little remained on the shelves but personal prescription bottles for asthma, coughs, and indigestion.

Dr. Amiel said: 'Do we return these to the kids tomorrow?'

'Oh, no. They'd just lose them. Mrs. E. says we're to stick close to the counselors at the station when they turn over the kids. Then we deliver the bottles to parents. It's a good time for presents, even cash, because they're all relieved to see their daughters in one piece.'

'Not that we've had much to do with that.'

'No, I guess not. God was on our side, and Mrs. E., of course, who agreed to send the one really sick kid home. I think she might have had influenza. I wonder how she is.'

'No idea. Strange we never heard. Maybe the Ehrlichs did and didn't say.'

Lunch at the cottage was creamed chipped beef on toast, salad, hot rolls, tarts, and excellent coffee. Grete had brought the rolls from the bakery, where Ib was seated, holding a bottle of ale against his sweating forehead.

'Drink less, sweat less,' she had told him. He said nothing, covered the tray of fruit tarts and rolls with a napkin, and thrust it at her.

Mr. Ehrlich had returned from Liberty with the final grocery order, the mail, and the *New York Times*. He sat down beside Oscar.

'Paper here says there's a group been formed called the March of Dimes. It's to raise money for polio victims. Head of it is Basil O'Connor. Remember him?' he asked Mrs. Ehrlich.

'No,' she said in a tone suggesting such information was beneath her. She took a roll, buttered it thickly, and put it, whole, into her mouth.

'Franklin Roosevelt's law partner.'

'Any other news?'

'Well, yes, Andrew Mellon died yesterday.'

'I thought he *was* dead,' said Nurse Jody.

'It always seems that old people are already dead,' said Dr. Amiel sagely. 'When John D. Rockefeller died last May, I thought *he* was dead.'

'How old was Mellon?' Mrs. Ehrlich took another roll, her hand reaching into the basket at the same time as Oscar's. He took two.

'Eighty-six.'

'Wow,' said Oscar, his mouth so full of food he found the exclamation hard to get out.

'And Rockefeller?'

The doctor tried to remember. 'I'm not sure. Almost a hundred, I think. Something like ninety-seven or -eight.'

'Wow,' said Oscar, and swallowed hard. '*That* old. And rich too. Like Grammer.'

Everyone looked reverently toward the door behind which Grandmother Ehrlich was resting, her lunch having been brought in to her by Grete. To the campers the old lady was something of a legend. Rarely was she seen in public, from the time she was helped from the camp sedan to the bungalow until tomorrow when she would be moved into the car by the combined efforts of the doctor, Mr. Ehrlich, and the driver, Carmen.

Now and then the campers would catch sight of her white head through the bungalow window. Some thought she was a ghost, others decided she was a witch. The doctor had always called on her in early evening to administer her nightly high colonic enema, because the nurse was thought by Mrs. Ehrlich to be incapable of such a complex procedure.

Dr. Amiel suspected the old lady was very close to the end of her life. Sometimes she knew him, often she did not seem to. He guessed she was over eighty, old enough for her many afflictions: diabetes, rheumatism, heart trouble, and that common sign of extreme old age, a greedy appetite.

Occasionally a peculiar light would pierce the gray fog that inhabited Grandmother Ehrlich's mind. Once, as he was administering her enema, he heard her speak. She enunciated each word clearly, as though she were delivering a sermon:

'Birth, constipation, and old age are mortal diseases,' she said.

'What?' he asked, not believing that a full sentence had come from the old lady. But already her light blue eyes had clouded. She was gone, returned to a place where the present did not exist, he imagined, a past intelligence where philosophic observations could be formulated and then forgotten.

She spoke to him one other time. He had arrived early at her bedroom because he'd promised to drive Dolly to Liberty for crepe paper and wanted to get the enema over quickly. He found the old lady seated at her window wrapped in a quilt despite the heat, watching the campers line up for dinner. Her eyes were angry.

'I know about those children,' she said. He nodded, and waited.

'They come from the devil. Most of them. Only a few children came from God. None of mine came from Him.'

Obliged by loyalty to his employer, Dr. Amiel said: 'Oh, come now. I think Mr. Ehrlich is very good to you. How many children do you have?'

She made no reply. Perhaps she hadn't heard.

116

Then she said: 'We are all very sick of ourselves.'

Those were the last words he was to hear her say.

Of course he knew he would not be there, but he found himself imagining the scene at her deathbed. She would mumble something, perhaps something profound, but no one would understand. The Ehrlichs would be eager to have the departure of the aged woman over with (for he had noticed their impatience at the care she required). They would not be at her bedside. Her end might come while they were in Florida, or perhaps recruiting in New York in February. They would miss her last lucid moment. She would escape into senseless darkness, sick unto death and, as she had said to him, mortally sick of herself.


In early afternoon, no one was out on the line. It was rest hour, a time regarded at the camp as essential, ever since medical experts had said that tired children were more likely to contract polio. The adults at the camp took advantage of this mandated siesta. Mr. Ehrlich was lying down in his room, Mrs. Ehrlich in hers, both of them sleeping off the effects of lunch. Oscar was in the bathroom looking into the mirror in order to pick away the crusted pus that had formed on his eyelid. Muggs was in the A&C bungalow, the door locked behind her, advancing the braiding of Cindy Maggio's belt.

'She'll never know. It'll be done sooner and then I'll be rid of the brat,' she told herself.

Fritzie was in the counselor's room at the rear of her bungalow checking the chart ('Thank God this will be the last time,' she thought) on which her bunkies were required to mark their successful bowel movements every day. That chore finished, she wrote a postcard to her friend, Joe Lyons, to assure him that she was looking forward to their reunion in his fraternity house in a few weeks. The omnipresence of female society all summer had somehow increased her once tepid affection for Joe. Now she accepted much about him that she had hitherto disliked: his male overassertiveness, his unquestioning belief in himself and his natural, God-given masculine rights, his conviction (had his mother provided him with this?) that he was unrivaled among men.

Fritzie wrote: 'Can't wait to see you again.' She informed him, as an afterthought, of the time and place of her arrival in Hoboken. But she had little real hope that he would be there to welcome her back 'to the land of the living,' as she wrote.

Oblivious to their counselor's yearnings, her bunkies lolled on their cots. Muriel daydreamed about seeing Ruth the day after tomorrow and the resumption of their close, warm confidences, about the reunion with the part of herself she felt had been missing since Ruth went home. Loo lay with her eyes shut, her feet dangling over the edge of her cot, anticipating tomorrow night with pleasure when, she was sure, her gold medal would be awarded. It would be the one time all summer when glory would replace her constant embarrassment at being too tall.

Jo lay prone, stretching her completed lariat, using it as an exerciser to strengthen her arm muscles and wondering how she would attach a policeman's whistle to it. Before rest hour was over, she would have strained the thin leather to the point where the lariat would snap in the middle, reducing her to tears. Her sadness brought her thoughts to Ellie, the counselor on whom she had decided, just yesterday, that she had a crush.

Aggie, having nothing to do or think about, watched Jo, and thought she should have taken some arts and crafts periods this summer so she would have something to give her parents. But her regret was brief. She felt better almost at once when she remembered that they would still be in Europe when she

118

got home tomorrow, so there was no point in worrying about presents. Jo began a series of exercising leg movements. Aggie imitated her, one beat behind.

And Roslyn? She came out of the bathroom, where she had been fulfilling her duty, too late to record her success on the chart. Fritzie had already taken it down. Roslyn remembered her German *Fräulein*, who made her call out, after she finished evacuating: '*Ich bin fertig.*' She resisted the temptation to shout the words over the partition to Fritzie.

Roslyn lay down on her side, her eyes fixed on Fritzie's door, and pulled her Indian blanket over her. She considered whether she could safely give herself pleasure, but decided against it: she would be noticed. Instead, she reached under her cot to find the pile of newspapers. Riffling the pages made noise. Jo, who was loudly slapping her legs with two pieces of her lariat, said piously: 'Shhh.'

Roslyn leafed through a number of pages, enough to ensure the crackling noise would further annoy Jo. Then she put them back under the bed, sighed heavily, and fell asleep.


Rae and Will were on Rae's bed in the tiny bungalow, far up the line, reserved for the head counselor. It was the only bungalow without resident campers. They lay on their backs, their eyes on the rough ceiling beams, their hands clasped. Heavy despair had settled over them both. For the first time in many years they were about to live apart. Will's new teaching appointment was in northern Vermont. Rae was to stay on in her secure job as head of the physical education department at Hewitt College in Maryland.

The summer had been a long, loving, painful preparation for their separation. But now they found they still were not ready for it. They were beset by worries about the future. Rae thought Will would surely find a more proximate friend, and forget her. Will thought of the young, ambitious students who would admire pretty, amiable Rae, and seek her company, for whatever reason. They moved their heads to look at each other, their eyes filled with their troubling questions. But they said nothing.

Then they turned on their sides, facing each other as though they were about to make love. But they made no moves to do so, so great was their mutual anguish at the thought of the future. After years of passionate lovemaking, they had arrived at the realization that their bond was more than physical. They knew that, in a way they did not quite understand, they belonged together. They considered themselves to be found persons among the many lonely, lost people they knew. For them, the usual isolation that accompanies sexual deviation had not existed, or, at least, they were aware of it only as a couple. But now they were afraid that it would afflict them when they were separated and alone.

'It's all too much,' Will said. Tears came to her eyes.

'It is. It is,' Rae said, smiled at her friend, and then put her hands up to cover her own face.

They lay still, filled with the anguish of threatened, requited love.


Dolly and Dr. Amiel locked the costume-room door behind them. She stretched out on a wide, flat pile of pirate costumes. He took off his shorts and climbed on top of her, smiling down at her closed eyes and expectant mouth.

'Glad to have you aboard, Doc,' she said in her low stage voice.

'Glad to be aboard, Sarah Bernhardt,' he said.

He teased her with slow, soft movements. She motioned that she wished greater speed.

'It's probably the last time,' he thought. 'I'll do what she wants.' As he moved, he closed his eyes and considered how he would say goodbye to her.

She was too caught up in the rising action within her to think about what she would say to him when they were finished. The moment came, too fast, too acute to bear or to last, a point of pure joy for them both at once. Tired, surfeited, they rested a few minutes and then were ready to return to themselves.

The doctor thought: 'Curious, isn't it? My need for someone is over so fast, and then I go back to needing only myself.'

He slipped down onto his side to avoid falling off the platform of costumes, resolved to get what he was planning to say over with.

'Dolly, it's been swell. Really, really great. I'm sorry it's over.'

She said nothing.

He took a deep breath. 'I've been meaning to tell you.'

She waited. Then she said: 'What?'

'That I'm married. My wife's name is Ann. She's coming to New York from St. Paul, our hometown. On the third.'

'Her name is of no interest to me whatsoever. Or where she's from.'

'Oh, I know. That was stupid of me. I didn't know what else to say. But I wanted to tell you . . . about being married.'

Dolly smiled. 'Nice of you.'

'I hope you don't think I've been dishonest, or led you on, or anything like that.'

'Not at all. Why would I think that?'

'Well, why are you smiling like that?'

Dolly sat up. 'Well, I'll tell you. It's somewhat of a coincidence. I'm married too. I was going to tell you today.'

Suddenly, the doctor felt offended. For a moment he had had the edge, the higher road of bravely confessed guilt, and then he had lost it, too fast. Now he resented what he considered *her* dishonesty, oblivious to his own silence on the subject. She had practiced a deception upon him. The thought clouded his mind.

'Oh,' he said. Then he asked what he realized as he said it was a foolish question:

'Who to?'

'An actor. Name of Eliot. Lives in New York. With me.'

Then she laughed and added:

'He's from Connecticut.'

'His name and place of origin are of no interest to me. Whatsoever.'

Their sparring struck them as silly. They laughed, hard, then harder, until they lost control and rolled off to each side of the pile onto the floor. When the doctor was able to speak, he said in a voice that cracked:

'So what? So we're married. So what?'

'As long as it's not to each other,' said Dolly.

As though stirred by the same wind, they pushed themselves back onto the makeshift bed and began, slowly, to demonstrate their disdain for their histories by making love again.

Early in the summer, the senior campers had carved out for themselves a secret place in the woods behind Bungalow Twelve. There they went to gossip and to smoke. A narrow footpath, which they had attempted to obscure with broken branches and packets of old, wet leaves, led to it. It was about forty yards into the woods, a distance the senior captain, Leona, described as one City block when she gave directions to new seniors at the start of the summer.

Following the partially blocked path, one came upon a hollowed-out spot surrounded by close, tall pines. Seniors of years past (some were now stern parents who forbade their offspring every secret girlhood pleasure, especially cigarettes) had furnished the place with upturned small barrels and boards set upon stumps, created seats elevated from the always-wet ground. Smokers crowded together, inhaling with obvious relish the fragrant smoke of their Lucky Strikes and Murads, and exhaling proud smoke rings from their mouths, taking pleasure in the act of smoking itself but even more in the delicious secrecy in which it had to be performed.

Roslyn had found out about the place. One late afternoon, as she was drying after her bath, she had watched a thin line of seniors make their way back there. The next day, when she was quite sure they were occupied elsewhere and no one could see her, she went to the spot, telling herself she was desperately in need of a quiet place in which to think. It was in that little hideaway in the pine woods that she discovered the wonderful quality of stillness.

Sometimes she took a book with her, as protection against the predictable boredom of her own thoughts. But she rarely read. She became absorbed in nothingness, the absence of unnatural sound that filled the place. A few birds were there; they came to seem part of the silence. No silly camper voices, no bugle to get her up or make her go to bed, no whistles, no counselor orders, nothing that required obedience or evoked rebellion. Small animals seemed to stay away from the place. For the first time in her life she knew what it was to hear silence, to be able to feel herself sinking soundlessly down under her skin to a hidden core where she felt free to imagine things, to envision herself as an adult. Often it was a long time before a senior came to interrupt her creative inactivity and chased her away.

Life in a city or at a beach (as she had discovered last summer with Lion and those crazy Flowers kids) or in a crowded camp was never quiet, not for a second. Some people seemed to flourish under distracting roars and cheers and clatters. But, sitting in the hole in the woods, Roslyn came to realize the great power of silence. At times she tried to stop breathing or thinking, to experience the purity of silence without interruption, without the clash of ideas in her head.

When this was not possible, she would sit erect on a barrel, the seam of her serge bloomers caught in the place from which she kept expecting the show of blood that she planned to refuse. She would move slowly, rocking back and forth, to bring about the wonderful flashes of pleasure she had long ago discovered that area of her body could yield.

This was her unique, blissful secret. For she was certain she was the only girl in the world capable of producing, by herself, this exquisite sensation. It was her private discovery, one she added to her store of hidden knowledge, together with finding out about forbidden books. In her mother's bureau drawer, under her crepe de Chine underwear, Roslyn found a book called *The Rise and Fall of Susan Lenox*. She 'borrowed' it, put the cover from one of her old Nancy Drew books over its seductive jacket, and read it at night in place of *The Mill on the Floss,* which was assigned reading for English class.

On this last day of regular activities, the seniors having gone on their hike, Roslyn decided to go to what she called, with a literary reference that pleased her, the secret garden. She was trying to store up the protection of silence against the noisy banquet of tomorrow evening and the loud, insincere (she believed) farewells, the clatter of the train, the parental screams, the omnipresent uproar of the City. She wanted to say goodbye to this best of all camp places, and a permanent farewell, she hoped, to the camp. She vowed not to allow her parents ever to persuade her to come back, even if her aunt *did* pay for it.

This time she carried no reading matter with her, planning to have a dramatic little ceremony; she wanted to thank the place for its hospitality in her times of need, for her education in the joys of quiet. She wanted the place to know that she believed she would never again have to suffer from loneliness if she could find a quiet spot like this to be alone.

Pretending she was Natty Bumppo, she tried to walk the narrow path silently, one foot directly in front of the other, avoiding any twigs that might snap. Suddenly she stopped at the edge of the clearing: Fat Oscar's rump loomed up ahead of her.

Trying not to breathe audibly, Roslyn watched him replace a barrel and then stamp wet leaves around its bottom. He turned to leave, and caught sight of her watching him from the path. His face reddened, he rushed past her, not looking at her, saying nothing. She thought she heard him make a sound, like a grunt or a sob. She waited until she thought he must have reached the rear of the bungalows and then started down the line, but she made no move to leave the place. She was too curious and too angry. She sat down on the bench, furious that her holy space had been violated by that piggy boy. Then she reminded herself that all this property belonged to his family. So how could he violate it?

With her foot she pushed over the barrel Fatto had moved. A cascade of belts, compacts, lariats, purses, pocket knives, whistles, scarves, and dollar bills poured onto the packed leaves. Roslyn sat still, stunned. Her sacred grove had turned into a terrible cache of crime. Purloined objects had invaded the moral purity of a place that before had been polluted only by smoke. Her plan for a final, mystical rite, a requiem and a benediction, was wrecked, her peace of mind gone. And what was worse: she knew that if she reported her discovery the last hours of camp would be even noisier, full of accusatory voices, vengeful tones, blubbering confession.

'Jeepers,' she thought. 'I won't say anything to anybody.

125

What do I care? *I* didn't lose anything. And all this is junk. What does that dumb fat boy want it for?'

She stuffed Fatto's loot back under the barrel, replaced his leafy camouflage, and walked back along the path, Natty Bumppo style, to her bungalow to wait for her turn in the bathtub.

But it was hot, too hot to hang around in the bungalow. Roslyn went down to the lake and stood on the dock. She heard Hozzle tell her assistant, Ellie, to give surface-diving tests to two campers who were trying, for the third time, she said, to earn their junior lifesaving badges. Roslyn understood their difficulty, because she had the same problem; clearly, they both disliked holding their breath underwater. But there was another thing, she noticed. They were girls with big hips, so it was hard to pull themselves down with their weak arms. And then, with all that fat, how could they ever hoist those weights up from the bottom of the lake?

Hozzle looked as if she had given up on them. But Ellie seemed patient, more patient than she would have been in July, Roslyn surmised, when she'd overheard Fritzie say Ellie was waiting to hear if she had been moved off the waiting list and accepted into the freshman class at Sweet Briar College. Yesterday Roslyn had heard Ellie yelling all over the place:

'I'm in! I'm accepted!'

Roslyn envisioned Ellie going home, celebrating with her parents, and then going hog-wild at Peck & Peck buying cashmere sweater sets and tweed skirts.

Roslyn saw Ellie wave the dopey girls out of her way. She surface-dived to move the window-sash weight, a white towel tied around it, closer to the shore.

'Eight feet,' she said.

One girl dove down, pulled hard, and came up, red-faced,

gasping, and empty-handed. The other tried, with no success. Ellie moved the weight again.

'Seven feet.' She told them to try again.

Ellie watched them closely as if she expected them to drown. To Roslyn they looked more frightened than determined.

She looked away to see Hozzle standing at the edge of the 'crib,' a floored area where beginners could put their feet down. The swimming counselor seemed to be surveying the lake as if she really loved its clear green water, the surrounding hills, the oversized blue bowl of sky. Roslyn knew that Hozzle taught water sports and lifesaving in a pool at her college. She wondered if she had ever felt smothered there by the enclosed, wet, chlorinated heat.

Hozzle stood unmoving at the edge of the crib as if she were in command of the almost round lake—the one imperfection the small cove at the end, like a blowout place on an inner tube. Standing as still, Roslyn watched someone far away paddle out toward the cove. Birds, whose names she did not know, flew low over the water. She saw the two surface divers disappear again, only to come up too fast to have reached the bottom.

Hozzle looked disgusted. 'Jesus, they feed kids too much these days. They're bottom-heavy. They probably have too much air in their buttocks,' she said to herself.

She walked over to where Ellie and the two girls were drying off.

'Who's out there canoeing? I thought all the boats were in.'

'No idea,' Ellie said, anxious to be away from the waterfront. 'What'll I do about these two blimps?'

'Pass 'em,' Hozzle said. 'What the heck. God forbid they should ever have to save anyone's life.'


Muggs stopped a junior counselor who was patrolling the line to make sure every camper was lying down on her bed.

127

'Any of the bunks started packing yet?'

'Yes. Number Four. You know those freshman counselors. They had their kids packing last week, I think. They can't wait to get home.'

'Okay. I'll take a look in there while they're resting.'

The A&C bungalow was locked when Cindy came back after rest period.

'That bitch,' she said aloud to no one. She tried to kick the door in, but it did not move. Jean came up behind her. Cindy was peering in the window.

'Anybody there?'

Cindy turned around. 'Who're *you?*'

'Jean.'

'Well, Jean, no one's in there. And I'll tell you what. No one'll *be* in there today and I'll lose my goddam belt again and that bitch Muggs is so rotten she'll never open the damn place again. *Ever.*'

Jean stood open-mouthed, amazed at this outpouring of forbidden words. She decided this must be the girl from Brooklyn, the one Roslyn had told her about,

'The one who swears,' she had said.

Jean said to Cindy: 'She said tomorrow morning. I just thought I'd try to see if it was open. Maybe we'd better come back tomorrow.'

'Shit.'

'*What?*'

'I said shit.'

Jean was frightened. She thought a moment and then she said:

'I'll come back tomorrow. I've got to get started on my trunk. Then I have to finish my test at the lake.'

128

Cindy waited until Jean was out of sight. Then, taking careful aim, she spat on the middle windowpane, and moved her finger through the saliva. She wrote:
MUGGS THE BITCH

The afternoon moved slowly. Tired, sweaty seniors returned from their hike, mosquito-bitten and thirsty. The water in their canteens had been used up in the second hour of their hike. They lined up at the water cooler on the porch of the Amusement Hall. After they had drunk their fill, they poured water over their heads.

The juniors swam, celebrating their luck at having a cool, wet double period at the lake, all except a few wearers of red beginner's caps who were still confined to the crib. Their feet were planted nervously on the wooden floor, water to their waists and their terrified hearts pounding in their chests when they lowered themselves into the water to try the dead man's float.
Jean swam toward the middle of the lake with her friend Sally, both wearing their newly earned white caps. When Hozzle blew the whistle to check on the whereabouts of the swimmers, the two clasped hands and raised them ostentatiously into the air to demonstrate their obedience to the buddy system and their proud distance from the shore.

Will sat in the high chair at the tennis net refereeing the final match between a Blue and a Gray mediate. Both girls were grimly determined to win. Will, distracted from the furious play by thoughts of Rae, made two miscalls in a row. There were loud protests from the players. Will realized her mistakes almost at once. Her eyes filled with tears, affecting her vision and her judgment. She knew well she had been wrong, but she refused to change the calls. She ordered the girls to get on with the game.

Rae crossed PERIOD 3-4 and PERIOD 5-6 from her schedule sheet. Her heart ached, an unusual pain for her. She was one of the few persons who was not glad that camp was ending. Summer had always been a long, sun-filled, orderly idyll. She was happy when the campers seemed content, the counselors relaxed, Mrs. Ehrlich pleased, and all minor crises, if they had to arise, resolved quickly. This summer one small difficulty still remained, she reminded herself, but Muggs, usually a reliable problem-solver, had been assigned to locate the missing stuff, so all would be well.

'Then why do I feel so rotten?' she asked herself, and then she remembered. Willie. . . .

And Roslyn: unaware of the currents of emotion, the wounded sensibilities, small passions, and large indignations, raging among some of the campers and counselors, she sat on the edge of her cot, bent over at an angle, thinking about her pain. Her stomach hurt, as it always did when she felt life was going badly for her. She was exhausted by the handball game, by her large lunch and long nap, by her distaste for the prospective awards banquet. She was in despair about *everything,* she told herself: going home to Brooklyn, school in two weeks, leaving Fritzie.

She decided to write her beloved a letter to leave on Fritzie's bed, a final declaration of love, proving her undying fidelity and illustrating her new, elaborate, grown-up prose style. Everyone else had left the bungalow for a swim. Blessed quiet filled the room, even the empty space under the rafters. She found her Linen Weave Writing Pad under her cot, put the lined blotting sheet under the first sheet, and wrote:

DEAR FRITZIE—

Not quite right, she thought.

She crossed it out neatly and wrote under it:

DEAREST FRITZIE.

The progress from the positive to the superlative seemed an important step to her. Perhaps Fritzie would notice it.

In her complex and involuted new style, she put down what she most admired about her counselor: her cheerfulness, her fairness, the way she seemed to like everyone (she did not write that, privately, she would have preferred less equality and a stronger affection for *her*). She listed her virtues, avoiding the true reasons for her love: her bright, charming face, her smooth womanly voice, her lavish grin, the tight curl of her black hair at her neck and around her perfect ears, her black-as-night eyes that shone like polished coal. Most of all, the way her starched middy blouse pulled across her lavish bosom.

Now that she thought about it, it was Fritzie's person that she loved, not her character. But she could not bring herself to write that. She ended the list with 'your lovely personality.' It occurred to her she might use the popular idiom for 'sexy.' She would tell her she had 'it,' but she refrained for fear it would sound too, well, forward.

Then, wishing to appear literary and learned, Roslyn thought of complimenting her on not having 'a superiority complex' like some others she was prepared to name. It was a phrase she had heard applied to Aggie, only in reverse: 'Aggie has an inferiority complex,' someone had said. Roslyn had only a dim idea of what that meant. It was clearly an affliction as widespread as influenza and polio. She decided the whole thing was too uncertain, so she omitted its opposite in her catalogue of Fritzie's assets. She signed the letter with three X's to signify kisses and then wrote, "Your bunkie, Roslyn Hellman."

She looked under her bed. Finding no envelopes in the dust, she folded the letter in thirds, clipped it shut with a rusty bobby pin, and laid it on Fritzie's pillow.

On every field and court, games came to an end. By five o'-clock, Will and the other referees had assembled in Rae's bungalow to report the results. Hozzle brought her list of names of those who had passed their lifesaving tests. Points were awarded for this feat and added to the team scores. Muggs told Rae she had inspected trunks in seven of the sixteen bungalows and found nothing.

'Oh my. Well, keep looking,' she said. Everyone filed out to prepare for supper. Rae totaled the last points. Once again the Blue team had won.

'Five times in five years,' she told herself cheerlessly. 'Hurrah for the Union Army.' Thinking that Mrs. Ehrlich would not approve of this inequity, she went into the bathroom to run a bath.

Wearing a clean blouse and her somewhat worn blazer with its tarnished CCL insignia on the pocket, Rae walked to the directors' bungalow. She wanted to ask about borrowing a camp car to go to Liberty tomorrow evening after the banquet.

The Ehrlichs were having their early-evening Scotch and sodas in their living room. Oscar was drinking a milk shake. The Ehrlichs did not offer her a drink.

'Of course you'll all wait until lights out before you take off?'

Rae felt her carefully maintained patience with Mrs. Ehrlich wearing thin. Never in all her years at the camp had she left the camp, or allowed any other counselor to leave, before she was certain every camper was in bed and the under-cover readers had been warned to put out their flashlights.

She stared at Mrs. Ehrlich, who sensed danger in Rae's silence and said quickly:

'Of course I know you won't. That goes without saying.'

Oscar met Rae at the door. 'Can I come with you? I've never been to Liberty at night.'

'I wish you could. But there are five others I've promised already, so the car is full.'

In her soft, consoling voice, Mrs. Ehrlich said: 'Anyway, dear, they stay out until midnight. That's too late for you.'

Oscar glared at his mother and left the room. Rae watched him leave, noting his large behind and thinking that he could not squeeze into the backseat even if Mrs. Ehrlich had insisted they take him. Rae took the key from Mr. Ehrlich and thanked them both. She closed the screen door quietly behind her.

Halfway up the line she met Muggs. Rae sighed and stopped to listen as Muggs complained about Cindy Maggio's vulgarity in vivid detail, and about the defiled windowpane.

'Oh my,' said Rae.

'What will you do? That girl ought to be spanked and have her mouth washed out with soap.'

'We'll let her parents do that when she gets home.'

'Oh, sure. I can just see that. Where do you think she gets it from?'

'No idea. From them, do you mean? Well, maybe. Yes. Well, how is the search going?'

'Found nothing.'

'Lordy lord.'

'I'll keep looking.'

'Good. Thank you.'

Muggs saw the keys in Rae's hand.

'Going to Liberty tomorrow night?'

133

'I think we might, yes.'

'Would there be room for me?'

'I wish there were, but five others have asked to go.'

Muggs said nothing. The wings of her long, sad nose reddened. Rae's heart melted.

'But if you don't mind driving, you can have my place. I've plenty to do here.'

'No. No thank you. I really don't want to go that much. Besides, I don't drive.'

Rae felt sorry for her, but relieved. The Hewitt College group—Hozzle, Will, Rae, Tori (a motherly freshman counselor), and Fritzie, the one favored outsider—traditionally spent one of their last nights of camp together in the village, toasting the prospect of payday. Mr. Ehrlich would distribute the checks at the station, thus ensuring that everyone's contractual duty was fulfilled until the last moment. They would all drink to the end of eight weeks of arduous camper care, and to each other.

At the steps of her bungalow, Rae tried to think of some way to make up to Muggs for her exclusion. Nothing occurred to her.

'See you later,' she said.

'Yes,' said Muggs and walked on. She thought about the unjust rule against counselors bringing their own cars to camp. Her navy-blue Marmon roadster, old but still elegant and serviceable, had been stored in the New York City garage on Eighth Street all summer. The car had been her dearest companion ever since her father had taught her to drive it on her sixteenth birthday.

Having eaten an early supper in the Ehrlichs' kitchen, a meal of leftovers from lunch, Grete went to her room. Ib was not there.

She went down the hall to Carmen's room. He was in his upper-
deck bed reading the *Police Gazette*.

'Did you see Ib?'

'Not since morning. Why? Is the old goat missing?'

'Not missing. But not in our room, where he usually goes to
drink after the bakery.'

'Any booze missing? Find it and you'll probably find him.'

Grete drew herself up. She resented other people's referring
to Ib's drinking, regarding it as an insult, somehow, to her and
to her union with him.

'Not your business, dago.'

'Then why ask *me* where he is?' Carmen went back to his
paper.

Grete decided she would look no further. She went back to
her room, thinking: 'He is asleep somewhere, like always,
whenever the ale comes over him. Let me hope, someday he
falls asleep with his head in the big oven and I will be free.'

She settled into the chair to read her book, *Elements of Good
Cooking*. Grete had decided to go to a cooking school this winter. A good occupation, she thought, in this country of big
appetites and much money. She was studying a recipe for
chicken fricassee when Mr. Ehrlich knocked on the door and
then opened it.

'I have your check.'

'Very good.'

Mr. Ehrlich stood in the doorway and handed her a sealed
envelope. Grete opened it, read the figures, and smiled at the
director. After eight weeks she had earned two hundred and
ninety dollars, more money than she had seen in one sum since
last summer.

'Thank you, sir. Very much.'

'Don't spend it all in one place,' he said and laughed at the
cleverness of his admonition. So inconceivable was the thought

of doing such a thing that Grete stared at him, unable to understand what he was laughing at.

Mr. Ehrlich held out another envelope.

'This is for Ib. Where can I find him?'

'He is away a minute. I will give it to him.'

Mr. Ehrlich hesitated. Once he had overheard a nasty exchange between the two in the bakery. Embarrassed by what his reluctance might mean to Ib's wife, he handed her the envelope.

'Be sure to remember to give it to him.'

Grete was indignant. 'Of course, sir. Why would I not?'

He could think of no reason. He nodded vaguely.

'Goodbye, Grete. If I don't see you tomorrow, thank you for all your good work. And thank Ib. I hope we will see you both next summer.'

'Thank you, for these.' She waved the two envelopes and granted him one of her rare, tight smiles.

Mr. Ehrlich remained in the doorway. 'Do you happen to know where Carmen is?'

'In his room. There I saw him just now.'

'Okay. Well, again, goodbye.'

'*Also.*'

Left alone, Grete opened the second envelope and saw it was for the same amount as hers. She rolled the two checks into a tight ball, put them into the crease between her breasts, and buried the envelopes in the trash basket. She intended to forge his signature, and deposit them both in her account: Ib would only squander his. She would tell him Mr. Ehrlich was sending their checks in the mail to the City.


All summer long, Oscar's secret sport had been spying on the seniors. They were all about his age and seemed to him to be uniformly beautiful. In the late afternoon of this day he saw them returning from their hike, looking overheated, as his mother always said when he was flushed. Still angry at his rejection by Rae, he decided to follow them up the line for a last look at their wonderful bodies. He took his usual path through the grass behind the bungalows, where, he thought, he could not be seen by anyone.

He often looked into the rear windows to see the seniors in their baths. His penis stiffened and moved upward at the sight of their white bottoms and their black or gold triangles of hair in their crotches as they stooped to test the water and then stepped over the high side of the bathtub. He stood still, watching through the edge of the curtain until they came out, rosy from the heat of the water, their breasts like oranges, sometimes held in their hands, sometimes falling in lovely large circles on their chests.

Some mornings (if he got up in time) he spent a satisfying hour behind the bungalows, taking up his peeping post when the girls were using the toilet. He watched them seated, enjoying, he could tell, the pleasant sensations of defecation. Everything about the camp he had hated—sullen foreign help, officious counselors, the nasty, suspicious doctor and the nastier nurse who gossiped to his mother, campers who called him Fatto behind his back and even, sometimes, to his face, the heavy, constant presence in his life of his parents—was compensated for by the wonders of these visions, by his chance to spy on the mysteries of the female sex he so desired to understand.

Lying on her cot, staring out of the window behind her bed, Roslyn saw Oscar's fat shape disappear behind the back of the bungalow. She had seen him there before and had a pretty clear idea of what he was doing. Waiting her turn for a bath, she thought he might look in to watch her when it was her turn.

'So what? The jerk. He can look. I'm nothing to see, anyhow,' she said to herself.


Everyone in camp had saved one clean middy blouse and one pair of relatively unsoiled bloomers for tomorrow night's banquet. Roslyn's last blouse was creased but unspotted. She put on her blouse and then lay back on her cot, feeling very good because, wonder of wonders, there had been hot water left for her bath even after that hog Loo had her turn. She thought about the City, the wonderful, crowded, smelly-with-bus-exhaust City . . . maybe she would get a ticket next week to see that play *Room Service* at the Cort Theater that got a good review in the *Times*. Her mother had sent her a roll of newspapers containing the theater and financial sections of the *Herald Tribune*. Here, even though it bored her, she read about the effect on consumer purchases of the recent and terrible stock market collapse.

'Don't I know,' she said to herself. 'Not even a decent tennis racket this year.'

But there was still the theater. 'Maybe I'll get a standing-room ticket over Labor Day. Most New Yorkers will be in Connecticut or at Jones Beach. The theaters won't be crowded.' She had read that Gertrude Lawrence was opening in September in a Noel Coward play. Roslyn's need to be always the star of all the activities in her own life had fallen off inexplicably. Now she worshiped the stardom of others, especially people on the stage. Gertrude Lawrence! She had read that Noel Coward was acting in it too.

In the winter of the Crash, when her days had taken on a

Brooklyn grayness, and when she had the requisite two nickels for round-trip fare, she would leave school at noon on Wednesday, matinee day, without permission, ride the subway to Times Square, and look about for a theater, *any* theater, with a large first-act crowd on the sidewalk under its marquee. Often she was able to get into the theater with patrons returning from their smokes. She stood at the rear of the orchestra behind the last seats, or found an empty seat as the lights went down, and watched the rest of the play.

School seemed far away, seven or eight days, she thought. Meanwhile there were a few good things to go home to: the wonderful, palatial movie houses that she loved, her bicycle, the Automat, WQXR on the radio, the public library, and the Capehart phonograph which had somehow survived the things her family had sold after the Crash (like the De Soto) and their awful exile to Brooklyn.

Her heart sank when she remembered the problem of having no place to keep her records, housed as they were in their 'unsightly' brown albums (her mother's word for them), and the loss of Central Park and Riverside Drive to ride in. Now her beloved bicycle could take her only through Prospect Park, she thought, that flat, barren stretch of grass and trees not even near a river, and what was worse, full of lounging hobos.

But first she had to get through the next night's banquet in her wrinkled blouse, spotted green tie, and torn sneakers. Half awake, Roslyn foresaw it all, a fantasy re-created on what she remembered from two years ago:

'We will get the best meal of the whole summer, so we can go home and tell our parents how great the food was and they will think it was that way the whole summer. Roast chicken, bread stuffing, homemade cranberry sauce, and Cookie's pie with ice cream on top, *à la mode,* whatever that means. Exactly what we had at the banquet the last time I went. My name will be called: *ROSLYN HELLMAN*. I will be handed another stupid tin pin. Rae calls it bronze. She says it is given to me for some dumb thing or other, character maybe, or enthusiasm, or maybe catching the most snakes and salamanders.

' "Now for the Big Moment of the year," Rae will say in her serious voice that sounds like she is announcing the Armistice. Mr. Ehrlich brings in the silver loving cup. I wonder, as I did last time, why it is called "loving." Shaped like a heart, maybe? I remember I meant to look it up during the winter but I never did. I wonder if it is really silver or just fake like the pins. A cup made of silver paper or something like that. Mr. Ehrlich hands it to Rae. She holds it high up over her head, that silly smile on her face, and says:

' "This year the cup goes to the Blue Team. It is the twenty-fourth"—I don't know how many, maybe more, maybe only five—"time in a row. Will Senior Captain Leona Swados come up to receive it? And will all the Blues stand up so we can applaud their great efforts."

'Then Leona will go to the main table and take the cup from Rae and hold it over *her* head, pretending to groan at how heavy it is. All the Blues, from little screaming freshmen to grinning juniors (Jean will be one of them), and my sports opponents among the mediates, and the snobby seniors will stand up. I will be sitting down, of course, with the other defeated Grays.

'Some of the Blues will clap for themselves. Others will clasp their hands over their heads, and some will show how proud they are of themselves by putting their thumbs in their armpits and waving their free fingers in the air. It is all too awful. Then Leona hands the cup back to Rae. Of course, everyone knows it stays permanently in the Ehrlich bungalow. Next year it will be dragged out again and then it will have the captain's name and team and date printed on it. I hope I won't be here for *that*.

140

'Then we will all troop out into the dark night, smelling of pine, and mist coming from the lake, and under the bowl of stars I won't see again because the sky in Brooklyn comes in little squares and rectangles between the roofs of buildings. We'll trudge back up the line to our bunks and take off our grungy green uniforms for the last time this summer. Tomorrow morning we'll put on our uncomfortable city clothes, which will probably look okay to us after all the middy blouses and bloomers every day.

'Everyone around me will fall asleep very fast, worn out by the cheering, the food, the terribly long time it takes to give ninety-six campers an award for something or other, and those long, dull speeches by the directors. But I will lie here in bed, feeling very low, I know I will. I will have that black feeling of defeat I always get even though I didn't care about winning or getting a medal.

'I will search around for my flashlight, whose batteries are dying, and scrunch down under the blanket to read the one section of the *Times* I always save, from last November. It is full of wonderful stories, each one told in a single, neat paragraph, one to a subject, about New York's hundred neediest cases. I have read them again and again since last November. I will try to turn each one into life. I think these pathetic cases will be the raw stuff from which my stories will be made.

'I have a plan. I intend to memorize some of these neediest cases, taking characters and stories, plots, from them, so I can begin my novel this winter now that I am fourteen and old enough to start my career as a real writer, not just an imaginer like I used to be when I made up the lemming game last summer.... I will hear Rae calling me from the steps to put out my flashlight. She is one counselor who gives orders in a nice voice. I think she may understand she is dealing with a budding story writer, maybe a great artist. I will put out my light.

'In the dark, I'll think of my love and wonder if she has read my letter yet. What grateful words will she say to me, or write back to me? I'm scared at the thought of how she will take my declaration of love and lifelong devotion. I feel hot under the covers when I think of her.'

Roslyn is overcome by the unusual warmth that accompanies heated reverie. Easily, she slides into cool, obliterating sleep.

Everyone in Bungalow Eight was asleep except Laurie, whose birthday it had been, and Jean, who had been kept awake by the ugly bathroom sounds of Laurie 'upchucking,' the juniors' current term for vomiting. Ib's cake had been large, chocolate inside and out, with a white inscription and, because he had some heavy cream to use up, interlarding of whipped cream. The birthday girl, as Ellie, her counselor, called her, consumed three pieces.

Jean waited for her to come out of the bathroom and then went over to her bed.

'Feel better now?'

'Yes, I think so. Some better.'

'Great. Well, good night. Don't let the bedbugs bite. We're going home soon.'

'Thanks.' Laurie turned over, thinking how much she missed her mother. She vowed never to eat *anything* again.

Jean stretched out on the top of her blanket, cradling her beloved new tennis racket in her arm. 'Another long winter to wait,' she thought. 'All that school to get through. Ten months, and then I can come back. Jeepers creepers, alone with my mother all that time. And no swimming, either.'

As she closed her eyes, she smiled, remembering the game she played in the winter with her best friend from school who sometimes came over to spend the night. Chinese checkers. With all her athletic and water triumphs behind her, she decided that now there would be more: 'I'm good enough to beat her at anything.'

Consoled by the prospect of more victories, she fell asleep.


Roslyn woke from a violent dream. Balls were being thrown at her. Her head was the object of a game in a sideshow. Around her face a sheet was spread and held upright. She shook the balls away by waving her arms, and sat up. Her legs were caught in her sheet, but she was relieved that there were no softballs in the bed. What time could it be?

It was rare for her to wake up from the time she put out her under-the-covers flashlight until seven o'clock when reveille sounded. She had no way of judging the time. It was still dark: it could be six-thirty for all she knew.

Wide awake, she saw, in the light glow of a lamp, that Fritzie's door was ajar. That meant she wasn't in bed yet, so it couldn't be six-thirty. Midnight maybe? Roslyn found her flashlight under her bed. As quietly as she could she walked through the row of cots toward Fritzie's room. She passed Jo, curled into a C and snoring because, she had told them, her tonsils and adenoids needed to be taken out in the winter.

Fritzie's bed was flat. Her Westclox said fifteen minutes after twelve o'clock. Roslyn went back, passing Rita's empty bed. Mildred was asleep, lying in a long, straight line, her arms at her sides as Roslyn imagined a dead person would have them. Loo's uncovered feet hung over the end of her cot. They looked as though they were not connected to her. Roslyn did not bother to inspect Aggie.

Roslyn sat on her cot, feeling disoriented and, for no reason she could think of, afraid. Her stomach still ached, she realized, and she was tempted to lie down to relieve it.

Where could Fritzie be? The question put all thoughts of her physical discomfort out of her mind. She decided to go look for her.

Never before had she been on the line after lights out. It was cold outside; she had forgotten to put on her bathrobe. She started to go back for it and then remembered: it was packed. She decided she was cold because she was alone in the dark and because her stomach ached. It really wasn't that cold, it was *August,* for gosh sakes. Her flashlight's batteries were worn and weak, and the lamps intended to light the path were almost as dim as the one she held in her hand. The woods, the bungalows, the path made one dark country, until she saw a circle of light through the trees, down near the lake, almost at the bottom of the line.

'Maybe someone is swimming. Maybe Fritzie and the others are down there skinny-dipping. The seniors say the counselors sometimes do that.'

She shuddered at the thought of what it would be like to be without her bathing suit in an infinity of black night water, with no light to show her the shore, surrounded by one great expanse of scary nothingness.

'I would hate it.'

Roslyn walked until she came close to where the odd light was. It was made by the headlights of two cars. In them she saw that every counselor seemed to be there. They stood in clumps, talking to each other in voices so low she could not hear anything they were saying. No one took any notice of her there on the edge of the glow.

She saw the Ehrlichs in the center of one circle. Mrs. Ehrlich looked ghostly. She wore a white nightgown and over it a white lacy robe. Mr. Ehrlich was in his pajamas. In the weird brightness of flashlights and some candles the Ehrlichs looked to Roslyn like a pair of twin dwarfs, bobbing up and down as if they were wound up. Fat Oscar, the *thief*, Roslyn thought, stood close to his mother, shivering. He had on white shorts and a cardigan sweater. One of his eyes was swollen shut.

She saw Rae go over to where Muggs was standing and say something to her. Then Muggs looked grim. She turned toward the bungalows, to patrol the line, Roslyn thought, because all the other counselors were here. For a moment she thought Muggs had spotted her on the edge of the darkness, but no, she kept on walking, grumbling about something, but Roslyn could not make out what she was saying.

What was happening? Was this some final ceremony, something that took place at midnight at the end of every summer? Had she slept through it when she was here before? No. She realized it was not some silly farewell rite. One lighted car had pulled up close to the footpath to the lake. She saw SHERIFF painted on its white door. Two tall men wearing caps and uniforms got out, looked around them, and then went over to the Ehrlichs, whom they seemed to know. Roslyn moved in closer to the crowd of counselors and crouched on the damp grass under a clump of birches, lit by the funny light that made the others look very strange. Now she could hear.

'. . . she went down to look for him. She saw his . . . he was caught under a canoe,' Rae said to one of the sheriffs.

'Carmen and the doctor helped her lift him out,' someone else said.

She heard Mrs. Ehrlich's high voice: 'Our doctor says he's been dead . . . drowned . . . for about five hours. Maybe more.'

*Dead.* It was a word Roslyn knew, but a concept she could not hold for long. Always before it had struck at a distance. When it happened to John D. Rockefeller she had read about it, and also when the workers in Chicago at the steel plant who went out on strike were shot dead by the police last Memorial

145

Day. *Killed. Dead.* Words with no specific meaning unless a face or body known to her, like Lionel's father, was attached. Like the people in the hundred neediest cases who 'lost' a father or a child. *Lost,* another word for the vague, distant, mysterious dead.

Roslyn saw some people moving very slowly up the incline from the lake carrying among them what looked like a sagging, rolled-up rug, like the one in their apartment that was taken away to be cleaned every spring, 'to spare the Oriental,' her mother said. The truck driver, the doctor, Will, and two other broad-shouldered counselors Roslyn did not recognize carried the long bundle. They moved very slowly.

The procession came closer to the circles of light. Roslyn saw they were not carrying a rug but a bundle of wet clothes from which, at one end, two legs and feet without shoes stuck out. From the other end a man's head hung down. She thought it might drop off at any minute and come away from the clothes, because it swung about like a lamp in a wind. The face was almost black; it looked like ink had been injected into it. The eyes were wide open, and all she could see was white where colored eyeballs should have been. Who was it? Somehow the man looked surprised, or maybe scared. But he was dead. *Dead.* She felt as if she were about to explode with fright. Her stomach ached unbearably. Her heart burned. She thought her chest might be on fire.

At the end of the little procession walked the woman who worked for the Ehrlichs. Her face looked powdered.

'Poor Grete,' she heard Mrs. Ehrlich say. She went over and put her arm around her waist. The woman stopped and stood still, like stone, like an upright board, Roslyn thought. Then she knew who the dead man was: the husband of Grete. This waterlogged man was the baker who made sweet buns for breakfast, birthday cakes, great desserts.

The sheriff said to the bearers: 'Put him down.'

He bent over the dead man for a few moments. The other sheriff poked at the body with a fat finger, and then closed his eyes. A few counselors moved closer to see better, Roslyn supposed. But she crawled backwards over the wet moss, having seen too much, and then stood up, feeling sodden like the dead man. She believed she had suddenly been made into a new thing, a girl who had come close to a dead man and now felt bloated with inky water. No longer was she composed of healthy bones, firm flesh, and whole skin. She was terrified by the awful sight of midnight death, ten feet away from her. The vision of the baker had invaded her safe life, the absolute health of all these camp weeks, the protected days of her summer. Only once before had she been in the presence of death. But Lion's father had been enclosed in a wooden box so that the reality of a dead person had been no challenge to her belief in her own immortality.

How could anyone die in a camp where everyone was young? How did the baker dare to bring death into this safe place? How could such suddenness wipe out her certainty that she would always be alive? She wanted to go back to bed, to wipe out the unthinkable sight. She decided she would not let herself believe in its reality.

But the continuation of the procession toward the broad path down the line halted her retreat. She went on watching. She knew, in one sudden stroke of insight that made her headache and stomach ache worse, and her eyes tear, that it was all true, that the baker had drowned, died, in Clear Lake. She felt she had suffered an instant education. The surface of all her days and nights to come, all the places she loved in Manhattan, even the impregnable marble balconies of movie palaces could be invaded by this unthinkable thing: being *dead*. 'The young and strong, like me, just have longer to wait to find ourselves

147

dead,' she thought. 'We are on our way towards it. It could happen to me on the train home, or next week in the City, or while I am asleep tonight. I wouldn't even know.'

All at once she knew that for her (for was she not always the star of her own play? the main character of the drama?), someday, or maybe soon, she would not *be. Ever again not to be.* Eternity suddenly stretched out before her like the black lake, overwhelming her with terror for the one short moment she could bear to think about it.

'How can this happen?' she asked herself, talking aloud as if she were debating or arguing. At the sound of her own voice, her anguish increased. Why had no one told her this one awesome truth about living, that she would not always be alive? If her every breath was now going to be loaded down with threat, how could she go on breathing?

Again she turned to leave, furious, feeling already half dead with the new knowledge that lay heavily on her chest. Behind her she heard Hozzle say:

'He *did not* have permission. He never asked me. All the boats were in and stacked up for the year.'

Rae said: 'But did you see anyone out there? In the cove?'

Roslyn heard someone on the path behind her. Fritzie put a hand on her shoulder.

'What are you doing here? You know you're not allowed to leave your bungalow after lights out. You should have been asleep hours ago.'

'I couldn't sleep. I came looking for you. I wanted to find out ...'

Roslyn babbled her excuses as Fritzie moved her up the path, paying no attention to what Roslyn was saying.

It may have been the violent stab of mortality she had just received that made Roslyn rebel. She stopped walking so abruptly that Fritzie almost fell into her.

'Why didn't you answer my letter?'

'Come on, keep walking. I was going to thank you for it tomorrow.'

'Thank me?'

'For all the nice things you wrote about me. I appreciate it.'

Roslyn's heart sank. It felt as though it was pressing down against her stomach.

'But I said I loved you. Didn't you read that?' she said with what seemed to her an extraordinary burst of courage.

'Roz, don't be silly. You don't really love me. You're a silly kid with a crush. Everybody gets them sometime or other. Pretty soon you'll meet some nice boy and then you'll know what real love is. Like I do now.'

'You couldn't ever love me back?'

'Of course not, silly. I like you, but I love a guy named Joe Lyons. A *man*. Girls don't love girls. Come on now, keep walking.'

The presence of death, first, and then denial of the reality of her love: lights seemed to have gone out in her life. 'To her I'm silly,' she thought. 'She doesn't even *like* me, let alone love me. She doesn't believe in what I feel. She doesn't understand *anything about me.*'

They arrived at the bungalow. 'Get back to bed. Tomorrow's a very long day. Then, soon, you'll be home with your parents and forget all about this . . . nonsense.'

'But Fritzie,' she said, unable to think of anything to counter her rejection. She wanted to make one last effort on her own behalf, to take one chance at persuading her of her love. Fritzie pushed her up the steps.

'Don't fret. See you in the morning.'

'Aren't you coming . . . to tuck me in?'

'No. Don't be silly. Go to bed. Good night.'

Roslyn could not bring herself to say good night, to say

anything. She hated Fritzie for her denial of her suffering, for her indifference to *real* love, for her easy dismissal of her declaration. Yet she knew, as she sat on her cot in the dark, that she herself did not understand what it was she was feeling. She *thought* she wanted what Fritzie said she did not really want, what she could not have, what she could never have. She should not want it, and someday, would not.

'How does *she* know?'

The sheets felt cold and damp. The dark in the bungalow had deepened. She thought it was possible that she would never fall asleep again. The nightmare of the baker, his head fallen back as if he had broken it in a terrible effort, maybe, to stay afloat, and the awful blow her love had suffered, might keep her awake forever, scared, shocked, disillusioned. While she considered the cost of eternal wakefulness and the pain of unrequited love, she began to feel drowsy.

'I hate her. I love her,' she thought, and fell asleep.

After talking to Grete, Mr. Ehrlich told the ambulance driver to take Ib's body to the undertaker in Liberty and then have it cremated, the ashes to be sent by parcel post, insured, to the apartment in New York of the bereaved widow, as he described Grete to the driver.

'Send me the bill,' he said.

Irritated at having been called out of bed at this hour, the driver said, 'Oh, sure, but I'd better stop at the coroner's place first. He's the one to okay that.'

Mr. Ehrlich apologized for his ignorance. 'Of course, do what you have to do. But be sure to say he went out on the lake without permission from anyone here. We're not responsible.'

The ambulance pulled rapidly out of the camp grounds.

Mrs. Ehrlich, full of pity for the white-faced Grete, invited her back to the bungalow for hot chocolate. Fritzie, Muggs, and Rae were standing within earshot, so she invited them as well. Then she passed the doctor, who had been called to examine the body and, to his dismay, had ended up helping to carry it, and the nurse. Dr. Amiel's jacket was wet. To stop himself from shivering, he had his arms wrapped around his chest.

'Might as well,' Mrs. Ehrlich thought. She invited them too.

Soberly they all filed into the dining room. Mrs. Ehrlich gave the doctor a sweater of Oscar's and then started into the kitchen. Grete got up and gestured that she would get the hot drinks from the kitchen. Mrs. Ehrlich sat down heavily in her chair at the end of the table. No one spoke as they waited to be served.

Mr. Ehrlich brought a plate of cookies from the pantry. Oscar reached for one. The others declined Mr. Ehrlich's offer, hindered by the thought that these might be the dead baker's final products. No such scruple restrained Oscar. While Grete poured cocoa from an agate pot, he reached for a second cookie.

'That's enough, Oscar. You'll get fat,' his mother said.

Oscar frowned. He withdrew his hand, which held three cookies.

'Leave him alone, Lena,' Mr. Ehrlich said. 'He's a growing boy.'

The doctor smiled. Mrs. Ehrlich looked annoyed. The others addressed themselves to their drinks. Grete brought her cup and sat down beside Rae, who turned to her at once.

'We're all very sorry, Grete. If there's anything we can do for you here, or back in the City . . .'

'Nothing. But I thank you.' She looked grim, the only expression she could manage to disguise the immense relief she felt.

'I am free,' she thought.

She had been instantly, unexpectedly liberated, saved by accidental death from a further extension of her unbearable

151

life. Reaching to her chest, she fingered the checks in her brassiere. She said:

'One thing maybe, Mr. Ehrlich. You could write my poor husband's check—to my name?'

Mr. Ehrlich looked startled. 'Yes, of course. I can do that. Did he have his check with him?'

'No. I have it.'

Grete reached down, brought out a folded check, and put it on the table. Everyone stared at her. Grete started to gather up the cups.

'I . . . did not see him to give it, after you paid us. I was waiting. I did not know he went on the lake. I would have said, don't go. He does not . . . did not know to swim.'

'Sure. I'll write another one right away.'

He took the check, followed Grete into the kitchen, and leaned against the counter to write.

Grete rinsed and stacked the dishes. For the first time since she had worked for the Ehrlichs she left the dishes unwashed.

'Those pigs. Let them do them,' she thought. She took the check Mr. Ehrlich held out to her, said: 'Thank you. Good night,' and left by the back door. She was eager to get away to her room to enjoy in privacy her miraculous release.

Mr. Ehrlich sat down at the table.

'Better get to bed, Oscar,' he said.

Oscar stood up. His heavy stomach protruded between his white shorts and his shirt. He reached down to hitch his pants up over it.

Muggs gasped.

Mrs. Ehrlich said: 'What's the matter?'

Muggs put her hand over her mouth.

'He's got—he's wearing Cindy Maggio's belt.'

'That's his belt,' said Mrs. Ehrlich. She looked hard at her son. 'Isn't that your belt, Oscar?'

'Sure is,' he said, pulling his shirt down to cover his stomach and the belt. 'I bought it . . . in Liberty.'

'No,' said Muggs. 'It's hers. I taught her how to make it. It was stolen . . . well, taken from the A&C bungalow.'

Mrs. Ehrlich stood up. Her loose flesh seemed to shake in anger.

'Are you saying my son stole that belt?'

'No. Well, yes. I guess I am saying that.'

Rae decided matters were getting out of hand. 'Come on, Muggs, let's get back up the line. It's almost two o'clock. We have a hard day tomorrow.'

Fritzie got up quickly to put her hand on Muggs's shoulder. She too sensed the danger in Muggs's insistence on what was apparent to everyone, including, she thought, the Ehrlichs. Oscar had stolen the belt and probably everything else that was missing.

Rae said: 'Good night,' hastily, as if she was speaking for everyone, and pushed Muggs before her out the door.

'We'll be going too,' said the doctor, gesturing to the nurse.

Mrs. Ehrlich's face was pale. 'No, wait. Talk to him, Doctor. Find out why he did it.'

'No, I don't think so, Mrs. Ehrlich. You talk to him. Or Mr. Ehrlich. You're his parents.'

Mr. Ehrlich stood up, knocking into the table. He was very red in the face and looked at Oscar as if he were about to hit him. He opened his mouth, seeming about to explode until his speech came, high and rapid:

'*I am not his parent.* I am his uncle. Mrs. Ehrlich, er, Lena, is my sister. She is Lena Ehrlich Hayman. Oscar is not an Ehrlich. He is a Hayman, son of Isaac Hayman, a terrible man . . .'

'Shut up, you fool,' said Mrs. Ehrlich.

Mr. Ehrlich went out the door. Oscar moved to follow him.

'Stop, Oscar,' Mrs. Ehrlich said. The boy turned. He stared at

153

the floor. The doctor and nurse stood, frozen in their places.

The doctor said: 'I'm sorry. I didn't know. I thought you were ...'

Trapped by the shock of the revelation, they all formed a tableau of stunned silence during the interrogation that followed.

Mrs. Ehrlich said: 'Have you been taking things from the bungalows, Oscar?'

Oscar said nothing.

Dr. Amiel felt compelled professionally to act. He said to Mrs. Ehrlich:

'Ask him why he took the things.'

'Oscar, tell me why you took things.'

Oscar went on staring at the floor. Then he said, in a voice so low they had trouble hearing him: 'I wanted to have things of the girls'.'

Mrs. Ehrlich held on to the table to steady herself.

'Why, in God's name?'

'I don't know. Just to have them. And wear them.'

'Did you take other things?'

'Sometimes.'

'Like what?

'Things hanging on the lines ... behind the bungalows.'

'Things? What things?'

'Panties ... and well, um ... underwear.'

'Anything else?'

'Money, sometimes. Only a little. Not much. There wasn't much around.'

'My God, Oscar, with all the allowance you get?'

'I thought I'd buy them things, presents. In Liberty.'

'Who is "them"?'

'My friends. The seniors.'

'Which seniors? I never saw you with any seniors.'

'Maybe not now. But they would be my friends if I had more money.'

Dr. Amiel could stand it no longer. He took the nurse's arm. 'I think we'd better be going.'

Fritzie, as though released from a trance, followed them to the door.

Mrs. Ehrlich said: 'Doctor, please find Rae early in the morning and tell her Oscar will return everything he's taken to her bungalow tomorrow morning. First thing. I'll see to it.'

'I'll do that. Good night. It's almost good morning.'

Mrs. Ehrlich said, grimly: 'Yes. Almost.'

Walking up the line, Fritzie was absorbed in the night's revelations. Mr. Ehrlich's disavowal of the paternity of Oscar and his relation to Mrs. Ehrlich added to the drowning of the baker: she felt exhausted by the weight of the disclosures. She needed to get to bed. On the steps of her bungalow, Dolly was waiting.

'Glad you're back finally. I couldn't sleep. Not after what happened,' Dolly said. 'It was like a scene in a Eugene O'Neill play.'

'That was nothing. You should have been at the cottage just now for the sequel. Well, come in, but not for long. I'm bushed.'

Roslyn woke up when the dramatics counselor's foot struck the leg of her cot.

'Sorry,' Dolly whispered. Roslyn sat up.

Fritzie stopped at the bottom of the cot to look at her. Roslyn decided to avenge her rejection by ignoring her.

'Go back to sleep,' Fritzie said. The two counselors went into Fritzie's small room and closed the door.

Roslyn lay awake, trying to hear what they were talking about in there. This day and night had given her a taste for the instructive practices of peeping Toms and the joys of overhearing. By such illegal means, she now knew, she could be educated in what was going on among adults. All this was good to learn for a girl who was going to be a writer, maybe more useful than memorizing stories of the hundred neediest cases.

Not being able to hear what Dolly and Fritzie were saying ('They are *purposely* whispering,'), she was patient, absorbed in the summer's education, enumerating the virtues she had acquired. Patience, for one thing. If she lay here alert, listening hard, sooner or later Dolly and Fritzie would forget and speak loud enough so she could hear. Sure enough. In a few minutes, half awake, she heard Fritzie say an amazing thing: *the Ehrlichs were not married. They were brother and sister.*

'Why do you think they never told anyone?' Dolly said.

'I'll tell you what I think. I bet they thought it looked better for them to be married, to have people think they're married. For the parents, you know. A couple might seem to be more reliable caretakers for kids.'

'I always thought it strange they looked so much alike.'

'Married people sometimes grow to look alike, though. I've noticed that. Oh, God, I hope I don't start to look like Joe Lyons. He's getting bald and has that big nose. Maybe I won't marry him. Even if he asks me, which he probably won't.'

Roslyn felt a new sadness wash over her. She thought of beautiful Fritzie, of what a desecration it would be if she married Joe whatever-his-name-was and grew to look like him, whatever he looked like.

But that thing about the Ehrlichs: she couldn't wait to get home to tell her parents. To put her mother straight, who always said they were a perfect couple to run a children's camp.

Then she heard Fritzie tell Dolly they had found out that Oscar was the camp thief. ('Ha. I knew that, before they all did.') She felt great pleasure at hearing that the news had spread, although she regretted that she had not been the unique mystery-solver. The little holy family of her parents' invention was falling apart.

'But why would he want those things?' Roslyn began to fall asleep as she listened to Fritzie tell Dolly why he stole. He was what she called a fetishist. Roslyn decided to look up the word when she got home. She thought: 'That stupid, awful Cindy Maggio. Why would anyone want anything of hers?'

The last full day of camp was anticlimactic and rainy, full of lackadaisical activities because all the contests were over and the spirit of fierce competition had died away. Somehow, word of the baker's drowning had reached most of the campers. The older ones found the news terrifying; the young ones were affected mainly by the disappearance of their favorite desserts. The other revelations of the night before were confined to the staff and counselors, and to Roslyn, who told none of her bunkmates about her discoveries, relishing her sense of being the only camper privy to great secrets.

Rae waited in vain for Oscar's appearance with the purloined goods. She spent much of her time rallying the dispirited cook and kitchen helpers to prepare for the banquet, and enlisted Grete's help in the bakery, surprised by the good humor and willingness of the bereaved widow.

And the banquet: it went off exactly as Roslyn in her reverie had thought it would. She was pleased to have predicted its progress so accurately, and went to bed tired and happy, feeling she had successfully fulfilled her role of prophet.

The ride to Liberty in the dark took more than an hour. Will sat in front, Rae drove. They said nothing to each other. Behind were Hozzle and Tori (the diminutive was all that survived of her name, Victoria), a stocky, middle-aged, warm-hearted woman, rightly considered by Mrs. Ehrlich to be a perfect substitute for the little girls' mothers. Fritzie was between them. Being crammed together made for good-natured complaints, much shifting of buttocks, and outbreaks of hilarity in the backseat. The laughter seemed to drive Rae and Will into deeper silence.

No one was at the bar in Keating's Saloon. Ignoring the tables intended for ladies, the five counselors took stools together. In the half-dark their uniforms as they perched there gave them the look of crows on a wire. As always, the talk took on the semblance of a play, with the bartender using his customary lines.

Jerry Keating: 'Hello, girls. What'll you have?'

Tori (with a strong tone of satire as she imitated Jerry's choice of noun): 'Beers for all. Right, girls?'

Hozzle: 'Right for me.' The others nodded.

Fritzie: 'Yep, I'm feeling very free and rich tonight.'

Tori: 'But are you old enough to drink here, girlie?'

Fritzie: 'You bet your life I am. Old enough to do anything. And I can't wait.'

Hozzle and Tori laughed. Rae and Will said nothing. A circle of gloom seemed to surround them. They all drank deeply of their beers. Aware of their troubled friends, the others fell silent, their gaiety extinguished by their friends' moroseness.

Rae reached into her blouse pocket for a pack of Murads and handed it to Tori. She took one and passed the pack. Will lit everyone's cigarette and sank back on her stool to stare ahead at the row of bottles reflected in the mirror, on which was mounted a DRINK DR PEPPER sign.

Fritzie decided to try again. She took a drink of her beer and looked at Rae:

'Everything went okay tonight, I thought.'

At last Rae smiled. 'I agree. Thank you.'

Hoping to draw Will into a better humor, Fritzie said:

'I was glad to hear that everyone seemed to know the words of the camp song. It only took eight weeks.'

Tori (singing): 'Clear Lake, to you we sing our praises . . .'

Will said nothing. She stared at the Dr Pepper sign as though she had complied with its instruction and was awaiting further word. The tubes that formed its frame contained a bubbling colored liquid which seemed to interest her more than the talk.

Conversation moved from generalities to the particulars of the day behind them. Everyone ordered another beer. Rae, determined to hide the truth, told them that all the trunks were packed, and all of them had been searched. Nothing had been found.

Hozzle: 'Who searched the counselors' trunks?'

Rae: 'Muggs.'

Hozzle (who had lost twelve dollars to the thief): 'Ah. And who searched *hers?*'

Rae (laughing): 'Some of the missing stuff is from the arts and crafts bungalow. She must be sick of looking at all those things. As for the money, I have a suspicion, somehow, that she *has* money. A dollar here, two there, would hardly make any difference to her. But if you think I should, I will.'

Hozzle (grumpily): 'Twelve dollars is more than one or two here and there.'

Rae: 'Okay, I will.' Fritzie looked at Rae but was silent.

They ordered another beer and drank in silence. Rae paid for them. There was a small protest from Tori, but Rae waved it off.

'You've all been a great help to me, all summer. I'm grateful. My pleasure.'

Will looked at her, still saying nothing.

Fritzie: 'Speaking of paying, when do we get our checks?'

Rae: 'At the station tomorrow afternoon.'

Fritzie: 'Do they think we'd take off tomorrow or something if we got paid on the last day?'

Rae (shaking her head): 'It's the way they've always done it.'

Tori decided it was time for a new subject: 'I heard on the radio this morning they're not going to make Pierce Arrow cars anymore. The company's going out of business.'

Fritzie: 'Damn. That's too bad. I always thought that was a great car. And I adore the swell-looking guy in their ads.'

Rae: 'It's the kind of car I always wanted. In place of my junky Plymouth that's always breaking down. What about you, Willie?'

Will: 'Makes no difference to me. Anything's better than not having a car at all.'

Rae thought of the years she and Will had shared the old Plymouth. Rae owned it and did most of the driving, because, they agreed, she was the better driver. She wanted to say to her: 'Take the car, love. I'll get another.' But she knew she could not afford it, not at the beginning of the semester. She was silent.

Jerry Keating: 'How about one for the road, girls? On me.'

Rae said: 'Not for me, thanks.' The others said yes and thanked him.

Aware of what the approaching academic year meant to their friends, Tori, Hozzle, and Fritzie made no reference to any future beyond the next day. Fritzie felt the fire of her high spirits at the thought of seeing Joe (maybe tomorrow—who knows?) dampened by Will's depression.

'Why don't we have a midwinter reunion in Hagerstown, maybe around Christmas?' Tori said in a halfhearted attempt to lighten the atmosphere.

Fritzie: 'Swell.' Privately she doubted she would be there. She and Joe had talked about skiing in Vermont.

160

Will: 'I'll try to come,' knowing nothing in this world would keep her away if Rae was going to be there.

Tori stood up and said she ought to get to bed early, because tomorrow . . .

They all looked at their watches. Rae put fifty cents down under her glass for Keating's tip.

He thanked her and said: 'So long, girls. See you next summer. Don't take any wooden nickels.'

'We won't,' said Fritzie dutifully.

At the door they called back, almost in unison: 'Goodbye, Jerry.'

'Bye. Erin go Bragh,' he said to their backs. As he wiped the bar he shook his head at his wasted allegiance.


The ride back to camp, always before part of the final celebration, turned into a dirge. Separation sadness affected them all, making them aware of their approaching loneliness, of the end to the short, comforting comradeship of the summer. Even cheerful Fritzie felt low and threatened. Squeezed in between hefty Hozzle and Tori in the glum darkness of the car, she wondered whether Joe had met someone during his summer out West, where he had worked on a dude ranch. Sinking lower, she decided he probably had.

'I will have to get to know some new guys on campus, now that he has probably ridden off into the Western sunset with a cowgirl in Montana.'

She felt tears on her cheeks and closed her eyes, filled with sudden affection for the unfaithful Joe.


A heavy, late-summer rain fell as the camp awakened to Friday, going-home day. Reveille was late because Ellie, the bugler, had been up 'until all hours,' as she put it, rehashing

Wednesday's extraordinary events and the minor excitements of the banquet. She had overslept, and so had everyone else.

The rain darkened the sky. The campers in their olive-green raincoats sloshed unhappily through puddles to the Mess Hall almost an hour late for breakfast. There was no point in raising the flag for the half-day, so they went directly to their benches inside. Most of them were silently celebrating the thought of going home; only a few, like Jean, felt depressed about their return.

The counselors were in foul humors. There were no fresh-baked muffins. The cook had made cocoa but by now it was cool, the coffee weak, the milk stale-tasting. The campers asked for buns and were told there were none. They all ate day-old bread and jam, cold cereal, and hard-boiled eggs. Unbroken gloom sat among the breakfasters. Only Grete, running back and forth between the kitchen and the dining room, had risen to a good day, her fantasies suddenly transformed into sunny reality. Helping the cook to boil more eggs, she smiled secretly into the rising steam.

Roslyn had always liked rainy days. For one thing, she didn't have to play games or go swimming. But today the rain matched her bad mood. She had awakened with a worse stomach ache and gone to the bathroom. There it was, blood in the bowl, blood on the paper, blood between her legs and all over her pajama bottoms.

She had been caught unawares. It had come too fast for her to rally her planned defense. Depressed by her failure, she stuffed toilet paper between her legs and walked carefully to her packed trunk to find the 'things' her mother had made her bring. She was prepared, but defeated.

After breakfast she sat glumly on the bottom step of the bungalow, her bare feet in the mud, avoiding as long as possible the cleaning-up efforts of her bunkmates going on behind her. Red salamanders were out in large numbers, scooting through puddles and paddling with their miniature webbed feet in the muddy alleys between the bungalows.

Roslyn stretched out her hand in readiness. She was one of the camp's best catchers of small amphibians. She captured one now, holding the small, wet body close to her face. She watched as it raised its thin, diamond-shaped head to look at her, she thought, as if it knew it was a prisoner of her curiosity and was equally curious about her.

She considered how she would describe the little amphibian in science class this winter. 'This salamander, the Catskill Mountains kind, has little black eyes, set way back in its head, which is shaped like a pen point. Its arms'—if that's what they're called on a salamander—'have five fingers'—called what?—'one of which is a small thumb like ours. But on its legs'—called what?—'there are only four fingers.

'I don't know why there should be different kinds, but there are. My mother told me they are green in Florida. But in the Catskills where I had to spend my summer vacation they are bright red with spots of brown on their backs, especially after a rain. Then they change. The brown spots get bigger and spread out until they cover the red and the salamanders are brown everywhere and you can't tell them apart from the mud they like so much. Some people call them chameleons because they change color so fast. That may not be the right name for this kind of salamander.'

On the spur of the moment, Roslyn named the salamander in her hand Emma after Caleb's mother, whom she remembered liking because she was so silent most of the time. She thought about the beach at Far Rockaway, about how she had lectured to the others about lemmings, describing their curious habits. She wished she knew more about whether the little creature in her hand had the same self-destructive instincts. Yes, she remembered something. She had heard that if she held it by its paper-thin tail it would not like it and would abandon it in her hand.

'Come on in here and sweep under your bed,' Fritzie called. Startled, Roslyn clamped down on Emma, who panicked and moved. Roslyn grabbed again, and looked. All that was left of Emma between her fingers was the flat tail. The salamander had leaped into a puddle without it, and disappeared.

Roslyn looked for blood at the end where it had been attached to the wet slippery body. There was none. A bloodless detachment, she thought. She wished she had been able to manage something like that in the bathroom this morning. She carried the tail into the bungalow, handling it with great care, and laid it on her bare pillow. Fritzie had stripped her cot while she was out catching salamanders.

'Icky. What is *that?*' said Loo.

'Emma the salamander's tail. She left it with me as a going-home present.'

'You're cruel,' said Jo.

'Yes, you are,' said Aggie.

Muriel, who had been lying on her bare cot, came over to see the tail. She looked as if she was going to cry.

Fritzie put a broom into Roslyn's hand and said:

'Come on, kids. No time for anything but cleanup if you don't want to miss lunch before we leave.'

'If lunch is anything like breakfast, that will be okay with me,' Roslyn said. She put the tail, now shriveling, between two pages of her notebook, as if it were a treasured fall leaf, and stuffed the book into her overfull trunk. She doubted she'd need to take notes on the train ride home.

Fritzie folded sheets on Loo's bed, next to Roslyn's. Loo had gone to the bathroom. Roslyn sat on her cot, holding the broom, and whispered to Fritzie:

'Is it true they're not married?'

'*What?* Who?'

'The Ehrlichs.'

'My God. You are something, Roz. Where did you hear that? Of course it's not true.'

'I just did. But it is true, isn't it?'

'No.' Then Fritzie realized Roslyn was grinning at her. She whispered angrily: 'Don't go blabbing that to everyone.'

'So it is true,' she thought. 'My love Fritzie is lying to me. She's not as good as I thought she was.' Roslyn shuddered at this newly revealed flaw in Fritzie's character.

While Fritzie sat down hard on the top of her trunk to get it closed, Roslyn went out on the porch to nurse her disappointment. 'Maybe that's the way it will be all my life. All my loves will turn out to be imperfect. Everyone will have something that I will come to hate them for. But that's okay: I'll hold on to their weak point so I can feel better when they don't love me back.'

She decided love must be like a salamander with an expendable tail, joined so tenuously that it comes off if you reach out to grab it, and then the rest of it slithers away and disappears into the mud. Or like the lemmings who (probably in despair, she thought now) dive into the sea and drown. These similes, imperfect as they were, made her feel very grown-up. She had become capable of creating figures of speech, a literary practice more adult than copying newspaper plots.

After her trunk had been forced shut and locked, and the dust balls removed from under her bed and swept into the middle of the floor, out the door, and down the front steps to join the muddy path, Roslyn reclaimed her observation post on the steps. It had stopped raining, and a weak, almost fall sun was trying to shine. She saw Fatto walking up the line toward Rae's bungalow, carrying a gym bag.

Fritzie was sweeping the porch behind her. Roslyn saw her

look at Fatto and then look away, pretending she hadn't seen him and his bag.

'Don't worry,' Roslyn said smugly. 'I already know about him.'

'My God, Roz. Is there anything that goes on in this camp that you don't know about?'

'It's my job to know things.'

'What job?'

'Writing. I'm a writer.'

'What have you written, may I ask?'

'Well, nothing yet. Except in my head. But I'm getting ready.'

'Well, that's good to know. I'll be more careful around you from now on.'

'Someday I'm going to write about you.'

'For God's sake, don't.'

'Well, maybe not you so much. I don't happen to know much about you. But about my feelings for you.'

'That too. But you'll forget all about that by the day after tomorrow. Even maybe tomorrow.'

'Never. I'll never forget.'

'Okay. You can show me your feelings now. Go and put your shoes on so you can help me move the trunks to the porch. Carmen will be coming by in a little while to get them. And wipe the mud off your feet before you put your socks on. Your mother will think you never washed.'

Furious, Roslyn stamped into the bungalow. 'She was making fun of me again, rejecting me.' She vowed that if she ever came back here (God forbid, as Fritzie would say), she would concentrate on snakes. She was already fond of their sleek, green, shining bodies and wet, white underbellies. She would launch a campaign against anyone catching them in order to use their skins as belts. Instead she would make pets of them. They ought to be good for new similes and metaphors.

166

Grete put her belongings into a large packing case. She tied it with heavy twine and wrote MISS GRETE OLSSEN and her address on both its top and its bottom.

'For sureness,' she told herself.

She went down the hall to Carmen's room. His belongings were neatly folded in a still-open camp trunk outside his door.

Carmen opened the door.

'Oh say. Meant to come by. Sorry about Ib.'

'It is all right. But thank you. I came to ask. Do you want his clothes? I think they fit you.'

'Sure. I'll take them.'

They went to Grete's room.

'Over there,' she said and pointed. 'In the corner.'

Carmen scooped up two bundles and carried them to his room. When he came back to thank her, Grete was sitting on her bed, her feet up on the rung of a chair. She was drinking from a quart bottle of ale.

'Jumpin Jehoshaphat. Didn't know you ever drank. And so early in the day.'

'So early? Yes. I am just finishing this bottle. Ib's from Wednesday. I am thirsty.'


Oscar said to Cindy Maggio, who was taking a damp suit off the line: 'Here's your belt. I found it.'

'Where?'

'In the grass somewhere.'

'Son of a bitch,' she said.

Before she could get out the accusation that came to her mind, he had started down the line. At Rae's bungalow he paused, swallowed, and wiped his forehead. He went in. Rae was packing. Another counselor whose name he did not know was sitting on Rae's bed watching her.

'My mother made me come to give you this.' He handed her the gym bag.

'What is it?'

Oscar swallowed again and said nothing. As she started to open it he left, clumping down the steps. He went around the bungalow towards the woods.

Rae pulled out a tangle of purses, belts, lariats, underpants, and money.

'Jesus Christ,' said Will.

Rae looked troubled. 'How can she expect me to return all this stuff?'

'You could set up a booth in Hoboken and invite the owners to claim their stolen property.'

'A good idea, in part. Hoboken, no. It would make a bad impression on the parents. But I'll find Muggs. She can say she located the stuff somewhere. The kids can come to her for their, uh, their lost-and-found possessions on their way to the buses.'

Will reached into the pile and separated a ten-dollar bill and two ones.

'I'll bet these are Hozzle's. I'll give them to her on my way down. It'll make her happy for the rest of the winter.'

Rae smiled wanly: 'I wish we were going to be.'

'Going to be what?'

'Happy. For the winter.'

'In that I join you, my friend,' said Will. She reached over and brushed her finger against Rae's cheek.


At two-thirty the buses were parked at the camp gate, behind the trucks loaded with trunks and cardboard boxes. Counselors shepherded their bunkies down the line. Rae, looking weary and dispirited, her familiar clipboard in hand, inspected each bungalow as it was vacated for campers' possessions, made a check on her list, and then moved on.

Mrs. Ehrlich was nowhere to be seen. Mr. Ehrlich gave the bus drivers their orders to depart when their bus was full, and waved to the campers, who were singing camp songs as they leaned out of the windows. Filled with the pleasure of departure and thoughts of dinner tonight with their families, they waved back happily to the director.

On the last bus, the doctor and nurse sat together. Dr. Amiel had hoped to ride to the station with Dolly, but she had taken an earlier bus with Fritzie and her campers.

'Stuck with me, Doctor,' said the nurse when she saw him looking around.

'Yup. Guess so.'

'Glad it's all over?'

'Am I ever. All those infernal baseball fingers.'

'When does your wife arrive?'

'In a few days, I think. Why do you want to know?'

'No reason. Are you looking forward to her coming?'

'What is this, the Inquisition?'

'What about Dolly, your great love?'

'I will look back on all that with the greatest pleasure, Nurse Jody.'

'You bastard,' she said, her words heavy with the bitterness of the everlasting underling.

Dr. Amiel smiled at Nurse Jody.

'Yup,' he said, with professional arrogance.

Between them, Mr. Ehrlich and Oscar lifted Grandmother Ehrlich into the backseat of the sedan. Mrs. Ehrlich came out of the cottage carrying a gray lap robe, which she tucked around the old lady's legs.

'Where am I going?' she asked her daughter.

'To New York. To the apartment. I'll see you there.'

'Enjoy the ride,' Oscar said and stood back beside his mother. His face was very red, and one eyelid, rosier than the other, was swollen shut by his sty.

'Don't forget the checks, Lena.'

Mrs. Ehrlich said: 'When have I ever forgotten the checks?'

Mr. Ehrlich got into the car. Carmen started the motor. Mr. Ehrlich turned around and said to his mother: 'Just relax. You'll be fine.'

'When?' she said.


The station platform was crowded with noisy reunions. Parents listened delightedly as their daughters reported their athletic triumphs, their achievements in the water, their medals and pins. The parents exclaimed over how brown their daughters were, how healthy they looked, how they'd grown. When the fathers said goodbye, they pressed ten-dollar bills into the hands of the counselors they considered responsible for these satisfactory states.

Fritzie saw Joe Lyons's bearded face far down the platform. She resisted the impulse to run to him, because Muriel, unable to locate her parents in the confusion, clung to her arm, and Roslyn, who appeared to be more interested in Fritzie than in finding the Hellmans, held her hand. The Kresses found Muriel. As they hugged her, she stood very still, not raising her arms to them, her eyes wide with recognition that what she had guessed, had *felt,* was true. She noticed her parents' somber clothing among the other summer-clad parents, their stricken faces, the absence of her sister. . . . Fritzie handed Muriel's health report to Mr. Kress, and then stood back, still held captive by Roslyn.

Roslyn whispered to her: 'Where's Ruth?'

Fritzie said: 'I don't know.'

170

Roslyn thought: 'She's lying. Why isn't she here? Why are they wearing black? I bet I know.'

Alert to fictional possibilities, Roslyn decided Ruth was very sick. Then too, she might be dead. The awfulness of this thought went through her, and made her hands shake. She wasn't brave enough to stay around the Kresses any longer, to learn the truth. *Maybe I don't have what it takes to be a writer.*

She called over to Muriel: 'So long. See you next year.' She knew at once it was a stupid thing to say, but she couldn't think of anything else.

Muriel appeared not to hear her. She was crying into her mother's shoulder. The Kresses paid no attention to Roslyn or Fritzie.

Roslyn walked away with Fritzie.

'Is your boyfriend here?'

'My fiancé? Yes, he's here.'

Roslyn decided to make one last grand gesture.

'I hope you'll be happy.'

'Thank you, Roz,' she said, and, feeling she owed the girl a bit of kindness, she kissed her on the cheek.

Roslyn stood still, as if she were suffering under her touch, and stared at her counselor.

Fritzie laughed, said goodbye, 'See you next summer,' and walked away down the platform toward Joe Lyons.

'Not bloody likely,' said Roslyn aloud.

'It's something,' she thought. 'She likes me. I still love her. Emma may grow her tail back and be whole. My stomach still aches a little, and that silly pad between my legs is beginning to make me sore. But I'm beginning to feel better.'


From a distance Dolly waved to Amiel. He waved back and then turned to the Maggios. Mr. Maggio, holding on proudly to two red woven belts, shook the doctor's hand vigorously.

'I want to thank you, Doctor, for the good care you gave my girl here.' He slapped him twice on the back and then handed him an envelope.

'It's a small token of my appreciation, Doctor.'

Mrs. Maggio nodded to the doctor. Despite the warm day, she was wearing a fur stole, a large string of pearls, and gold jewelry.

The doctor thanked Mr. Maggio and said: 'It was nothing, sir,' a literal truth, since Cindy Maggio had never been sick. He gave her father the health report and looked around to see if the circle of counselors around Mrs. Ehrlich had thinned out.

Three abreast, the Maggios walked toward the ferry slip.

'Never once was in the goddamn infirmary,' said Cindy to her father.

Mrs. Ehrlich watched the family group get on the ferry. She had been informed by Rae that the junior camper's vocabulary had been more colorful this year than last. She resolved not to call on the family this winter in order to remove Cindy and her language from the camp roster.

But she need not have worried. The Ehrlichs were to be saved by a kindly Fate. Through the newspapers, they learned that the Maggios had gone abroad to visit relatives in Sicily soon after the closing of camp. There was a gathering of the large Maggio clan. While they ate hugely of pasta and drank much *grappa,* an investigation into Mafia activities in the United States revealed that Constanzo Maggio, Cindy's generous father, had been involved, in a suspicious manner, in Brooklyn politics. The borough's district attorney informed Sicilian officials, through federal representatives there, that the Maggios would not be welcomed back into the country. Cindy Maggio's vulgarity would no longer be a threat to the sheltered minds of junior campers.

Dr. Amiel took his envelope from Mrs. Ehrlich and shook her hand.

'Have a nice winter in Florida. I've enjoyed the summer.'

'I'm glad.'

'Where's Oscar?'

'He made the first ferry. There's a movie in the City he wanted to see. Called *Public Enemy,* I think.'

'I hope he'll be all right. Try to get him to lose some weight.'

'Yes. But you know him. I'm not worried about that. It's . . . his behavior. What am I going to do about that?'

'Why don't you take him to a psychiatrist?'

'That Freud stuff? I don't believe in it.'

'Well, maybe you're right. I hope his eye clears up,' he said, anxious to get away from Oscar's multiple troubles and to make the ferry. 'You take care. Say goodbye for me to your . . . to Mr. Ehrlich.'

'Thank you. I will.'


For a few moments after the doctor left, Mrs. Ehrlich stood alone, feeling deserted and defenseless, without her supportive head counselor, without useful Grete, without her brother or her son. She saw Muggs coming toward her. Immediately she resumed her old confident stance.

'Goodbye, Mrs. Ehrlich,' Muggs said. She was dressed in a handsome blue skirt and blouse that Mrs. Ehrlich thought looked as if it had come from Saks Fifth Avenue. Her heels were very high, displaying the elegance of her arches.

'I'm sorry about the belt business. Maybe I shouldn't have said . . .'

'Maybe not,' said Mrs. Ehrlich coolly. She handed Muggs her check.

'Are you making this ferry?' she asked the counselor as she started to turn away.

'No. I'm driving back.'

*'Driving back?'*

'Uh, well, yes. The chauffeur brought my car.'

Mrs. Ehrlich stared. For the first time since she had hired her, three summers ago, she remembered about Margaret Stewart. Not just the arts and crafts counselor, or the betrayer of her son, but one of New York's rich girls. Maybe she should have had her to dinner one night. . . .

Margaret Stewart said, waving the check: 'Thank you for this,' and smiled. Her receding chin seemed even more in retreat.

Mrs. Ehrlich said: 'Yes. Good. Well, goodbye,' and turned to greet the Hellmans.

Dr. Amiel made his way through the diminishing crowd to the ferry. He felt healthy but depressed, sunburned and well exercised but, for some reason, sad: sad about Dolly, apprehensive about his internship at Bellevue, which began in a few days, dejected at the thought that the noose of his marriage was about to descend upon him. He found a place at the rail on the upper deck and leaned against it to watch the boat make its slow, decorous way across the Hudson to Manhattan. For some reason, he suddenly remembered Grandmother Ehrlich.

'I'm sick of myself,' he said into the sea breeze, and laughed.

After all the farewells and pleasantries were over, Rae and Will made the last ferry. They went to the lower-deck rail. Will started to shake as she saw the water swirling about the prow of the boat. Rae took her arm.

'Willie dear. Let's go into the cabin.'

They took a bench at the back. A boy offered them hot dogs and soda. They refused, and sat very close to each other.

'Where are we staying?' Will asked.

'At the Lafayette. In the Village. I thought we'd blow a little of my ill-gotten gains on some luxury.'

'For how long?'

'Not very. We won't be able to afford it. Three days, maybe.'

Will shivered.

'What's the matter, love?'

'I hate being on water as much as I hate being in it,' Will said.

Roslyn had a superstitious concern: she wanted everything to come out even. If she lost something, she worried that she would not find something else to make up for it. When she used up all the envelopes in her stationery box, she worried about what to do with the orphaned writing paper. Sometimes she wrote longer letters so there would be no leftover sheets.

On the last day of camp, the shaky balance between good and bad things tipped for her. Things had not come out even. Everything she had seen, felt, heard, and overheard this summer was bad: thievery, death, rejection, uncontrollable bleeding, and what she surmised was the fate of Ruth Kress.

Crossing the river, the Hellmans and Aunt Sophie stood at the prow of the ferry. Roslyn held on to the chain that separated the cars from the drive-off ramp. Jean carried her hockey stick and tennis racket under one arm and held on to Roslyn with the other. Jean had just given her the belt she had made. Roslyn put it on over the top of her cotton skirt. She was pleased that Jean had done such a nice thing, but still it did not balance all the other . . .

She felt her father's hand on her shoulder. She thought: 'We are sailing the ocean blue—well, the river. Our parents are glad, at the moment, to have us back. Jean's got her gold medal around her neck. She keeps looking down at it. She's proud. I'm carrying nothing. I threw my tin pin into the woods before we left. But it was nice of her to make me a belt, the one good thing that's happened, well, maybe after the kiss on my cheek. I don't think I'll ever wash it off.

'I can smell the salt of the ocean. It's a Riverside Drive smell. Whenever I come upon it, I know I'm going to the City. I felt like I'd been expelled from it. It was like this when we came back from Far Rockaway. A coming-home odor. New York City used to smell of fall streets, delis, and fresh morning newspapers, the wind from the river and the dust of the gutters, movie theaters and lighted stores. Then it all disappeared with the Crash. Brooklyn is another country, but then, there's always the subway.'

Left behind were the pine-woods and clear-lake scents and silences that, for the rest of her life, would define *country* to her. Sweet, wet, heavy, sharp, they were the smells of a world outside the City, the aroma that would fasten itself to her memory of first love and the inevitable disorders of deception, death, and anatomy.

In the Catskill woods, at a summer camp on a clear but lethal lake, in late August 1930, Roslyn had made rapid advances out of her girlhood. She had left it behind in exchange for the pains and torments of being a woman. And, like everyone else in the world, she had learned that she was vulnerable to everything. And like so many others, she would come to know that she was one of life's neediest cases.

# 3

# Telluride

*A self-governing community of about twenty-five male students, chosen for their promise and achievement to attend Cornell University. Free room and board are provided, in return for assuming responsibility for the operation of the House, and for continued academic performance and agreeable communal behavior. The House: a simple, solid brick building, erected in 1910 in the Prairie style originated by Frank Lloyd Wright.*

CALEB FLOWERS SPENT the first months at college desperately sick for home. His dormitory, North Baker Hall, had provided its students with only three public telephone booths. So, every other evening, after dinner, he lined up before one of them to wait his turn. He could go just so long without speaking to his mother and sister in Far Rockaway.

For their benefit he affected a tone of cheery good humor. Yes, his room was fine, his roommate was swell, his studies were going very well, his social life was good, well yes, it was okay.

'And how are things going at home?' he would always ask, striving to keep his voice strong yet concerned and tender.

He listened patiently to their reports, the tenor of which never varied: everything was fine, Kate was studying hard for her midterms, Emma was reading a new novel by James Hilton ('somewhat nasty,' she reported), they missed him very much and were eagerly looking forward to Thanksgiving holiday and then Christmas recess and then spring vacation and, of course, the summer. . . .

When Caleb had shut the glass door behind him and gone to his room, he would break down. Beleaguered by the rigidity of daily academic assignments—forty pages of this, three chapters of that, a paper for the day after tomorrow—he could not rid himself of the memory of his mother's wonderfully lax and undemanding ways of living, her patient and selective deafness, her uncritical admiration of him. But most painful were the haunting recollections of Kate, his loving, beautiful sister, whose ethereal presence was constant and troubling.

His roommate was an athletic fellow from upstate New York who wanted Caleb, and everyone else in Baker Hall, to like him. Boris, who asked to be called Bo, was agreeable, obliging, and sociable: everyone was invited to their room at any hour. He was a jovial host to strays and popular freshmen alike. Caleb, unaccustomed to rowdy horseplay and constant, surreptitious drinking (for prohibition was still practiced by the Cornell administration even after its repeal the year before by the national government), felt out of place and alien in their populous room.

On the evenings of his telephone calls he was always relieved to come back to find his room empty. He could indulge his tears and rid himself privately of all traces of his childish sorrow. He felt guilty about his sadness, believing no other man of college age on the entire campus could be found indulging in this foolish state. It drove him out of Baker and across the field to the library, because he knew that his room would soon fill up with boys playing Tommy Dorsey and Paul Whiteman records over and over on the Victrola, drinking gin and pineapple juice, and talking about the girls undoubtedly waiting in the parlor of Sage Hall for the boys to call.

In the first year, as a result of his retreat from sociability, Caleb achieved high grades, placing him on the Dean's List and guaranteeing the renewal of his tuition scholarship. And what was more, and most surprising to him, one day he found in his mailbox an invitation to spend his sophomore year as a resident of Telluride, the prestigious house for distinguished undergraduates, graduate students, and a few chosen faculty.

Curiously enough after his long year of homesickness, Caleb decided to spend the summer in Ithaca, putting files in order in the office of the *Cornell Daily Sun*. He told his mother he needed the experience because he was considering a career in journalism, a decision he had not given a thought to until he uttered those words to her. His real reason for not going home, until two weeks before the fall semester began, was more self-serving. He was not willing to suffer through another period of bruising displacement after indulging himself in a long summer's feast of familial comfort and affection. Better to have no taste of it at all, he decided, than to starve once again for its richness.

To satisfy his conscience, he went to Far Rockaway for the last weekend in August.


Emma found his news hard to believe. Caleb showed her his letter.

'Room *and* board?' she said.

'Yes,' he said. 'It's a wonderful house. Lovely parlor, big rooms, a porch, fireplace, everything. I'll have a room to myself, I think. But it doesn't matter. Everyone there takes his studies very seriously. No drinking or fooling around with girls, and such.'

'It must be much in demand. How many boys live there?'

'Men, mother, *men*. Not boys. This year I'm told there will be about twenty-five.'

'How did you come to get in, Caleb?'

'Well, Mother, I heard about the house, so I applied. In my

spare time at the paper, I wrote the essay they asked for and took it over to West Street, where the house is, not far from where I lived this year. Then I went back a few weeks ago to be interviewed. Last Tuesday, just before I left, I got the letter.'

'It's wonderful. Isn't it wonderful, Kate?'

'It is wonderful,' said Kate soberly. 'Congratulations, Caleb.'

Kate had found Caleb's late return home that summer very difficult. Her summer had been uneventful, an unmarked transition from a dull senior year in high school. She had waited eagerly for his vacations, planning the time for his return, hoping to renew the warmth of the friendship she had not been able to transfer to any other person at school.

But his short stays at home had been painful failures for her. Caleb seemed afraid to come close to her in the old way. When she looked at him, as she could not help doing because in her eyes he grew more beautiful every time she saw him, he met her eyes and then quickly looked away, as though he did not wish to be inspected in this way. Or perhaps he did not wish to return her glance, to see her as she was growing up to be. Or perhaps, she thought, he was feeling a reluctance to face her, because he no longer shared the same need she was feeling.

He was interested in her plans, no longer in her person, she believed. But she wanted so much to lie in his arms in the old way, to hear his wonderful stories, to play his lady, his amorous companion, his love, his wife. Since he had gone away, she had found the realities of her life disappointing. She went on reading myths, fairy tales, and sagas, rereading the romantic fiction from which he used to draw his games, but now she found them painful to review in his absence. Only the memory of the part they had played in their shared past sustained her.

'Where will you go next year, Kate? Where have you applied?'

'That's the trouble,' Emma said. 'Nowhere. I keep asking

her, but she won't decide. I've suggested Cornell, to be near you, but she won't do anything about *that.*'

'I like it here,' said Kate. 'I don't see why I have to go to college. What would I study? What do I want to be?'

'You once said you might like to be a teacher,' Caleb said. He felt no enthusiasm for her attendance at Cornell but had no wish to reveal his opposition. He felt he had cured himself, after great pain, of his long boyhood obsession with Kate. Now he was afraid to test his belief by her proximity to him.

'No, not anymore. Besides, it costs a lot to go. I don't have a Regents scholarship like you. And I'm a girl. So I can't get into some house that gives you free room and board, can I, Caleb?'

'No. It's only for men.'

Emma said: 'But, Kate, I've told you. I can manage.'

'But I told you, Mother, I don't want to go.'


By denying to them what she secretly wished for, Kate thought she was punishing Caleb for his desertion. She wanted to repay his cavalier indifference to what he should have longingly re-membered during the winter of his first year at college. Now, if she insisted on staying at home, doing nothing but living Emma's somnolent life, and Caleb went about making his suc-cessful way in the world, she might elicit some pity from him. He might be moved to comfort her in the old, wonderful way, even to return to her the one thing she cared about in this world: his love.

But it did not happen. Claiming he had much settling in to do in his new quarters, Caleb left Far Rockaway a day early. He could not disguise his eagerness to get to the new house, to begin his college life afresh, and to register for Professor Harry Caplan's classics course. He had heard, he told his mother and Kate, that it was difficult for a sophomore to get into it. Also, in the privacy of his single room, he wanted to try out the phonograph Emma had given him as reward for his freshman grades.

Kate said goodbye. She waited for him to offer to kiss her when he approached her. They looked at each other awkwardly, he at the top of her head, she at his hands, each trying hard not to recall the old ardor of their embraces. Emma hugged him and told him to come home soon.

The Greyhound bus ride to Ithaca went very quickly. He occupied himself with savoring his relief at his escape from his family and anticipating the new semester and the new place he was going to live.

In the next two years the lives of the Flowerses were uneventful. The scenario they had all tacitly agreed to when Caleb first left home was followed without change. While his classmates played and drank and dated, and his housemates at Telluride talked and studied and advanced to fellowships in scholarly fields, Caleb spent much of his time taking solitary walks, because he had been told by an English instructor they were very good for the development and clarity of his mind. He took extra courses in literature and stayed in the library's reading room almost every evening until it closed at ten o'clock.

His only recreation, at the end of his Saturday-evening walk, was in the Carnegie Room in the student union, where he listened to records of his choice in order to wipe out his ignorance of classical music. He enjoyed posturing as a picturesque solitary, seeing himself in the role of a reclusive, romantic, moody Heidelberg student, preparing for his emergence into the world of the intellect. Thus engrossed, he was not surprised to discover that, unlike almost everyone else in his class and at Telluride, he had no interest in the coeds in his classes. Single-mindedly, he worked for high grades and the favorable notice of his instructors.

With outward grace, Kate accepted her assigned roles as housekeeper and her mother's caretaker. But when Caleb came home on holidays, he was aware that she seemed sober, even on occasion morose. She spoke less than he remembered, especially to him, and moved about the house performing her chores as though she felt herself to be almost invisible.

Emma, always oblivious to the small dramas being played out in her presence, now noticed very little of Kate's retreat from Caleb or of Caleb's forced cheerfulness. With few demands upon her attention, she aged fast and became almost totally deaf. She seemed to have retired into the envelope of her self: her appetite and her pleasure at Caleb's occasional presence her only visible responses beyond the tray placed before her to hold her meals.

Silent as falling snow, she sank into somnolence and weight.


Late one evening, at the start of his senior year in Telluride, Caleb was called to the telephone. Expecting it to be Kate, he was startled by the masculine voice.

'Remember me? Lionel Schwartz? From that summer at the beach before the Crash?'

'Of course. Where are you?'

'I'm in Baker Tower. I've just got here. I called your home, and your sister told me where to find you.'

'Wonderful. It'll be great to see you again. Let's have dinner together. How about tomorrow? Are you free? Can you come here?'

'Where is here?'

'Telluride House. On West Avenue. Not far from you. Where are your classes? Mostly in Goldwin Smith?'

'No. Down the way. I'm in the College of Agriculture.'

There was a pause.

'Oh. Yes,' said Caleb. 'Well, if you're coming from a class on the Ag campus, take Tower Road back to the library, where the clock tower is. I'll meet you there on the steps. Five-thirty okay?'

'Fine. I'll be there.'

'Oh, and wear a tie and jacket. We're required to dress for dinner.'

'Okay.'

'See you then.'


Caleb and Lionel shook hands awkwardly on the library steps. Saying very little, they sat for a few moments on a stone bench to recover from their feelings of strangeness. Caleb recalled the Lion of old, the shy boy who had built residential structures in the sand. Lionel remembered the big handsome boy who had pulled his sister out of the surf when they all played lemmings. They began to talk of those summer days, contributing their most baneful memories of every event. Caleb was sure that Roslyn Hellman had been the curse of their existence. Lionel remembered Kate as Caleb's devoted and intrepid follower.

'Shall I call you Lionel, or Lion, as we used to?'

'Lionel. I've always rather liked Lion. But my mother hated it. She said it didn't suit me. Perhaps she was right.'

Lionel was still very slight. His bones seemed to be lighter and more flexible, his skin thinner and more blond than Caleb remembered. His hair, eyebrows, and lashes were still almost the color of his skin, his lips slender and very red, shaped like an equals sign, Caleb thought. His shapely head seemed not to have changed; he had the same small, flat ears that looked as if they had been drawn on his head, and the same fine, narrow, straight nose. Caleb could not prevent himself from staring at him. It was astonishing: he looked very much like Kate.

'How is your sister?' Lionel asked, as if he had read Caleb's mind.

'Kate's fine.'

'Where is she going to college?'

'She didn't go. She's at home with Mother.'

'Working in Far Rockaway?'

'Um, no. Not really. My mother hasn't been well. Kate does a great deal for her.'

'Oh, I'm sorry. I remember your mother clearly. She was very nice to us that summer.'

There was a long pause. Caleb thought briefly about Kate, that yearning look in her eyes, cooking, doing the laundry, bathing and dressing Moth, walking to the store. Lionel thought about Emma giving them lemonade on the veranda on Larch Street.

Caleb looked at his watch. 'We'd better start over to dinner.'


After dinner, which was served by student waiters to the well-dressed, mannerly residents, Caleb took Lionel into the sitting room, where many of the diners had moved into the heavy leather chairs. They were drinking coffee, smoking cigarettes, and listening to a senior geology student describe the stratification of rock at Cascadilla Falls.

A little way into the talk, Caleb and Lionel looked at each other, displaying a silent, shared boredom with the subject. But they stayed in their seats until the discussion period began.

'Like to see my room?' Caleb whispered. Lionel had been listening intently to the questions. Everyone in the room but him seemed engrossed in some arcane detail of the talk.

On the way upstairs, he asked: 'Are they all geology students?'

'Oh, no. William is the only one. We all have to give a talk now and then about what we're studying. But we do find our-selves getting interested in each other's work. That's why they're asking all those questions.'

'That's something. In Willard Straight, where I had dinner last night, all I heard talked about was how St. Louis would probably end up playing Detroit in the World Series. And a lot about the local football team. They call it the Red Tide. Or some such thing. All very boring to me.'

'What are you interested in?'

'Architecture. I've always been. I'm in Ag because it costs very little and I can get some electives over here. But I've got to take a lot of other stuff—physics, botany, economics, food and nutrition, that kind of thing—in order to stay in the college. And you?'

'Classical and medieval literature. There's a great man here, Lane Cooper. I've been lucky to have two courses with him.'

'What will you do with that, as my mother would say?'

'Nothing, I suppose, unless I go on.'

'Will you?'

'Who knows? I'd like to. But it's not easy to get fellowships now. People are fighting for them.'

'Are you in ROTC?'

'God, no. Are you?'

'Well, yes, I've enrolled in it. We're required to take Military Science and Tactics. So it made sense to take that too. It's good exercise if nothing else.'

'Do you have to take a language?'

'No, I don't think so.'

'Too bad.

'Do you?'

'I've had French all along, three years of it. Last year it was French poetry with a fellow named Lang. Alexander Lang. Have you heard of him?'

'No, I haven't.'

'Well, he's awfully good, a wonderful teacher, in fact. Speaks such perfect French that it's hard to believe he was born here, in Scranton, Pennsylvania, he told us when someone asked what part of France he was from. He's been at Cornell for three or four years, but he goes to France every summer, the day after school closes, I've heard.'

'I may have seen him in Straight. What does he look like?'

'He's funny-looking, tall and sort of very thin with quite long, yellow hair and a little pointed brown beard.'

'Oh yes, does he wear a flower in his buttonhole? I think I have seen him.'


In this desultory way they talked on about college matters, Caleb sitting on his bed with a pillow propped up on the wall behind him, Lionel sunk down in the leather seat of the crate-like wooden chair.

'Frank Lloyd Wright comfort,' Lionel said. 'But it looks very nice.'

'Who is that?'

'An architect in the Middle West who designs all the furniture in his houses to match the design of the house. Sometimes he builds it all into the house itself.'

Under the surface of their rambling conversation there moved a subterranean current of wonder. Lionel had discovered a curious, unexplainable attraction to Caleb's rugged, sun-browned face and solid, almost square-appearing body. He wanted to touch him, to stroke his straight brown hair back from his forehead. And Caleb: to his amazement he found himself watching Lionel's every move, more aware of the easy, graceful motions of his head and hands than he was of his talk. Was he thinking of Kate? he wondered. Or was he now trans-

187

ferring his boyhood regard for her to this boy, no, man, who looked so much like her?

At ten o'clock, Caleb suggested that he walk Lionel halfway back to his dorm. Downstairs the rooms were deserted, and outside on West Avenue only the shadows made by the lamps standing high and parallel to the great oak trees crossed their path. At the doorway to McFadden Hall, Lionel turned to Caleb.

'This is about halfway. You don't need to come any farther. It's been great. Thank you so much for asking me.'

Lionel reached out to take Caleb's hand. Impetuously, almost without a thought (afterwards, on his way home alone, he was to question himself about how it happened, how he came to do it, what had prompted his injudicious move), Caleb ignored Lionel's outstretched hand and put his arm around him, pulling him awkwardly off balance and close to him. Startled, Lionel put his arms up to return the gesture. In the dark night, beyond the reach of the dim West Avenue streetlight, they hugged each other and, by a kind of extraordinary mutual agreement, stayed in each other's arms longer than the occasion called for or the parting justified.

There are times in every life when a gesture goes beyond thought, when two persons reach instinctively into the future at once without giving thought to the present and with no reference to the past, indeed, to anything that has gone before. At such a time the actors are not prepared for what they have done, are not aware, until it has happened, that they will do it. And yet, so significant is the movement that it turns lives against their expected direction, away from the purposes they had intended to serve, and toward an unforeseen, even dangerous future.

Such was the nature of the embrace that Lionel and Caleb exchanged. Embarrassed and frightened, they separated, nodded formally to each other, and walked away in opposite directions, making no plans to meet again, saying nothing beyond an abrupt good night. It was as if they had been caught in a riptide of feeling that had come upon them with no warning. There was nothing for them to do but to struggle against its hold without trying to understand its cause, and, most of all, its effects.

Lionel found it hard to sleep that night. He finished reading the assignment in his botany text, turned out the bed light, and lay for a long time without closing his eyes. On the blank wall of his room he thought he could see the outline of Caleb's body. The warmth he had felt coming from the hug of their parting made him shiver now in his bed. He could not bring himself to advance beyond feeling into sense.

'I don't know what to make of this,' he thought.

He decided he could not deal with it in his tired, confused state.

'Tomorrow,' he said to himself. 'Tomorrow I'll go back over it and see what I did. What he did. What we did. What it all meant.'

Caleb's excitement was so great that he could not go back to his room. He turned off West Avenue onto the New Road and walked down Central Avenue to Cascadilla Creek. At the bridge over the falls, he stopped and leaned against the railing. The place was congenial to his mood, for the rush of water under his feet matched the maelstrom in his head. The cool air of the September night, mingled with the cold mist that rose from the falls, dried the perspiration that had formed on his face and neck. Looking down made him feel sick, so he turned and braced himself up onto the stone wall, sitting with his back to the fierce white water below.

Caleb's surprise at the embrace was not as great as Lionel's. He was aware that it was at his instigation it had happened. He might be called the perpetrator, he thought, the leader, the officer who ordered the action, and Lionel merely the foot soldier, the enlisted man. Now that he considered it, at a safe, cold distance from Lionel, in this vertiginous no man's land removed from the heat of the moment, he saw that it had all begun when first they met on the library steps and he had been struck by how much Lionel looked like Kate, how his soft-appearing blond skin and bright blue eyes, even his fragile-seeming body, were echoes of hers. So much did he resemble her that, most startling of all, he seemed to be of her sex.

This confusion of images, superimposing the picture of his once so beloved sister upon the presence of the boyish Lionel, left Caleb without the resources to sort out what he was feeling, what he had felt all evening as he sat across from Lionel at dinner, and in his room, and then walked with him toward the dorm and, in that one moment of unfathomable impulse, reached out and took him into his arms.

He knew what it was, not a hug, not a simple, comradely embrace, but the response to a need to hold Lionel close, a desire he could not remember feeling before, except perhaps from a distance, for other men. Never before had it struck him so immediately, so keenly, as tonight. He thought of lying in his sister's bed impelled toward her by the strangeness of his desire and her innocent but willing presence. First his sister. Now Lionel . . .

'What is it with me?' he said to himself. 'Why am I so . . . odd? How in God's name will I end up?'


After a week, during which he had studied hard and spent more time than usual running around the Schoelkopf track, racing against the times he had set for himself, Caleb could no longer put off his need to see Lionel again. He called the number in Baker Tower but could not manage to get through; the lines were always busy. When he finally reached someone, an anonymous voice took the message that Caleb Flowers had called and wanted Lionel Schwartz to call back, preferably at dinnertime.

He waited five days, coming to dinner early and staying long at the table in conversation with anyone willing to linger, in order to wait out the time a return call might possibly be made. But it did not come. Disheartened, he gave up and decided to walk to Lionel's dorm to see if he could meet him coming in or going out, or even find him in his room at the end of the day.

Miraculously, Lionel was there, and he came down after a floormate went to tell him of Caleb's presence downstairs in the common room.

To Caleb he looked wonderful. His cheeks and lips were very red and his damp hair darker than usual: he had just showered and shaved. His starched white shirt was open at the neck, and he wore freshly pressed brown wool trousers. His brown-tipped shoes gleamed in the light from the chandelier.

'You are a sight for sore eyes,' Caleb said, and laughed at the triteness of his sentence. 'Why didn't you call?'

'Why didn't you?'

'I did, days ago. I left a message with someone here for you to call me back.'

'Well, the someone never told me.'

'Never mind. Would you like to have dinner with me?'

'I would. But I've got to warn you. This late in the month, money's an object. I'm on a tight budget. I don't eat big dinners. Hamburgers are usually all.'

'Are you hungry?'

'And how.'

'Well, consider this an invitation to a big dinner. I'll pay.'

Lionel laughed. His pleasure at seeing Caleb was obvious in his grin and the brightness of his blue eyes.

'I'm at your service, sir,' he said. 'Let's go. Where?'

'Have you been to the Senate yet? It has good food. But it's a bit of a walk.'

'No matter. Any food is good food to me, if there's enough of it.'

'There will be. I'll see to it."

They made their way down the hill to North Aurora Street. Lionel had not been in the city of Ithaca before; he found the streets confusing. Caleb took short cuts; to Lionel, who was looking at Caleb and not watching where they were going, the way seemed circuitous.

They found seats in a corner at a large table. Caleb expressed his hope to the waiter that since they were so early, they would not have to share their table with anybody else. The waiter took their order for a quart of ale and two large plates of spaghetti with meatballs. He said he hoped so too, but you never knew.

Caleb had planned to tell Lionel that he had thought about him often, perhaps too often, in the past week. But he found this difficult to say, fraught as it was with dangerous implications. Instead, he described a fascinating lecture he had heard Morris Bishop give on the lays of Marie de France.

Lionel appeared to be listening, his eyes fastened on Caleb's face. But his thoughts were the same as Caleb's unuttered ones: he wanted to say how much he had missed seeing him during the week, how his face had inserted itself between the pages of every book he read, along the paths of the Ag campus he had walked, on the empty blackboard behind the lecturers he had listened to.

Lionel countered Caleb's narrative with one about his freshman English class:

'English 8. I was real lucky. I ended up in a section taught by a professor named Strunk. The men who usually teach Ag students, like Adams and Baldwin, had filled-up sections. So they put two of us in Strunk's Arts and Sciences class. First thing he told us was to go to the bookstore and buy what he said was "the little book." I had no idea what he was talking about, and no one else in the class did either. But the clerk in the bookstore knew all about it. It turned out to be a book on writing and grammar. That sort of thing. The professor is the author and the publisher. It cost fifty cents.'

'How lucky, That's great for you. I had Strunk for freshman English too. And I had to get the little book. I learned a lot from him. He's very funny in class, and very nice to students, although he holds to a hard line about how to write. Now, every time I use an adverb or extra words in a sentence in a paper I feel guilty.'

The waiter set their dinners down and called their attention to the two frosted glasses he had brought. Caleb thanked him coolly, as if he had expected them as a matter of course, opened the ale, and poured two full glasses. They drank until the glasses were half empty and then stopped to look at each other.

'Very good,' said Lionel, raising his glass higher as though he were toasting Caleb. 'Very refreshing. Thank you.'

'I like ale better than Piel's beer, which is what everyone drinks here,' Caleb said, to make conversation. He was beginning to wonder how much more there was to say that did not bear on what he hoped was going on silently between them.

'I wouldn't know. They're both new to me. Since my father died, my mother never has anything to drink in the apartment.

193

I think she believes it's disrespectful, or something. Of course, after that happened there was very little money for anything. These years have been rough.'

'I'll have to see that you get used to the pleasures of the glass. Even hard liquor, which *my* mother seems to prefer on occasion, according to my sister, who disapproves of anyone having even one drink of anything. Speaking of girls, do you ever see Roslyn Hellman?'

'Now and then. We don't get together much. She lives in Brooklyn and was going, I think, to college there, to a new branch of City College.'

'What's she like now? I remember her as bossy and pretty stuck on herself.'

Lionel shook his head. 'Do you? I guess I've always admired her, so I didn't see that side of her. She's tall, as tall as I am, thin, you know, and sort of flat-chested. She has black hair and wears it short, cropped off, sort of boyish. She's the only girl I know who wears men's shirts and ties.'

'Does she live at home?'

'Yes, to her disgust. She doesn't get along with her mother. She told me she wanted to go to New York University so she could live in the Village and get away from home, but there was no money. So she's stuck out there in Flatbush.'

'You people in Manhattan always think of the other boroughs as distant and dismal swamps, don't you?'

'And how,' said Lionel. 'I can't conceive of living out there among the savages.'

'What about in Far Rockaway? Same thing?'

Lionel laughed. 'No, I've always thought of that place as rather civilized because the Flowerses lived there and, of course, *I* spent a summer there. That must have had some taming effect on the place, I'm sure.'

Caleb smiled. 'Well, I concede it's not a great place to spend your life. I'd like to see Kate get out, but at the moment . . . Anyway, you never run into Roslyn?'

'Rarely. We've gone to the movies a few times, and once, recently, by accident, we had dinner at the same table in the Jumble Shop in the Village. She had been at some student union meeting with a friend, and I had been looking for a book in the Eighth Street Bookstore. I think it was something on the Bauhaus. They didn't have it, but they ordered it for me.

'It was strange. We talked for a while about applying to colleges, and about money, or the lack of it. She told me that a friend of hers who'd gone to Spain with the Abraham Lincoln Brigade had died of a shot to his head. Her eyes filled with tears and I asked her what battle it was. "No battle," she said. "He was shot in the head in a cantina by a soldier friend who was fooling around with his rifle. They were drinking wine."

'Then she broke down. I asked her if he was someone she had been in love with. "No, not at all. But we were friends. I cry when I think of the idiocy of it. So much for going off to fight against fascism and for democracy," she said. I haven't seen her since. I learned about her going to Brooklyn College from her mother when I called and she was out. She never called me back.'

'More spaghetti?' Caleb asked. 'They give you a second portion here if you want it. Free.'

'Not for me. Believe it or not, I'm finally filled up.'

Caleb paid a dollar and fifty cents for the two dinners and thirty cents for the ale, and gave the waiter a twenty-five-cent tip. Some of the pale liquid remained in the bottle. He corked it and put the bottle under his arm.

As they walked up the hill, Caleb put his hand on Lionel's shoulder.

'Shall we finish the bottle at Telluride?' he asked.

'Fine with me.'

It was close to nine when they arrived at Caleb's room. He had found two clean water glasses in the scullery and poured the ale into them.

'Not much left,' he said.

'I don't think I'm up to much more. I've got two classes tomorrow morning.'

'Are you tired?'

'A little. Are you?'

They stood around the table that served as a desk, taking small drinks of ale and exchanging bits of talk, their eyes on each other. It was clear to them that the offhand questions and trite answers, the sips of ale, the talk about professors and classes, were of no importance beside the grave matter that inhabited their thoughts. Lionel was reluctant for the evening to end. Caleb sensed his unwillingness and shared it.

'Like to lie down and rest before you take off?'

Without replying, Lionel moved over to the bed and lay down. He placed his hands under his head and closed his eyes, feigning rest, Caleb thought. Perhaps Lionel was waiting for him to join him. He did, lying on his side so he could watch Lionel's face until he opened his eyes.

Lionel reached for Caleb's hand and held it. It was this touch, the warm union of their fingers, the slight pressure that Caleb exerted in response to Lionel's move, that brought the two of them to the point of acute knowledge. A curious climax had been reached, an epiphany without preparation. Having never thought about wanting to love one another in this way, suddenly they had no doubt that this was what they felt, what they had wanted all along.

Still, they made no further move toward the other places on each other they wished to explore, although they knew well they were held on the bed by weighty urges to touch, to put their mouths together, to wipe out the distance between them by placing their erect members into orifices in a way they had never before considered.

In the long silence that seemed to gather itself up into bubbles above their heads and then form into soundless clouds, they filled the room with their breathing and their heat. Without moving, they lay like the gilded human statues in the circus who, in their sculptured stillness, portray the living dead.

At last Caleb could bear it no longer. He freed his hand to open the small buttons of Lionel's fly, and wrapped his fingers around his firm part.

'Is this all right? Do you mind?' he asked.

Lionel did not reply. Instead he broke Caleb's hold on him, slid down to his crotch, unbuttoned him quickly, and moved close to take him in his mouth.

'Will you like this?' he asked in a voice so soft Caleb had to strain to hear.

'And how,' Caleb said, echoing Lionel's favorite expression and offering colloquial proof of his delight at the proposal.


The winter semester seemed to them to be over very quickly. They had tried hard to apportion their time so that they did not meet too often. They kept up their studies, perhaps because their pleasure with each other became so intense they could not bear to meet two evenings in a row.

Caleb grew lax about calling home regularly. He found himself thinking about Kate now and then, and always when he looked at Lionel lying beside him: his fair skin, his thin, boyish pliant body, the way his hair curled about his ears. He still wished to think of a way to free her of her dutiful tie to their mother, but the joys of his present state kept him from doing anything about it.

Lionel limited his contacts with his mother to reassuring postcards at odd intervals. Caleb had become the kingbolt of his existence. He could not proceed in any direction without considering what Caleb's wishes might be. The machinery of his daily life and his plans for the future ran smoothly on the paths laid down by Caleb; he could imagine no separate existence for himself.

Neither of them gave a thought to anyone else. There was so much new subject matter to be explored; they were totally absorbed by it. They found the contents of their minds and their persons, and the miracle of their union, worthy of all the time they could be together. The sensual delights and the warm comradeship they had discovered occupied every moment they were not sleeping, in class, in the library, or, in Lionel's case, in the laboratory or on the drill field. Lionel had been promoted to corporal in his ROTC platoon; Caleb took great pleasure at the sight of Lionel in his trim Army uniform.

To the dismay of both mothers, to whom they reported that they needed the time to study in the library, and to Kate's intense sorrow, the two men spent Thanksgiving recess and the Christmas holidays in Ithaca. Because college housing was closed during those times, they rented a small, sunny room in Snyder's Tourist Home on North Aurora Street. Almost no one else remained in town during those times; Mrs. Snyder accommodated them for one dollar a night. Caleb willingly paid the bill. In early morning he went out to the bakery down the street for rolls and coffee and brought breakfast back to their room. They ate in bed, interrupted only by the now customary pleasures that punctuated the hours of their free days.

They luxuriated in their contentment. In the afternoons, and before their late suppers in Johnny's Coffee Shoppe (open day and night, its sign said proudly) or at the Senate, they read the texts assigned for the next semester, sometimes exchanging books to see what the other was reading, in much the same way as their sexual activities teeter-totted between them, one accepting and the other providing, one giving when the need was for donation and the other receiving, with grace, the alms of passion.


At Easter, the spring break lasting two weeks, they agreed to spend the last weekend apart, in New York and in Far Rockaway. Separation was painful. Since the fall they had not been apart except for a few days. They had grown used to each other's presence.

Lionel took home a folder full of notes to write a term paper. Caleb filled his bag with books. They proceeded on the theory that the busier they were, or at least appeared to be, the easier it would be to plead unfinished work and so be able to leave early for Ithaca.

Sadie Schwartz had grown even more resentful, Lionel found. Being alone had not improved her embittered disposition. During his few days with her in the small apartment on West Seventy-seventh Street, she seldom left his side or the room in which he was trying to write, except to prepare their meals, make his bed, and empty his wastebasket. Lionel understood that she was demonstrating, silently, how essential he was to her happiness, how necessary she was to his comfort.

To underline her sacrificial approach to life, she told him that a neighbor in the apartment house, a widower named Ben Janowitz whom she had met seated in the sun on the Broadway benches, had suggested to her that they might marry. But it was impossible, she had told him. In deference to her concerns for Lionel and to the memory of her beloved Lester, she had turned him down.

Lionel sighed, and made no response to this blighted prospect for his freedom.

On Saturday (he had been home three days) he could bear her constant presence no longer. He telephoned Roslyn Hellman and asked her if she would like to see a play with him in New York.

They had not met in more than a year. In front of the Maxine Elliott Theater they embraced and then stood back to inspect each other. Lionel was chagrined to see that Roslyn seemed to be taller than he; Roslyn noticed only Lionel's fair hair and skin, and wondered if he yet was able to grow a beard.

On line to get standing-room tickets—*The Children's Hour* was a successful play with no seats to be had on Saturday night, especially the fifty-five-cent ones they could afford—the two old friends brought each other up to date on their lives. Roslyn was full of stories about the inadequacies of her parents. She had no good words for Brooklyn College, which was still struggling to become established. Some of the buildings were still without heat in this terribly cold winter.

'I hate living at home,' she told him. 'But I have no choice, what with so little money and all. Even so, I had to wait more than a year to enter. Butchers aren't paid the way brokers were, you know. But my parents are thinking of moving to Miami Beach next year, where my aunt and uncle have a winter house. It's cheap there, no heating bills to worry about, no winter clothes, all that sort of thing. My father thinks he might find some sort of part-time work down there. I think they'll be able to manage. Some of their friends have started to vacation down there in winter.'

'That's wonderful,' said Lionel, inching closer to the box office. 'Then you'll be free.'

'Well, yes, free, but pretty poor. I'll have to get a job while I finish college. I'll have to find a cheap place to live, in Brooklyn yet,' she added, in a tone that suggested she would then be condemned to Siberian exile.

They were lucky: they got the last two standing-room tickets and found themselves in the second row of standees with a good view of the stage. The play, set in a girls' boarding school, started slowly. Standing close, the two friends shifted about, trying to get into comfortable positions. But when it became clear that the evil pupil had thought up a vengeful accusation against two of the women teachers, their attention was fastened to the stage. They hardly moved again.

After the climactic second act, they went into the lobby, hoping to spot some departees whose seats they might claim for the last act.

'It's an interesting play, isn't it?' said Lionel, his eyes on the crowd.

'Yes, very. And surprising, shocking in a way, for Broadway. Do you think the two women, well, you know, really love each other?'

'I think the one does. The one who wants to marry, I suppose, does not.'

Roslyn was silent. She had a sudden vision of herself walking beside Fritzie years ago, through the black night woods of the camp, waiting to hear her counselor's response to her passionate letter.

'Don't you agree?' Lionel saw himself sitting on the parapet over Cascadilla Falls waiting for Caleb to come to take him to dinner, worrying that he would arrive emptied, suddenly, inexplicably, of the measure of love he had expressed the day before.

'I do, of course I do. But how do you think it will end?'

'As plays like this usually do, I suppose. The one will marry that guy, and the other will look around for someone else. Most of these plays end happily, or they wouldn't be hits on Broadway.'

Lights flickered, signaling the start of the third act. They went back in, to stand in the newly opened spaces in the front row of the back of the orchestra. Vicariously, painfully, they entered into the ruined life of the woman on the stage who was unable to bear any longer the truth about herself.

The suicide of the homosexual teacher that brought Lillian Hellman's play to its conclusion stunned them. They walked to the corner of Forty-fourth Street and went into Child's on Broadway to have coffee before Roslyn took the subway home.

At first they said nothing, stirring cream and sugar into their full cups, mopping up the overflow with napkins, and trying to ignore conversation. They were still captives of the emotions the play had aroused in them.

Lionel broke the silence with the only noncommittal question he could think of: 'Are you by any chance a relative of the playwright's?'

Roslyn laughed, relieved that the spell of introspection had been broken. 'Not that I know of,' she said. 'It would be nice, though. She's very good, don't you think?'

Lionel did not reply. In his mind, he had moved far away, into the bedroom in Telluride that first evening when he and Caleb had lain together on Caleb's bed. In the silence that followed, they both felt a desire to relate their histories to the other. Roslyn wanted to say that she had once had a crush on a camp counselor. Lionel wanted to say, 'I am gloriously, madly in love with Caleb Flowers.'

But neither of them said anything, perhaps because they were unaccustomed to the luxury of baring their souls. Or it may be that they feared the burden of confession, the bestowing of any part of themselves on the other to carry away from this evening.

The surface of Caleb's return to his family was pleasant. His mother seemed to be in good spirits. Her deafness had increased to the point that communication was difficult, but still, she smiled whenever her eyes rested on him and reached out to touch him whenever he came close to her. He felt wanted, he sank back into the old security of being the beloved son.

Emma was now obese and had lost her mobility. Stationary in her overstuffed living-room chair from early morning, her swollen feet elevated on a stool, her now rarely opened library book on the table beside her, she seemed to Caleb to be Buddhalike in her apparent contentment. Her eyes were always on him, waiting for him to sit beside her and tell her tales of life at college. At other times, she appeared to be waiting impatiently for Kate to serve her meals on the card table pulled up to her chair in front of the fireplace.

It seemed to him that his mother had buried the history of her early life in layers of fat. Nothing could be sensed of her inner being. He saw only the constant, inappropriate smile she never allowed to vary. Her thoughts, if indeed she entertained any, were invisible, protected from expression by her overabundant flesh and the tight harness of deafness.

At dinner, Caleb and Kate sat beside her at the card table, the small square of space overcrowded by their plates and cups. At these moments they must have appeared to be bound together, he thought, united as they had been before his departure, into a claustrophobic family circle.

The newspaper photograph of the Great War soldier no longer sat on the mantelpiece. Caleb wondered who had removed it, but he did not inquire. It was as if Private First Class Edmund Flowers had vanished from the house on Larch Street he had purchased for his family, and from the memory of his mammoth, now-silent wife. The myth that had first entertained him and Kate during their early years and then had been wiped out on the train ride home from Lester Schwartz's funeral was never mentioned again.

Kate had been determined to make Caleb's return an occasion of celebration. She cooked his favorite food and, when Emma had gone up early to bed, she sat beside him on the sofa. Almost timidly, as if she had never done this before, she reached for his hand. He took it in his, but when she turned her delighted eyes upon him she saw he was looking at the mantel, not at her.

After a moment, he took away his hand and reached into his breast pocket for a crumpled pack of Camels. To Kate the removal had the effect of a blow. She flushed and looked down at her hands, which she now folded decorously in her lap. Caleb did not notice. He thought he had succeeded in making his move a simple indication of his intention to smoke.

'Do you know who I met at school? Lionel Schwartz. Remember him?'

'Yes. I remember playing with him one summer. I remember we called him Lion. Then we went to his father's funeral in the City.'

'Well, he's now a freshman in the Ag school. He's . . . he's very nice. We see a lot of each other.'

'Does he look the same? I remember him as skinny and very blond. Odd for a Jew, Moth once said.'

'Just the same. He's quite handsome, and very bright. He wants to study architecture.'

Kate was silent. She realized too late that she had revealed her animus against a friend of Caleb's by her racial reference, but she could not help herself. Three years apart from her brother had failed to lower her fevered feelings for him. To the contrary, his absence had intensified her longing for his old, warm, promising presence in her life.

In Kate's most fervent fantasy, Caleb would come back to her, a wise and needy Odysseus. He would return to Far Rockaway to take his old place in her bed, sharing the games of imagination she had been forced to play alone as the faithful Penelope, the patient Griselda, and the famous brides of Christ, like Saint Theresa, who sought solitude in which to wait for their Bridegroom to claim them.

Kate fantasized that she would no longer have to resort to lonely release. He would be there as of old, still feeling and looking so much like her that he seemed close to being her twin, a mirror-image lover. She knew that she was too old for such pretense, that Caleb had changed. His hair had darkened, he was far taller and broader than she, but there was always the rest . . . the imagined consummation of their love.

Suddenly she thought to ask: 'Do you have a girl up there?'

'A girl? No.'

'Not even one?'

'Not even one. I don't go in for that sort of thing. I have too much work.'

'Don't you ever go out to dinner, or to the movies in the evening, things like that?"

'Well, yes I do. Often, with Lionel.'

Kate was flooded with relief. There was no girl to separate him from her. He would return. She was afraid to inquire about his plans for the future. But she felt sure now that he would come back. She had only one more school semester to wait. Like Penelope, like Griselda, she would wait patiently.


After spring recess, Lionel settled down to finishing his papers and lab reports. Caleb, his course work almost completed and his senior thesis, on Geoffrey Chaucer's life in the customs house, delivered to a faculty reader, was forced by the approach of graduation to think about what he would do next. He had applied to stay on for another year at Telluride, citing his desire to go to graduate school in the English department, but he had not heard from the chancellor about it.

In April they found an evening they could both spare from work. They met at the closest bar, the Chapter House, down Stewart Avenue and close to Williams Street, where they had roomed for a short time during the recess. It was a favorite rendezvous spot because few students were there in the late evenings, and the townspeople who frequented it paid no attention to them. They sat in a corner where there was almost no light and shared a bottle of ale.

The pretense they had managed to maintain until now was that the future had no existence, no reality. It would not arrive, not for them. In their state of felicity with each other, the thought of an interruption to this condition was inconceivable. Caleb knew, although he did not say this to anyone, that his plan to stay on another year was based on his desire to prolong what he had found in Lionel: friendship, wonderful physical pleasure, and a conviction that he was capable of love apart and away from his boyhood tie to his sister.

Lionel asked if he had heard anything about the English fellowship.

'Not a word. But I only sent my application in to the master's program last week. I asked about a scholarship, but I'm not too hopeful. Depends pretty much on who else is applying, especially from the outside. We'll see. It might be a while before I hear. But I did hear that there's a job I could get as a book runner in the library. That would pay some of my expenses in case nothing else comes through.'

Lionel smiled. 'If nothing else comes through, as you say, for the rest of my life but us, I will be content,' he said in his high, soft voice that made his usual formal diction even more pleasant to Caleb.

'Right. Oh so right,' said Caleb, wanting to touch the light down on Lionel's fine cheek but knowing he could not do it in this public place. Instead, he put some coins down under his napkin and stood up.

'Time, gentlemen, please,' he said to Lionel in his newly acquired English accent. 'I've got an exam tomorrow.'

They walked slowly up Stewart Avenue until they came to Boardman Hall. Then, as was their custom, they took a dirt path through the quadrangle to the steps of Goldwin Smith. In the safety of the shadows of the long, dark stone building they said good night, their arms around each other, their faces and lips pressed so close they could hardly breathe.

It was then that they saw the light streaming from an upper window of the building. Caleb stepped out of the shadows to look up.

'That's Professor Lang's office. Probably working late. It's the only light on in the whole building.'

'I'll be on my way, love,' said Lionel. 'You don't have to walk me home.'

But of course, as always, Caleb did. On his way back, he saw that, glowing dimly now at this distance, a light was still lit in Goldwin Smith.

The doors to Goldwin Smith were roped off when Caleb arrived the next morning a few minutes before eight o'clock, when he was due to take his final examination in Latin literature. Two campus policemen stood at the sawhorses and a group of his classmates formed a close semicircle around them. A police car and an ambulance were on the grass.

'What's going on?' he asked a serious-looking red-haired fellow who was staring up at the second floor of the building. 'Can't we get in?'

'No,' said the boy, not looking at him.

'Why not?'

'They're bringing someone out. I saw them carry a stretcher in.'

'Someone sick?'

'I heard it's someone dead.'

'My God. *Dead?*'


Because of the lateness of the hour, Professor Caplan, standing outside with his students, canceled the examination and rescheduled it for the following day. By the time Caleb arrived back at Telluride he had learned the name of the dead person and the cause of his death. Alexander Lang, assistant professor of French, had hanged himself early in the previous evening, and was found by the night watchman who had gone at midnight to check on the light showing from his office.

By the end of the day, Caleb had heard, from graduate students and a resident instructor, the whole, terrible story. All afternoon the parlor of the house was filled with members coming and going, all talking about one subject: the morning's tragedy. Caleb had not been able to bring himself to leave the room, although he said very little to anyone, and never mentioned that he had taken Lang's courses. He listened to every rumor, to every suspicion that was aired, to every reasonable and wild supposition about why Lang had taken his life.

In front of Willard Straight, the student union, where they had agreed the night before to meet for hamburgers, Caleb shook hands with Lionel, a long shake that represented their compromise with decorum.

'I've heard, yes. It's all over everywhere, even as far as the Ag campus,' Lionel told Caleb as they went into the cafeteria.

'Do you know that he hung himself?'

'Yes. It must have happened about the time we saw the light.'

'What have you heard about . . . why? Why he did it?'

'Nothing except guesses and rumor. Someone in the lab said he was miserable here and wanted to get back to living in Paris. But I don't see how that's a reason for taking his life. He won't get abroad any faster this way.' Lionel laughed at this, and then stopped abruptly when he saw Caleb's face.

Caleb stared at Lionel and said nothing.

'Do you know more details than I do?' Lionel asked.

'One other thing.'

'What's that?'

'I heard from someone that he left a letter to be sent to a friend in Paris. The police read it.'

'They *did!*'

'In order to establish for certain that there was no foul play, or some such thing.'

'Did they say what it said?'

'The story I've heard, from a guy at the house who is in his department, is that Lang was being blackmailed by a student who had been, well, he was referred to as . . . his friend. Lang could not stand the . . . the possibility of disgrace and dismissal. That's what this student reported in the parlor. The fellow named in the letter as the blackmailer is a French major.'

'Do you think that's true? I mean, could this guy be making it up, you know, to get attention?'

There was a long silence while Caleb considered the possibility of irresponsible rumor-mongering and Lionel, horrified, tried to absorb the possibility that what he had just heard was true.

They finished their supper in silence. Then Caleb stood up and said he had to work on a paper. Lionel understood by this that he wished to be alone, so he said good night. For the first time they parted without making a plan to meet the next evening. An unaccustomed sense of threat seemed to have come into their alliance.

A week later, when Lionel could stand the strange separation no longer, he walked to Telluride at nine in the evening and asked the student at the desk to see if Caleb Flowers was in his room. The student went up, two steps at a time, and then came down to report that Mr. Flowers would be down in a minute.

Lionel felt cold. He had a premonition that something had gone badly wrong between them. A week without any communication was unheard of. His feeling of dread grew stronger when the message from Caleb was not that Lionel should come up but that Mr. Flowers was coming down. What unspoken thing, what inexplicable change, could have taken place without his being aware of it?

Lionel was at the window looking out at the stretch of bright green stubs of new grass at the side of the house. It was a very late spring; patches of snow had disappeared only recently. He was not aware that Caleb had come into the room until he was standing beside him. Making a great effort not to look around at him, Lionel continued to stare at the new lawn. He felt that Caleb was doing the same thing.

For a time that seemed interminable to Lionel, they continued to stand in these unnatural poses. Even when Caleb began his anguished monologue, Lionel could not turn to look at him. He felt as though he were being addressed from a great height or through a thick wall:

'I've been having a horrible time. I would have been in touch before. But I needed time to understand what I was feeling, what I was thinking, I guess is what I mean. I'm not sure I understand all of it now, but I see I can't put it off any longer. I've got to tell you, even if I'm not sure of it, and even if, tonight or tomorrow, I may change entirely and go back to my . . . our, I mean . . . old way of thinking. You see, Lionel, I know now I can't go on with my life. Our life. I love you, but I don't want to go on with our love any longer. I'm afraid. I can't. The price is too great. I learned that from what happened to Professor Lang. Nobody out there understands what we are, what we do, what we want. They didn't understand about him or why he died or why he felt he had to die. I've got to live the way everybody else does so I can do what I want. I want to teach and to get the degrees I need to do that and to get an appointment to a good college. I want to be able to go home without lying about myself and my life to my mother and my sister. Especially my sister, who thinks I'm some sort of god, and would never understand or forgive me if I told her about us. I need to have a family. Even if I see them seldom, I have to be able to say they're there and to know they're there. I need people to love me and think well of me. When I stood in the parlor and heard the things they were saying about Lang, I knew I could not bear it if such things were to be said about me. I haven't the courage to live his life. It's not possible for me. I am too much of a coward. I must do what is expected of me as a man—you know, earn a living, marry, have a family, become part of the world out there that tells everyone what kind of life to lead, what is acceptable. *We* can't decide that. I'm afraid we never will be able to. I want to be successful, and there is only one way. I have to be like everyone else. I have to surrender to the majority rule, because I am not brave enough for rebellion or resistance. This is a very long speech, I know, but I want to say it all and be done with it. I can hear old Strunk telling me to 'omit useless words,' but I can't do that. I need all the words I have and more to say these things to you. Please do not hate me. Or hate me if you have to, but try to understand why I've come to this point. Strunk would tell me to "avoid fancy words." But I have to use a few, like, I love you, and, I believe I always will, and, this has been the best year of my life, and, there probably will never be a better one. Oh to hell with Strunk.'

# 4

# Far Rockaway
# Revisited

*God setteth the solitary in families.*
—P<small>SALMS</small> 68:6

K<small>ATE'S</small> <small>LETTERS</small> <small>TO</small> C<small>ALEB</small>, while he was still at Cornell working for his master's degree, and later when he went to Yale, were pointed catalogues of the miseries of life in the old house where her mother lived her vegetable existence and Kate tended to her. In addition, Kate managed to suggest other subjects: her own loneliness and isolation, her sense of being her mother's captive, her need for her brother and the old love they had shared, her despair at his absence.

She wrote to him:

*My dearest Heathcliff,*

*Moth has a very bad cold. It seems to have settled in her chest. I worry that her cough is a sign that her lungs have been affected. The doctor came yesterday and told me to watch her closely for fever and 'extreme' lassitude, as he put it. It's hard to know about this last, because, as you have seen, even when she is better, she moves so little. I attribute that to her weight. But the doctor believes she has no desire to move, that she has given up on living. This may be so. The powders he left for her have made*

213

*her irritable. She is cross with me in the few hours she is awake. But then she sleeps long and heavily.*

*Tuesday morning I had trouble waking her. In her state of half-sleep, she said: 'Daniel, I'm cold. Come in the bed and warm me.'*

*I told her I was Kate and that I would get another blanket for her. She confuses names often. She must have meant Edmund, or Caleb.*

*It was last week, I think, that she said to me: 'Caleb, would you be good enough to rub my feet?' I did it, without telling her that you were not here and that I wasn't Caleb but Kate. I don't understand why all this is happening to her so early. She will be fifty-three next month (try not to forget to call on her birthday on the 12th, dear), which is old, I know, but not really that old, do you think? Her hearing is gone. I doubt she knows when I correct her or tell her you called.*

*She speaks very seldom (the quiet in this house seems to have expanded in your absence and with Moth's silence). But sometimes, in the midst of it she will say curious, almost poetic things. Yesterday she said, 'Look at all the remarks hiding behind the people.'*

*When I brought her breakfast this morning, she said, 'Close the door. I don't want to be responsible for it.' Strange and meaningless, but I think about her sentences all day and finally, oddly enough, make some sort of sense of them, my own sense, I'm sure, but still, a little sense. Another day she said another strange thing: 'After Epiphany I'll go back to the convent. It's warm there.'*

*I don't mind her thinking I am you. Do you remember, when we were alone together we used to notice how much alike we looked, how we were the same in so many ways, and often felt like the same person. But perhaps you do not still feel this way and would object if Moth were to call you Kate.*

*I think of you all the time and wait eagerly for the day you will come home.*

> *My love,*
> *Catherine*

Kate's letters continued to delineate in detail her mother's decline. She wanted Caleb, even at a distance, to help with the burden of their mother's state. Although there was little outward evidence of it, Kate believed Emma was suffering somewhere within the soundless envelope of her flesh. The physical burden of tending to her mother's many needs in order to keep her alive was Kate's alone. Her hope was to bring Caleb home out of love for his mother and, perhaps, for her. If she could make plain how oppressed she was, he might come back. She might then be able to win him away from the lure of college life and friendships she imagined he had succumbed to.

Although Caleb never mentioned the name of a girl on his occasional trips home, Kate wondered if that meant there was indeed one that he was hiding from her in silence so that she would suspect nothing.

She wrote:

*Dear Edward,*

*I feel very far from you and from all you are doing and learning. How close to becoming a Master are you? Will they call you that when you get your new degree, instead of Bachelor which I suppose you are now known as?*

*Here it is always the same, day after day. Sometimes it seems as if life everywhere has stopped because Moth's has, almost. I find it hard to believe that somewhere out there are people my age who are dancing and drinking and laughing with each*

215

THE BOOK OF KNOWLEDGE

*other. Or that you are having dinner in some interesting college place with Lionel—do you still see him? You didn't mention him when you were here at Christmas.*

*Last night I could not persuade Moth to go upstairs to bed. She sat rigidly in her chair, pulling bits of wool out of her blanket and holding them in her other hand. I asked her what she was holding. 'A crab apple tree,' she said.*

*All night she slept in her chair and woke disoriented and angry. Most of the time I don't know what she is thinking or feeling, because she speaks so little and often does not hear me when I question her. Her face becomes very red when she is angry, and her eyes seem to be more white than the blue we inherited from her. Then I worry that she will have a stroke. I think that the more immobile she becomes the more I am tied to her. There are times I feel she is lying on top of me, unable to move, and I am pinned down and smothering and cannot get out from under her.*

*And the silence in this house—there is too much of it.*

*I don't think I've written to you about the Reverend Mr. Reston. He is the Methodist minister and heard about Moth from the boy who delivers our groceries and came calling a few weeks ago. I shouted at her to ask if she wanted to see him, and she must have heard, because she nodded yes.*

*I waited on the veranda while they prayed together, or rather, I could hear him praying, and she, I think, must have just watched him as he knelt down and leaned against the sideboard. He was in that position when I came back in, his eyes closed, his mouth open. I thought he looked foolish.*

*He asked if he could come back again and I said it was up to Mother. She nodded as if she had heard, and actually smiled, and he smiled, to me and then to her. He is the sort of person who seems always to be smiling, even when he is praying. Strange.*

216

*I don't understand her willingness to have him come here so often—I don't remember her ever mentioning religion to us. I have no idea what religion she was, or we were, although I do remember she didn't much care for Jews. Maybe she was a Catholic. Once she said—long ago, I remember—that as a girl she had thought being a nun was very romantic. And I told you that in her crazy talk she mentioned a convent.*

*My theory is that she is willing to have Mr. Reston come again and again because, oddly enough, she wants the company of men. When he is here she is almost her old self, polite and agreeable. She appears to have forgotten the hurt our father dealt her. I have always believed that accounted for her silences and her removal of herself from us and the world outside. I believe she may even think that Edmund Flowers and you, of course, are somehow still here in this house. Perhaps Mr. Reston gives her the comforting sense of another male presence: I don't know.*

> *Come home soon, dear—*
> *Wallis*

*P.S.: I forgot. Yesterday I came upon her catching something in the air with both hands. She opened her hands to me and said, 'Here's some white bread getting uneasy.'*

*Dearest John,*

*The unexpected has happened: I have made a friend. Imagine that. Well, maybe he is not so much a friend as he is an adviser, or a patient listener. A young, black-haired priest in his Roman collar and cassock came to the door three weeks ago. I was startled because this happens so seldom. Mr. Reston, the grocery boy, the milkman, and the mailman have been the only visitors in a long time.*

*The priest was taking what he called a parish census. He had a lovely smile, that white skin the Irish have, and very black eyes with long lashes. When I said we were not Catholics, he smiled all the more and said, 'That's all right, I'm sure you go to some good church.' I said, 'I have to admit I do not. But my mother prays with Mr. Reston, the Methodist minister. She's not well.' He said, 'Well, if ever you would like to have someone to talk to or pray with I'm usually at St. Anne's rectory on Elm Street. You're always welcome.' He told me his name, Father Mahoney. Peter Mahoney. I thought of Abelard and wanted to ask him if he was his namesake, but I couldn't remember if Peter Abelard was in good standing with his church. So I said nothing.*

*How could he have guessed how lonely I am and that I might go there? Perhaps I looked starved for company or something. Well, anyway, I did go. One afternoon I told Moth I was going to the store. But first I went to the house, the rectory, that is, in which Father Mahoney lives. We talked for a while sitting in his brown sort of parlor with no rug on the floor and very hard-backed chairs.*

*He asked if I had any brothers or sisters. I told him about you, of course, not everything but enough so that he said, 'I can tell you love your brother very much.' Then he told me about his older sister, who became a Mother of the Sacred Heart (odd, isn't it, a nun and a Mother who is also a sister?). He said he loved her, she had been a mother to him after their parents died in a train crash. 'I was an orphan very young,' he said. I said I understood that, with Moth the way she was and having never known my father I sometimes felt orphaned. He told me that we are all born to be orphans in a way. So our sisters and brothers, sometimes friends that we make, take the place of parents and we are loved and cared for by them. He said it was the human condition to be only the children of God, and He was our true Father and parent.*

218

*Maybe this is so. I miss you so much. When you are gone and so far away I am truly an orphan.*

*Yours always,*
*Priscilla*

*My dear Hansel,*

*Sometimes I go to visit Father Mahoney twice in one week. He has given me a book by Saint Theresa about her life, which she calls 'the little way.' She believed God was present when one performed the simple acts of everyday life, like taking care of Moth, Father Mahoney said, cleaning up after she soils the chair, and spills her supper all over the rug. It seems to me to be a rather lowly way of thinking of someone as elevated as God, but it does make my life easier to accept when I try to think of it as she did. She thought loneliness was a holy state of being. I wish I could get to that point.*

*No more for now. I hear Moth. She has a little bell she rings when she wants something. Often I get upstairs to find her dozing and wanting nothing. Last night, when I asked her what she wanted, she said, 'I've been thinking about the grass. It bent over and smiled.'*

*Your Gretel*

Kate wrote to Caleb, under the old playful guises he had devised for them in childhood, whenever the burden of her life grew so heavy that only moving a pen across paper and sinking into fantasy relieved it. But as her visits to the rectory of St. Anne's Church grew more frequent, she relied less on letters to Caleb and more on Father Mahoney's sympathetic ear.

One Sunday she left Moth asleep in bed and, because Father Mahoney had been urging her, went to early Mass at St. Anne's. Emma had been awake most of the night with pains in her legs and had only fallen asleep at dawn. It was Kate's first visit to a church. Father Mahoney had told her there would be very few people there at five in the morning, and it was so. Five very old women, one old man, a hobo who slept across a pew at the back, two young men dressed entirely in black, and Kate made up the congregation.

Kate found the proceedings incomprehensible. Mysterious acts with a cup and a plate were being performed by the priest and a little white-robed boy at the altar. The priest's back was to the people, who, in turn, seemed to pay little attention to what was going on up there. The women held beads in their hands and whispered prayers to themselves. Everyone knelt and rose and knelt again as if they were being soundlessly instructed to do so by some authority from above.

Kate had been up most of the night attempting to relieve her mother's distress by rubbing ointment over her pulsing, swollen blue veins. The drone of voices, the dust that rose from the floor and the corners of the pews, the faint, sweet odor in the air, made her sleepy. She dozed off once and was awakened into a state of confusion by the sound of a bell rung by the boy on the altar. She thought her mother was ringing for her.

At that moment she happened to look across at the kneeling young men in black. Their faces glowed in the half-dark church. Their eyes shone as if they had been lit from within. Kate wondered what they were seeing that illuminated them in this odd way. The others too had ceased their private devotions and were looking hard at the priest, who had turned to them and raised a cup over his head. Suddenly, all the disparate parts of the ceremony, the persons standing up and sitting down, the priest and server, the statues and candles, indeed, the entire church, seemed to be concentrated on what the priest was doing. She could not fathom what was happening but she sensed it was something she wanted to understand. She resolved to ask Father Mahoney to explain it all to her.

*Dear Siegmund,*

*Yesterday, in a rare clear moment, Moth asked me to find a lawyer who would come to the house. She wanted to make a will. Father Mahoney gave me the name of someone he said was a good Catholic and a reliable attorney. Francis O'Malley came one evening last week. He is about the same age as Father Peter and looks almost like him, with that kind of Irish pug nose, broad face, and white skin. But his hair is red and he's thinner. Moth whispered something to him. He asked me to leave the room. Will-making, he said, is a confidential affair. I did as I was told.*

*I have no idea what she told him to do. For all I know she has decided to leave the house and the money we've all been living on from our father to the Ladies Garment Workers Union, which she once told me he hated more than anything. To spite him.*

*So, Mr. O'Malley is coming back in a few days with the typed-up will and bringing two people from his office to witness it. I am not allowed to be a witness because I'm family. Moth has gone back into her silence and says nothing to me about her will, so I have nothing to tell you. Maybe when you come home she will talk to you about it. She did say something curious after the lawyer left. She said, 'I don't believe angels have hot tears.'*

*Will you be coming home soon? I want you to meet Father. But more than anything, I want so much to see you. It seems very long since those few days after Christmas. Moth asks for you every afternoon in her odd way. She says, 'What does Caleb want for dinner?' or 'Did he say he would be late tonight?' I say no, you won't be coming, you are away at school, and she looks puzzled as if she is surprised to hear that. But she says nothing more and we eat alone together. Mashed potatoes, creamed spinach, a bit of cut-up well-done beefsteak, and always, silence.*

*Come home soon. I want to be able to hug the new Master and*

*congratulate him. And just once I want to be able to tell Moth
you will be here for dinner.*

*Yours, as ever,
Sieglinde*

*My dearest Lord Nelson,*

*The other day, because I miss you so much, I had to talk to
someone. So I went to see Father Peter. We talked for a while
about God and his church and the sacraments. Then somehow
we got on the subject of family, and I found myself telling him
about how close we were, how we used to lie together on my bed
and act our parts as lovers. I think he was surprised by that. He
asked me questions about what we did. But I said, Oh, nothing,
just make-believe sort of stuff.*

*But I think he suspects there was more than that, because he
said my deepest love should never be given to persons, especially
persons related to me, but instead it should be saved for God,
who will never fail me, never forsake me or be unfaithful, always
return my love. He will lead me away from sin, not into it the
way human beings do.*

*Have I told you that sometimes I go to early-morning Mass
during the week? Father Peter has explained to me the liturgy, as
it's called, and I've begun to learn the Baltimore catechism and
study some books about Catholicism. Some of it is very difficult
to understand, especially such things as resurrection, transub-
stantiation, the trinity, virgin birth, ascension, and such, but I
expect that it will soon come plain to me if I go over it often
enough. I visit Father in the rectory whenever I can get away, so
my 'instruction' (he calls it that) is coming along pretty well. At
home when I study the books he gives me I collect questions to
ask him. He seems to know the answers to all of them.*

*But, hard as I try, I cannot forget you. And us. And the lovely
times we had together. Nothing in my life, not even the assur-*

*ances of the Church and Father's friendship and kindness to
me, has ever mattered as much to me as that. As you.*

*Your loving Emma*

To her beloved brother, whom she addressed in one of her final
letters as Tristan, Kate (signing the letter as Isolde) wrote that
their mother could no longer manage the stairs. So she (with
the help of both Mr. Reston and Father Mahoney) had brought
down her large four-poster bed to convert the living room into
a bedroom. All the shades were pulled against the light that
bothered her weak eyes. The front door was locked; tradesmen,
men of the cloth, Mr. O'Malley, all used the back entrance.

Thus ensconced, Emma's vast downstairs presence turned
the house into a selpulcher, airless and redolent of confined,
lingering sickness. The parlor and dining room had become a
dark cave reserved for Emma's dying. It was also Kate's
prison. There she waited with admirable patience for her
mother to die.

'Dear Paolo,' she wrote (at Father Mahoney's suggestion,
Kate had been reading a redaction of *The Divine Comedy,* so it
was natural for her, as her now-assumed namesake, to feel she
had been confined in the second circle of Hell as payment for
her carnal sins):

*Last night I had the strangest dream. You were in bed beside
me, but when I looked down I saw that we had been combined
into one body with one neck, like Siamese twins. Our heads were
attached to it, and I lay there looking into your eyes. In the black
of your pupils (a strange word for the center of the eye, I've
always thought), I could see myself. Then I saw that everything
had changed. You were not you, but me. I had two heads. I had
become myself and you were gone someplace else. What was all
this about? I must have been crying in my dream, because when*

223

*I woke up my face was wet. I would like to hear any explanation
you might have, since my ignorance of psychology is very great.
But I remember you took a course in it when you were an under-
graduate, and you studied the interpretation of dreams.*

*Your puzzled, loving Francesca*

The last letter to Caleb was written in the week before Emma
died. Kate's current reading was in Greek mythology, in a
young people's edition she had found in the library. It had
introduced her to the story of the *Aeneid*. In her fantasy (for
she continued to take pleasure in escaping into fictional roles,
an actress playing all the tragic parts in plays), she saw herself
in the role of the broken-hearted queen of Carthage who took
her life when the Trojan hero deserted her. To Caleb she assigned the faithless consort's part.

She wrote:

*Dearest Aeneas,*

*I think it would be good if you came home within the week.
The doctor believes Moth will not come out of this coma, as she
did from the last. She has had another bad stroke. Even if she
does regain consciousness, he says there will be very little left of
her real self. It may be your last chance to see her alive, if indeed
you want to. I understand that your absences have to be longer,
now that you are teaching, than they were when you were a
student. But you can't stay away forever. I'm sure that New
Haven is an interesting place to be, and Far Rockaway never
where you would be if you had your choice. But still, it is time
now. . . .*

*I enjoy thinking of you as a Doctor. Somehow it seems higher
up than Bachelor or Master.*

*Your faithful Dido*

224

But the fact is: Kate never sent these letters to Caleb. She saved them in a handkerchief case, with a rubber band around them, and stowed the lacy packet in the bureau drawer under her neatly stacked camisoles. They were histories, or better, therapeutic exercises that she used to relieve herself of what she found hard to bear in the long days and nights of service and silence. She believed the letters had failed in her intention to communicate, except perhaps to herself.

On the last evening of Emma's life, when the doctor, who had never been quite certain of the exact nature of Emma's illness (he was to write on the death certificate: 'Senility, Obesity, Heart Failure,' as though it were a multiple-choice diagnosis), told Kate the end was very near, she telephoned to Caleb at Yale. He said he would borrow a car. He added: 'I'll be there as soon as possible.'

Then she went to sit beside her dying mother throughout the night, accompanied only by Father Mahoney.


At the edge. I can feel it. On the rim of nothing. Another breath, one heartbeat more, and I'll be gone. Oh I know. I can feel the cold that has moved through me. Almost all of me is gone into ice. From slow motion of blood, to feeling of lead in the fat, to stopping altogether. Almost over. My daughter sits near, I feel her here, her hand in mine. Perhaps my son is here too, come for the end. Can't feel his hand. They listen to hear the last breath I hold back from them, making them impatient. *Now.* Please. Hurry up, they are thinking.

No. None of my last little time for them. For me only. Gone where, all that time? Since that one time. Never to speak of it. But oh, the lies they are thinking, sitting there, in the porch swing, under the oak tree, beside my bed. Mistaken stories. In what I told them. The truth about Edmund they think struck me down. I know. Small inch of time I have. Dying of cold. Did I lose heart for life after the funeral? Pull back and in? Because of what I learned then? No. The mistake. A myth.

Oh, God forgive. Help me now through this last time. That once. What time was that? Oh yes, I remember: the man from the lending library who came those evenings. Very young. Edmund away in the war. Babies upstairs for the night. Knowing nothing about it. Dan? Yes, Daniel was his name. Lonely, oh God, I was lonely. Wanted me and yes, wanted him. True. We loved. Made love. Which? Both. The heat, the spark, the joy, the flow. Warm sleep. Oh that moment. Said he loved. Wanted him again and again. More. Then more. I was older. He did not notice. Came back, again. Edmund still in the war, and gone, not here. Loved Dan. Sinned with Dan. Never cared.

Oh god, it was good then. On and on. Until I heard Edmund was dead, killed. Said to Dan, he's dead now. I told it to, was it Dan? Yes, Dan. Never came back, he was afraid. I was free. Never wanted me free. Went to borrow books, Cain, Deeping, Morgan. He looked away. Hid behind his desk. Into the other room. Didn't come out. Never again to Larch Street. Children— hear me. Believe me. Love, all I had. Was with him. Before I knew about Edmund. The lady. In the black straw hat. Never mattered. Really. Never.

Colder. My ears and nose. Where are they? Gone already. Dan cut me away. Stopped up my flesh. Closed me off. Banked the fire. Had arson with him, not Edmund. Emma died first. Dan hiding in the stacks. Appearance is a lie. Love a surface, a deception. Don't believe it. Children never knew. Innocents. Caleb only man left. I loved him, boy-man. He loved Kate. Kate. Here? Have no one now. CalebKate. Who cared for me? This time? Caleb. Yes. It was Caleb.

Oh now, here it is. Where's my bell? Call Caleb. No, Dan. No. No one. Me. Alone. Gone to the past. Not here. Risen? Fallen?

Into the leaves? Who took the oranges? Where is the ocean?
alone. breathe out. last one, coldest. oh.


The will was read to 'the children,' as Francis O'Malley called
them, in his office. The house was left to 'my beloved son,
Caleb, in gratitude for his faithful care for me in my last years.'
The money, such as it was ('not very much now,' O'Malley
said), was to be divided between her two children, after all her
medical expenses and burial were taken care of. A few thou-
sand will be all, O'Malley told them, enough to pay the taxes
for this year and perhaps next. And his fee. After that . . .


They sat across from each other, rejecting without thought
their old positions. Caleb took his mother's place in the porch
rocker. Kate sat alone in the swing.

'You can have the house, Kate. You live here. I have no use
for it. I'm pretty sure of an appointment to the faculty at the
university in Iowa City. It's almost certain.'

'Thank you. That's generous of you. But no, I don't want to
stay here. It's too big, for one thing. And it needs a lot of work.
I've spent my entire life in it. I'm going away. You can sell it.'

'Going away where?'

'I'm not sure. I'll let you know.'

'Will you have enough money to go very far?'

'I won't need much. I'm not going far.'

Kate looked at her brother, willing him to look at her. Caleb
watched the swaying, heavy hydrangea heads at the edge of
the steps. He seemed determined to keep his distance and re-
serve.

Kate gave up her effort to make visual contact with him.
Instead she asked: 'Have you seen Lion lately?'

'No, not for some time. He sent me a postcard from Fort Dix. He has his commission and will be shipped out to some other station soon.'

'What about you? When will you be called up?'

'If I'm lucky, never.'

'How come?'

'Well, part of the teaching I will be doing, if I get the appointment, will be in the Navy preflight school—cadets, you know. In its wisdom, the Navy has decided they will need some acquaintance with the English language. Then, on the side, I've volunteered to edit training manuals at the college, that sort of thing.'

'Will you feel all right about not going?'

'Sure. I'm not the military type, you know.'

Kate resisted the temptation to say: 'More the caretaking type, perhaps?' But she recognized the danger inherent in such unaccustomed sarcasm.

Instead she asked: 'You are less the military type than Lion?'

'Well no, I suppose not. But my draft number is pretty high. By the time they get around to me I'll probably be married, a family man, all that. . . .'

Kate looked at the shadows of the hydrangea heads on the porch floor. The sight of their cloudy swaying made her dizzy. She could think of nothing more to ask. Caleb seemed to her to have already assumed his carefully planned, safe life, halfway across the country. Then she thought of one thing. . . .

'I shouldn't ask this, since you haven't mentioned it before. But . . . who are you planning to marry?'

Caleb laughed. 'Oh, no one yet. But almost all the instructors I know are married. If you are trying for a permanent appointment it helps to have a wife and children. Makes you seem more settled, more serious, I suppose.'

Kate said nothing. She was stunned by the cold-bloodedness of Caleb's future plans.

He took her silence for agreement with the logic of his project. The air seemed to grow heavy with her unspoken doubts.

Then Caleb asked: 'But you haven't said what you plan to do.'

'I'm not sure. I'm still thinking about it. Send me your address, and I'll let you know when I've decided. But you'll have to do something about the house. I'm hoping to be out of it very soon.'

'I'll put it into the hands of someone here to sell. We can divide the proceeds.'

'Please don't do that. I won't need the money. Keep it for ... for your wife and children. You'll need it.'

In this way, they disposed of their past. They put the house they had lived in all their lives on 'the market,' as the real-estate agent called it. Kate arranged to sell the furnishings, and donated their mother's clothing to the St. Vincent de Paul Society's thrift shop. Soon after all this was accomplished, Caleb settled in Iowa City, Second Lieutenant Lionel Schwartz was in England with his infantry company, and Kate, in the novitiate house in upstate New York, stood in the choir of the Sisters of the Order of the Virgin Mary, dressed in her novice's black jumper and head scarf, singing, with eighteen other young women, the morning's psalms, and awaiting the day when she would take her vows, as Sister Mary Christina, to the Order and the Church. She would become a Bride of Christ, saved at last, she believed, from all her old, unspeakable desires, from her past sins, from her unspoken resentment of Moth and Caleb, and from herself.

# 5

# War and Peace

*Life is what happens when you have other plans.*
—WALTER HAMADY

FOR THE GENERATION of men and women who survived it,
World War Two was the high tor of their lives. Old enough to
have felt and then remembered the impact on them of the
Crash and then the Depression, they were now of an age to
enter fully into the excitement of being 'called up' or volunteering for what everyone seemed to agree was a noble national
enterprise.

Young women, surprised at suddenly being admitted to hal-
lowed male places, were exalted by their promotion and by the
admiration granted them by the public for volunteering to
serve. They were given free travel to unexpected places, they
participated in the excitement of marching bands and patriotic
ceremonies. They enjoyed the heady comradeship of those
similarly committed, uniformed, and beribboned, and suffered
without complaint in shared, close lodgings and through insti-
tutional meals. All of this provided them with an Everest, an
unforgettable elevation, that gave never-to-be-equaled importance to their lives.

At twenty-six, very tall, her black hair cut into a severe bob, thin at the hips and almost concave of bosom, Roslyn looked handsome in her navy-blue ensign's uniform. Designed by Mainbocher to suit the androgynous American-girl figure in favor at the time, the uniform, with its cocky, antiquated seaman's stiff hat and gold-buttoned jacket, its severe dark blue skirt and white blouse (or light-blue or navy, according to the order for the uniform of the day), reduced all the usual varieties of feminine dress to a single, handsome, satisfying, undeviating constant.

Roslyn had arrived at this agreeable state of existence after a series of small civilian jobs. Working for a family of publications as an intern, she had been moved from one department to another until, with the shortage of men because of the draft, she was given a subeditorship on a magazine that customarily restricted women to jobs in the typing pool or, if they turned out to be exceptionally bright, in research.

After what she had considered her exile at Brooklyn College, Roslyn luxuriated in being in Manhattan, although she disliked her work. But the City was her happy playground, and she frolicked in it while the country prepared for its great civilian and military effort to win a second Great War. The very air in her corner of her beloved borough felt promising, lively, and patriotic. Behind her was all her professed radical past. Forgotten was her college recitation of the Oxford Pledge not to participate in any war, an oath she had taken surrounded by other student activists on the steps of the college's Main Building. She had moved beyond lip service to Marx and Trotsky into a pleasure-filled aestheticism that only New York City can generate.

Foreign sailors (the affectionate *pom-pom rouges*), German refugees, English expatriates who drank vermouth cassis in Third Avenue French bars, young men and their girls celebrated their liberty from family and academic restraints and waited, with very little show of impatience, for the calls to duty they knew would be coming.

Roslyn would walk home from work toward her one-room apartment on Second Avenue in the shadow of the Queensborough Bridge, stopping to drink at the Provençal or Lucie's with her very recent acquaintances, sometimes bringing one home to share her bed for a few hours, more often going on alone to the delicatessen to buy borscht and corned-beef-on-rye sandwiches for her solitary dinner.

On occasion she would go out after supper to a late movie, joining the crowds of other young persons who, like her, could not bear to see the wondrously free nights end. It had been on one such evening, in the queue waiting to see *For Whom the Bell Tolls* in a Broadway theater, that she noticed Lionel Schwartz, sleek, blond, and shining in his new, well-pressed lieutenant's uniform. He stood four persons ahead of her in line.

She moved up to join him, letting those she passed assume she was his date. She hugged him, and he returned her embrace, transforming their old cordial, civilian handshakes into the sort of instant wartime display of affection common in these days. They had not met in three years. Their youthful friendship had fallen away, but now, as with so many other young acquaintances of their generation, the circumstances of war, the imminence of mortality, and separations all around them propelled them into this unaccustomed demonstration.

'How great to see you again,' said Roslyn.

'And you. Are you living nearby?'

'Not far. A few avenues over. But I work for *Time* just down the street.'

They had reached the window of the box office. Lionel put down two dollar bills for two tickets. He handed one to Roslyn.

'Oh no, let me pay for mine,' she said.

'Not at all,' he said, making a gallant, sweeping, joking gesture with his cap. 'I'm now a rich second lieutenant.'

After the long movie was over, they came out of the Loew's State Theater, dazed by Broadway lights ablaze at one o'clock in the morning. Lionel said he had to get back to his post. Otherwise, he said, he would be glad to accept her invitation to have coffee with her at the Automat. Roslyn offered to walk with him to Grand Central Station: 'It's on my way,' she said.

They exchanged addresses and more news of their lives. Lionel asked Roslyn if she was still planning to be a writer.

'Well, I suppose . . . someday,' she said, showing some impatience with his tenacious memory.

Lionel said his mother was not at all well, 'beside herself' was the way he put it, and that he was scheduled to go overseas soon. Roslyn said her father's health had deteriorated. His diabetes had affected his lost leg.

'It's been very bad. The stump became gangrenous and had to be cut off, high up. Since then he uses a wheelchair most of the time, sits in it to take cash at the store, and uses it at home.'

'How is your mother?'

'The same as ever. Full of complaints about him, about everyone and everything. Money, weather, the stores in Brooklyn, my infrequent visits, what I wear when I do come home, my haircut. Everything. She takes the war personally. Every new regulation she thinks is directed at her. She rails against gas rationing even though they have no car. But it *has* cut down on my uncle's ability to drive them to Florida for their usual month's winter vacation, and *that* affects her.'

'That's too bad. I remember her as sort of young and very pleasant.'

Roslyn shook her head. "Twenty-nine changed everything for my parents. And yours too, of course. I remember your father as good-looking and a lot of fun. And did you hear that

Caleb and Kate Flowers' mother died last year? I remember *her* as a very nice woman.'

'Er, no. I didn't hear about that.'

'I saw a little notice in the paper.'

'I missed it,' said Lionel.

At the station they shook hands, no longer compelled by surprise to embrace each other as they had been by their first encounter.

'Good luck in your next assignment.'

'And you, in your job.'

'Did I mention I was thinking about joining the Navy?'

'*Really?* Why?'

'Something new and different to do, I suppose. And maybe interesting. They're looking for women who have worked in journalism to fill some desk jobs, to "release men for active duty," the flier I picked up says.'

'Well, then, the next time we meet maybe you'll be in uniform too.'

'It would be fun. Take care of yourself, Lion.'

Lionel laughed. 'I haven't been called that in a long time.'

'It was great to see you again,' said Roslyn. 'I really loved the movie. Ingrid Bergman is a wonderful actress. She looked great in that haircut. Thanks for the ticket.'

'It *was* good. I liked Gary Cooper. He's not much of an actor, but he's nice to look at.'

'Goodbye,' they said to each other at the same time.

They shook hands again. Lionel disappeared into the stream of uniformed men heading for trains to take them back to their posts. Roslyn walked on toward Third Avenue, thinking about the movie, Ingrid Bergman, seeing Lionel Schwartz in uniform with his soft, charming manner, thinking about getting to work on time today (it was almost two o'clock, she had noted on the station clock), thinking about the pleasure she would feel if she told her boss she was leaving, thinking about a new job, a new life closer to the bellicose heart of things, thinking, as she turned the corner at Second Avenue, about wearing a uniform.

In wartime, San Francisco belonged to the Navy. Sailors filled the sidewalks, the bars, and the restaurants, their caps at a rakish, almost celebratory angle, their wide-bottomed trousers whipping around their legs with the constant breezes from the Bay. Naval personnel hung from the sides of cable cars which made their arduous way up the city's hills and then came down with noisy, lighthearted abandon.

Roslyn's new station was on the sixth floor of an office building on New Montgomery Street. Almost from the July day she had reported for duty, wearing her spotless, pressed 'whites,' and gloves despite the heat, she knew she had been too optimistic about the promising interest of her assignment. Since her commissioning, she had served in two capacities on two posts. Both assignments were minor, pedestrian, and dull; she realized very quickly that the WAVES, an adjunct to the regular Navy, the Women Accepted for Volunteer Emergency Service authorized the year before by Congress (to the loudly expressed objection of regular naval officers and enlisted men), were to be assigned work that resembled, in most ways, exactly what the civilian world had to offer.

The Twelfth Naval District assignment came unexpectedly, and Roslyn arrived in San Francisco feeling very hopeful. She had been told it was a post attached to the Office of War Information and involved some sort of censorship work, Roslyn was not sure exactly what. On the day she arrived, she was introduced to the captain of the 'station,' ever after, she had been instructed, to be called the 'ship.' His tidy office looked out over downtown San Francisco and the bright blue bay, and was referred to as his quarters.

Roslyn went through the ritual of saluting Captain Ayres and presenting her orders. He looked at them briefly and then returned her salute and welcomed her aboard. Dutifully, she expressed her pleasure at being aboard. Then the officer of the day led her to a large room, almost like the newsroom of a newspaper, she thought, where twenty or so ensigns and lieutenants were seated in rows. He approached a desk at the far end of the room. Roslyn was two steps behind.

The officer of the day said: 'Lieutenant DeMarco, this is your replacement, Ensign Hellman. Lewis, Roslyn.'

A heavyset, swarthy lieutenant looked up from the newspaper he was reading, stared at Roslyn, and then stood up. It seemed to her that he rose very slowly and saluted her with some reluctance. One of his black eyes had a strange cast to it, as if he had damaged the cornea in some way. She returned his salute. The three officers stood awkwardly, saying nothing, suggesting they had nothing more of importance or interest to add to what appeared to Roslyn to be an unwelcome introduction.

At last, breaking the silence, Lieutenant DeMarco said:

'Well, Replacement, I suppose I should greet you with open arms and welcome you aboard and all that sort of thing.'

'Not at all,' said Roslyn. 'I can understand that you're not delighted to see me. Why should you be?'

At this point the officer of the day decided to interrupt the heavy air of unpleasantness.

'It's almost twelve. Would you both like to have some lunch down the street? My guests.'

'I think not,' said Lieutenant DeMarco.

Simultaneously Roslyn said: 'Thank you, no. I've got to move my gear into the room I've found.'

Lieutenant DeMarco sat down and returned to his paper.

Clearly annoyed, the officer of the day said to him: 'Your orders will be ready tomorrow, about four bells.'

Without looking up, DeMarco said: 'Whenever the hell *that* is. I'll clear out my desk this afternoon.'

'Good.'

The officer of the day, making no reference to Lieutenant DeMarco's behavior, walked with Roslyn to the elevator. 'We use it to abandon ship in case of fire,' he said. 'The captain takes his command very seriously.'

'Yes. I can see that. Well, I'll report early in the morning. Thank you for showing me around.'

'Not at all. It's part of my duty. See you then.'


When Roslyn got to DeMarco's desk the next day it was almost empty. In one drawer she found the burnt-out stub of a Camel cigarette, and in another half a Nabisco cookie. She sat in his seat and spent the day reading the handbook of censorship regulations. When her shift was over, she lined up at the elevator as she had been instructed, in full uniform, her hat squared on her head, her sweaty hands in her white gloves, her blue tie buttoned tightly under her collar. As she rode down in the company of three other officers similarly attired, one of them, a lieutenant junior grade, said to her:

'I'm Judy Bowes. Care to come along for a drink before you go home? I'm going up to the Fairmont for the usual before dinner.'

'I'm Roslyn Hellman.' They shook hands. 'Very nice of you to ask. I would like that.'

Roslyn was delighted by the invitation, thinking how nice it would be to spend the evening with this handsome and hospitable WAVE officer, to escape her loneliness and the return to her shabby rooming house. She might even be able to share with another woman (a fellow sufferer, maybe?) her thoughts about the oppressive misogyny of the regular Navy. Perhaps (was it remotely possible?) they might have more than that in common. . . .

At the Fairmont bar, Ensign Hellman decided that Lieutenant Bowes had taken pity on her, the new girl on the station in a strange city. It was not only that. Judy Bowes was a large, hearty, generous-minded woman who thought of the service as a kind of family party to which everyone was invited. She had been born in Atlanta and had about her the warm inclusiveness of her region. 'Y'all come' sounded in her broad Southern accent even if she did not say those words.

Waiting for her at the bar, with a stool reserved by his hat, was a burly, smiling naval aviator. He spotted her at once, smiled as he stood up, and gestured to the empty seat. Judy Bowes introduced Roslyn to 'my friend Lieutenant Commander Owen Hayes.' He invited Roslyn to take his stool and stood gallantly between the two women at the bar.

A tight row of navy-blue-clad shoulders pushed against each other as waiters tried to insert themselves between customers to give orders to the barman. Roslyn was pressed against the aviator on one side and a strange officer on the other, feeling, pleasantly, part of a great and noble whole, a phalanx of similarly destined persons laughing and joking together in the face of approaching danger. She remembered having felt this concord when they had all lined up at the flagpole, patriotic intermediate campers in their uniform bloomers, pledging allegiance with their hands over their hearts, the only moments in that traumatic summer years ago when she had felt part of anything.

The three officers downed their Scotch and sodas, one after another, until close to seven o'clock. It was too noisy to carry on any sort of conversation, so they sat looking ahead at their mirrored selves, sinking deeper into the solitude that often accompanies persons in a large crowd. Other officers and WAVES, straight from their stations, it seemed, came in to replace those who had left to go on duty.

'They're changing guard at the Fairmont Hotel,' Roslyn said, and Judy smiled.

'Christopher Robin went down with Alice,' she added.

'A soldier's life is terrible hard,' said Owen, and they all laughed, pleased with their common childhood memory.

Roslyn shared a cab with them until it reached Van Ness Avenue.

'I'll get out here,' she told them. 'I'm just up this street. Thanks for the nice evening.'

'Not at all,' said Judy in her sweet Southern drawl. 'See you at seven, God help us all. Bye.'

Roslyn walked up the hill to her rooming house, feeling the inevitable depression of the solitary person who knows the others have gone on to a companionable night. Her earlier mood, compounded of drinks and the proximity of young, uniformed society, fell abruptly. In her room she could hear the footsteps of two persons on the floor above her, the light heels of a woman, the heavy rubber-heeled tread of a man.

'Couples, always couples,' she thought, 'couples everywhere but in this room.' Not for the first time, it occurred to her that she had spent much of her life alone in the company of others, and that she had made little progress toward changing her singularity. Marriage had never been an option to her, perhaps because she had never sought it, and certainly because it had

239

never been suggested to her, she thought grimly, taking off her too-tight tie and her low, uncomfortable pumps. She felt no affinity for men, and the friendships with women she wanted had never been offered to her. After all the drinks, and the peanuts at the bar, she decided not to go out again for dinner. She took off her uniform and hung it carefully on a wire hanger, and lay down on the bed to consider her case: in exile once again, in a strange place, needing friends and doing work that would probably turn out to be routine, like all the other assignments in her disappointing life.

Six months later, settled into her job on New Montgomery Street, Roslyn learned that Lieutenant DeMarco had shipped out on a cruiser, the *Helena,* on its way to the Solomon Islands. Two weeks after that, Judy Bowes brought a cable to her desk.

'See this? Did you get a copy?'

'No, I don't think so. I've been working on press stuff.'

'Wasn't Lewis DeMarco on the *Helena?*'

'I think so, yes. Why?'

'This says the cruiser *Helena* was sunk day before last at Kula Gulf. All hands reported lost.'

'My God.'

After Judy left, Roslyn sat at DeMarco's desk, as she was to think of it now, her head in her hands, her eyes closed to hold back her unmilitary tears. For the next three days she felt she was working surrounded by an impenetrable fog invisible to everyone else on the station, sunk in the unshared misery that a catastrophe bestows upon the individual sufferer.

She had begun to recover, to accept the sinking of the *Helena* as part of the common condition of war, when she looked up at the end of her shift to find a young woman standing at her desk. She was carelessly dressed, as if her clothes had been thrown over her very thin body. Her short red hair did not fit under the cloche jammed down on her head, but stood out at all sides. Her eyes were wet and red.

In a voice so rough and loud that everyone nearby turned to see what was happening, she shouted at Roslyn: 'Now do you know what you have done?'

A terrible realization of who this angry and disheveled woman must be swept over Roslyn, but she said: 'No. What have I done?'

'You've made me a widow, you goddamn WAVE, and my child an orphan. That's what you've done.'

Roslyn stood up and tried to touch Mrs. DeMarco's shoulder, but she jerked herself away.

'Lew would still be here, sitting right here, if you hadn't . . .'

She lowered her head and wiped her eyes with a man's handkerchief she had pulled from her pocket. A yellow paper fell to the floor at the same time. She snatched it up and threw it at Roslyn.

'There. That's for you. You can read it over and over, like I have. Put it in with your medals and show it to your children. It's for you to keep.'

Roslyn was speechless before the force of the woman's furious grief. She caught the telegram and read that it began: 'The Department of the Navy regrets to inform you . . .' She did not read the rest but saw the signature: 'Frank Knox, Secretary of the Navy.'

Mrs. DeMarco was standing waiting at the elevator, sobbing into her handkerchief, when Roslyn felt able to move from behind her desk and walk toward her. When she reached the elevator, Mrs. DeMarco was gone. Judy Bowes came from her desk and put her arm around Roslyn.

'Pay her no mind, dearie. You're not to blame. It's the war. It's not your fault.'

Roslyn shook her head and said: 'Thank you. Yes, I know that. Of course.'

But all day (and for years to come) she thought about the lieutenant she had unseated and sent, without her being aware of it, to his grave at the bottom of the Pacific Ocean. She thought she saw an ironic connection between him and her friend who had died in Spain during the Civil War fighting with the Loyalists, shot through the head by a drunken American comrade. She now thought of Lieutenant DeMarco as her victim, dead of friendly fire from her WAVES orders.

For years she was to keep in her small, gray lock box, together with her discharge papers, a communication from James V. Forrestal, Secretary of the Navy, commending her for service to her country. He went on to inform her: 'The WAVES have released enough men for duty afloat to man completely a major task force.' Clipped to it was a newspaper summary she had saved, about women's contribution to the war. It was a testimonial to the bitterness about the war she was never to lose. According to the article, by releasing enlisted men and male officers for active duty, women had made possible the crewing of ten battleships, ten aircraft carriers, fifty destroyers, and twenty-eight cruisers.

'Especially the *Helena,*' she used to say to herself when she came upon the papers. 'Especially Lieutenant senior grade Lewis DeMarco. Released to die by Ensign Roslyn Hellman.'

# 6

# Futurity

*Why do we remember the past and not the future?*
—Stephen Hawking

It is true of all human beings that they are dualities, two persons: who they are in the red marrow of their bones and in the tiny convolutions of gray and white matter of the cerebrum, and in the unlocalized site of what is often called the soul; and what they appear to be to the world which has told them who they are. The lifelong conflict between the two persons, the struggle for the interior self to triumph over the exterior, given self: herein lies all the bloody warfare in the person, to be who we are and not what we have been made to be.

For everyone, the future is similarly divided, into what the Flowerses and Hellmans, the Schwartzes and DeMarcos envisioned it would be and, when unalterable reality settled down heavily upon them after their great expectations, the actuality, the inevitable truths that comprised their lives. Often, it takes a decade or more to solidify this duality. For the persons in this narrative it happened at the end of an extraordinary fifteen years in which the nadir of financial ruin and depression reached the zenith of war and prosperity. The present bifurcated into the future, *et eo ipso,* brought their histories to a close.

It is the last day of the war. Soon a huge military parade will start up Broadway, a victorious commanding general waving with both arms from an open car in a storm of ticker tape. At this moment, recently discharged Lieutenant Roslyn Hellman is sitting on a camp stool in an almost empty two-room apartment she has just rented in the East Village, drinking cold coffee from a paper cup, having returned once again to her beloved City after her long banishment in San Francisco.

She sits idly, projecting herself into futurity. Taking what she has learned about publishing during her years of apprenticeship before the war, she envisions the next years. She will acquire her own Vandercook press and place it centrally in this room. Aides working nearby will make paper and sew bindings by hand. She will print elegant limited editions of excellent poetry and her own prose. In this way she will avoid all the ego-breaking hassles of the publishing world, in much the same way as Walt Whitman and Mark Twain did, on occasion. She will enter the literary scene by the back door of her own imprint.

Then she will teach her craft to a young assistant, who will, in gratitude and affection, live with her in an apartment above the studio. They will spend their weekends in a small country house not too far from the City—somewhere in Westchester County?—and their vacations abroad—Scotland, Tuscany, the Greek islands, of course—but always they will return to the place central to her life and work, the City, the only City, New York.

Her press's name will be *In the House of Sappho,* the logo for which she will design herself. It will suit the flourishing enterprise. Because everyone involved with it, the poets and prose writers she will publish, the press operators and typographers, paper makers, binders, and, of course, her apprentice-companion and herself, everyone in the house, will be female . . . so Roslyn forsaw her future.

Did she also envision *the reality* of the future? Did she see that, on the other hand, desperate for company, money, and legitimacy in a new, changed, postwar City, she would marry a recently widowed osteopath whom she had met in a coffee shop on University Place? His practice was in Indianapolis. He was spending two weeks in the City taking his children to Radio City and the circus, to the top of the Empire State Building, for rides on the Staten Island Ferry, and to climb the Statue of Liberty.

In a suburb of the sprawling Midwestern city, Roslyn Hellman Cooke settled into the calm, matronly, unexceptional existence of a doctor's wife and the mother of two young stepsons. She wrote the monthly bulletin of the PTA, and served as recording secretary of the Garden Club. She cultivated roses and azaleas, she went to dinner parties and gave them for her husband's colleagues and their wives. She lived out her uneventful life in Indiana by choice, because she could not bear to revisit the City she had loved so much in her youth.

Every ten years or so she refurnished her large, comfortable, many-bedroomed ranch house, surrounded by other ranch houses of the same design. She moved without audible complaint through her long life, a tamed spirit who had buried her dreams of glory in her prize beds of tulips and cosmos. Occasionally, in a rare sleepless hour of early morning as she grew old, she wondered why it was that it had happened this way.


On the same day that Roslyn sat on the stool in the East Village planning her press, Dr. Caleb Flowers, assistant professor of medieval literature, was at his desk in the English department office of his college in Kansas City, reading, with no strong desire to learn from it, a recently published volume on the language of *The Canterbury Tales*. As he turned the pages, he fantasized about his future, seeing in his mind's eye an endless series of nights in which Lionel Schwartz would lie beside him as they both delighted in all the juvenescent pleasures of their arcane sex.

They will walk along the green banks of the Missouri River in early summer, their white, graceful hands barely touching. Their days will be rich with the soprano sounds from Lily Pons records, the lovely speech and sonorous sentences of French novels, many prints of Impressionist paintings decorating their walls. And, best of all, entirely free of onerous familial responsibility.

For the rest of their long lives, they will be, quietly, lovers, entirely acceptable bachelors in a gracious academic society, companions of the flesh and, when they grow older, of the mind, lying together in their secret, comforting bed. Then, pensioned and secure, they will go to live in Paris, in a community of their drinking, smoking, wildly conversing and sexually compatible fellows, the descendants of the aging, expatriate persons that Professor Alexander Lang must have known before his death ten years ago.

At that moment was Caleb able to see reality as clearly as the dream? For his fears and ambitions caused him to marry Meta Holmes, the daughter of the provost of his college, a plain-faced, pale, very thin, but most pleasant woman who bore him three sturdy, intelligent children. Working very hard while fighting a tendency to periodic depression, he was still able to publish two well-received books on medieval rhetoric. Every Christmas he traveled to whatever city the Modern Language Association happened to be meeting in, always accompanied by Meta, who enjoyed the society of other academic wives.

In middle age he bought the secondhand but very well maintained Cadillac he had yearned for all his adult life, and he serviced it himself until, many years later, he lost interest in it.

He became chairman of his department, and then dean of the college before he retired at seventy. Almost at once, as if he had been waiting for his freedom from schedules and academic semesters, he sank into a long depression from which numerous psychotherapists were unable to rouse him. He lived on, indifferent to automobiles, friends, his wife's kindnesses to him, and the genuine concern of his grown children. It should be said that, since the night he said farewell to Lionel Schwartz in the parlor at Telluride, Caleb Flowers lived unhappily ever after.

In the evening of that same day at the end of the war, the novice Kate Flowers kneels with her sisters in Christ for compline prayers. Her life has reached a crossroad, but, curiously, the two parts consist of present reality and dreams of the past. Scrupulously avoiding any thought of the future, she entrusts all such concerns to her Mother Superior, her confessor, and God Himself. As Sister Mary Christina, still some years away from taking her final vows, she is content to lead the orderly, prayerful, antiseptic, obedient, and almost pure life she has chosen. She is aware of no desire for any other.

But in her long, faithful life to come, she was never able to expel Caleb from her thoughts. Her guilt at their love could not be erased by prayer or self-denial. Even her general confession, made just before she was finally accepted into the Order, did not succeed in wiping out the memories that continued for a long time to warm her body on frigid nights in her narrow bed.

Every time she heard Deuteronomy read in chapel—'A curse upon him who lies with his sister'—she felt that heavy sentence upon her own head. To atone, she gave up writing to Caleb at Christmas, although she longed for a letter from him which never came. She prayed for him, without knowing what had become of his life. In her missal was a slip of paper on which she had printed a sentence from Paul's letter to the Romans. She read it often, with some anguish, without acknowledging to herself its private meaning: 'For just as in a single human body there are many limbs and organs, all with different functions, so all of us, united in Christ, form one body, serving individually as limbs and organs to one another.'

As time went on, Kate Flowers' life before the convent became the real world to her. By a firm exercise of her errant will, she found she could often live in it. Disbelieving in the appearance of things, as her mother had taught her to do long ago, she continued to cling to the only love she could remember, the only reality she thought she had known for certain. The past served her as both future and present while, on the surface and to her sisters, she was known for her goodness, her piety and charity, her fidelity to her vows.

Gentle reader, do not despair. There was to be one life that never descended into compromise or denial or unhappiness:

Captain Lionel Schwartz had been in the Army for more than four years. He had been awarded two Purple Hearts for his wounds and a Silver Star for bravery in the European theater. After V-E Day he was shipped out to the Far East, where he died of severe shrapnel wounds during the invasion of Okinawa.

For him there would be no long future, only an abruptly terminated present. Assigned in his young adulthood to play in a lethal, martial game with the black mallet, like the croquet one of his childhood, he was, at a stroke, dispossessed of his past and denied a future. But he went on living, in the confused memory of his institutionalized mother, driven mad by the news of his death, and in the elderly, depressed fantasies of Professor Emeritus Caleb Flowers.